D1139419

The
Collector's
Book of

Boys' Stories

The Collector's Book of

Boys' Stories

Eric Quayle

Photographs by Gabriel Monro

Studio Vista

To Garth Pearce

Author's note All prices quoted with dollar equivalents were
correct at the date of going to press.

Dates given in parentheses after the title of any work
indicate that the book in question was published in that
year but carries no date of issue on either the title page
or elsewhere.

Studio Vista
Cassell & Collier Macmillan Publishers Limited, London
35 Red Lion Square, London WC1R 4SG
Sydney, Auckland, Toronto, Johannesburg

ISBN 0 289 70412 X

Filmset and Printed by BAS Printers Limited,
Wallop, Hampshire

Contents

THE LOST PARROT.

An illustration by John
Barnard for Volume 1 of
The Boy's Own Paper, 1879

Introduction

Writing this book has been a labour of love. It was a task for which any bibliographer interested in juvenile fiction would eagerly have volunteered, despite the many difficulties involved. Twenty years ago, when I began collecting first editions of boys' adventure stories for a history of the juvenile novel, I had little idea of the obstacles to be overcome before a start could be made on the text. With few reliable bibliographies available, and with biographical information about the hundreds of minor writers who contributed the majority of titles young people read and enjoyed almost non-existent, the task seemed formidable. The compensation came in seeing my collection of first and other important editions of juvenile novels gradually commandeer shelf after shelf of book space, each vividly clothed in the brightly-hued pictorial cloth beloved by Victorian youth, until a whole room had to be set aside to house them. It is from these several thousand volumes that all the illustrations used in this present work have been drawn, an indication of the opportunities still open in this field to the present-day collector.

A few years ago it was possible to buy good copies of the first editions of the best-known titles of the major authors of the genre for sums ranging from £5 ($12) to £20 ($48). The revival of interest in Victorian fiction, and in the books read so avidly in the carefree days of youth, has meant that many of these same titles are now changing hands at well over three figures. Yet, even in these days of rocketing prices for almost every type of old book, it is still possible to acquire presentable copies of the works of most of the less well-known writers of boys' adventure stories, clothed in their evocative pictorial cloth bindings, for only a pound or two. Even less if you are lucky at jumble sales or accept the challenge of a bring-and-buy.

It is in this field of the minor, but none the less important, authors that the greatest opportunities present themselves to collectors of moderate means. The works of the big names associated with the juvenile novel, and titles that have long-since become household words, will nearly all be acquired in time, perhaps fortuitously in many cases, when one is offered a collection of volumes of school prizes or an auctioned 'box of books'. And, as your collection of boys' adventure stories gradually grows, you will have the satisfaction of knowing that each new acquisition adds a little to the sum total of bibliographical knowledge of a field of literary enterprise that is still comparatively unexplored.

I have used the phrase *boys'* adventure stories advisedly, for books specially written for girls are touched on only lightly and will later be the subject of a separate study. But the number of young ladies of the Victorian and Edwardian eras who admitted to learning more of their history and geography from the pages of their brothers' copies of the works of Ballantyne, Henty, and Mayne Reid, to say nothing of Mark Twain and Robert Louis Stevenson, makes this rather one sided history of the juvenile novel of significance to both sexes.

Some collectors will doubtless take me to task for laying such stress on the first edition aspect of book-collecting. They will point out that they are quite content with acquiring any early text of the authors they once read and enjoyed, and are still able to do this for less than a pound ($2·40) a volume in the vast majority of cases. They read the books they buy, as I confess doing with most of those on my own shelves, while many first edition collectors are content with the glow of possession and seldom put their noses inside the leaves of their treasured *objet d'art*. I admit the validity of this argument, while pointing out that to limit oneself to collecting only first editions (with notable exceptions stated elsewhere) is to embrace a discipline.

It is a formula that restricts the speed with which we can fill our shelves, and the keenest pleasures of book-collecting are found in the hunt, in finally tracking down an elusive quarry we have stalked for many years. First editions of the juvenile novel, as in any other field of literature, are obviously much more difficult to find than the run-of-the-mill reprints that once crowded the bookshops. To allow an absolutely free rein to one's collecting instincts, especially in that most fruitful of all periods for the juvenile novel – the Golden Age of the adventure story, bounded by

left
This three-volume quarto-sized series of adventure stories, dated 1899, was issued with full page coloured and black and white illustrations by Cassell and Company, London. It was the most ambitious venture of its kind during the Victorian era

right
From *Best Moving Pictures of 1922*. The film was the first introduction for many teenagers to the work of Charles Dickens

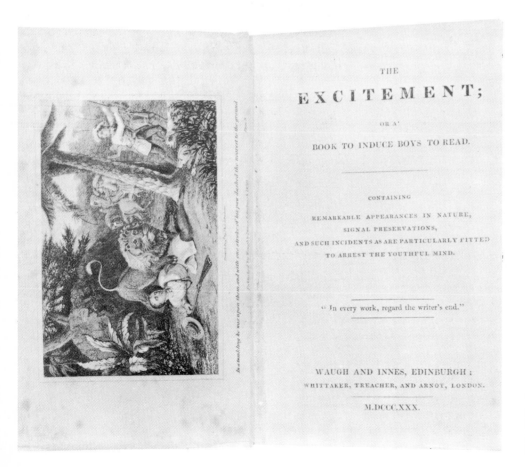

The first issue of the first annual specially produced for boys, a title that appeared each winter for over ten years

JACKIE COOGAN AS "OLIVER TWIST"

will almost surely double every few years – a prospect that must warm the heart even though a collector's primary consideration is for the aesthetic and literary value of the books he puts on his shelves.

Most of the pitfalls to be encountered and the points to look for when collecting first and other important editions of English literature have been set out in detail in *The Collector's Book of Books*, a companion volume to this present work. In it I have included a glossary of terms used in the catalogues of antiquarian booksellers and of specialist auctioneers. But the basic guide-lines needed to aid novice collectors, and to assist the uninitiated when seeking out titles and first edition dates, are all clearly set out in the book you are now reading.

To form a representative collection of first editions of the juvenile novel is to plough a fresh bibliographical furrow. This is still a comparatively unexplored field for the book collector, and for those with the critical ability to assess the relative worth, in literary terms, of the books they add to their collection, is inevitably to reap a rich reward. It is always the pioneers who gain the greatest benefits, both aesthetically and financially, in book-collecting as well as the kindred arts. Within a few years they earn the well-deserved plaudits of the eager followers of the trend they have set, as the late Michael Sadleir did by the publication of his *XIXth Century Fiction*. The indelible impact which thousands of juvenile adventure novels made on several generations of impressionable youthful minds is only now being fully appreciated. The inevitable result of this new awareness will be an upsurge of collecting activity and an even sharper rise in the prices of good copies of boys' adventure novels in the not too distant future.

the years 1880–1920 – is to court disaster. Perhaps not in financial terms, for early reprints of even the most famous titles can still be picked up for less than a pound or two, but in lack of shelf space and house room.

In this period of high activity, there were a number of writers who churned out a hundred – even two hundred – full-length titles, many of which, in the course of the next decade, passed through several editions. Much the same is true of other fields of literary activity at that time, notably detective fiction and the romantic novel. But there is a safeguard that immediately restricts exuberance and at least partly muzzles the squirrel instinct. By donning a first edition straight-jacket, which has the effect of preventing the collector reaching for too many inconsequential impressions of texts by his favourite authors, he not only protects his pocket and conserves his precious shelf space, but ultimately compiles a library of volumes symptomatic of their period of issue and in the form of binding in which their teenage readers originally knew them. It can confidently be stated that the value of a specialist collection devoted to first editions of the juvenile novel

Historical Background

Tales of adventure and stories of hair's-breadth escapes from seemingly certain death are as old as the history of the human race. From primeval times, when man first risked his life attacking creatures swifter and far stronger than himself, breathless descriptions of savage combat and the bravery of warriors and hunters in the legendary past must have held the young spellbound as they crouched around the blazing fire at their cave's mouth. These exploits are recorded in the pictures Stone Age Man drew and laboriously coloured on the walls and roof of his rocky homes. His struggles with bison and mammoth tens of thousands of years ago are still there for us to see, and his ultimate triumph over the most formidable of enemies is an adventure story etched forever in the stones.

Such stories have exerted a fascination since the earliest times. Affinities can easily be traced to those epic deeds of heroic and selfless gallantry 'far beyond the call of duty' that the Trojan War and its aftermath gave to young Greeks. Homer's *Odyssey*, composed centuries before the foundation of the Roman Empire, is essentially an adventure story in which he tells of the trials and tribulations and well-planned escapes of Ulysses during his ten years of ordeal on the high seas.

But it is to the historical novels and romances of the first quarter of the nineteenth century that the 'modern' adventure story traces its origins. Originally, the word novel meant a new or freshly told tale, thus distinguishing it from the legends, fables and fairy stories of tradition. It now denotes any fictional prose narrative, as opposed to a story told in verse, and the contents of the tale may be romantic, erotic, historical, adventurous, or what you will. Usually several of these and other elements are combined into an amalgam of sensations and ideas.

John Bunyan's *Pilgrim's Progress*, first published nearly three hundred years ago in 1678, earns the title of novel in some respects – and even that of adventure novel in others. But the first 'true' novel in English, in a style recognisable today, is generally considered to be that one time best-seller in kitchen and boudoir alike *Pamela; or, Virtue Rewarded*, 4 vols.

1741–42, by Samuel Richardson (1689–1761). I cite it as a milestone in the annals of English literature, but any work less like a tale of excitement and adventure it is difficult to imagine. Nevertheless, by the mid-eighteenth century there were aspects of literary endeavour that foreshadowed the historical and adventure novel which led ultimately to the books specially written to excite and stimulate an appreciative juvenile audience.

Up to this period, young people had little to read except adult books they had adopted as their own. Any personal literary possessions they may have had were nearly always in the form of debased, chapbook versions of well-known prose tales, or doggerel verses well laced with moral platitudes. Stories from *The Arabian Nights*, a series of tales first introduced into England in the eighteenth century from a translation from the French of Antoine Galland, brought a little light relief. From France there came also the fairy tales and traditional folklore stories collected by Charles Perrault (1628–1703). The frontispiece of the earliest editions had the legend *Contes de ma Mere l'Oye*, and from this title grew the name made familiar in the chapbook versions as the *Tales from Mother Goose*.

The chapmen and pedlars carried in their packs some of the first stories of adventure printed for a juvenile audience, but almost without exception these were versions of legendary tales that had been handed down by word of mouth since the Middle Ages. They appeared in the form of little pamphlets, usually no more than sixteen pages in length, illustrated with crude woodcuts and selling at anything from an old-fashioned halfpenny to as much as sixpence a copy. The Arthurian legends were special favourites, and it was to these tales of brave-hearted knights, risking their lives in order to rescue beautiful long-haired princesses from a fearsome variety of dragons and ogres, that teenage boys and girls turned in preference to the boring religious tomes they were forced to study even in their leisure hours.

The eighteenth century chapbook tales were often coarsely told, full of strange oaths and bloodthirsty scenes in which the thud of cloth-yard arrows mingled with the screams and groans of the fallen. They were

A Sea-lion Hunt.
From an old print.   Page 373.

The earliest adventure stories for young people consisted of passages extracted from the tales of travellers and explorers, embellished with woodcuts or copperplate engravings

as violent and as earthy as the hawkers who peddled them as wares in villages and small towns throughout the countryside. With nothing better to read for their amusement, children of all ages loved each and every one of them, the older members of the family spelling out the adventures of *Guy of Warwick*, *Tom Thumb*, *Springheel Jack*, *Tom Hickathrift*, *Friar Bacon*, *Robin Hood*, and a host of other heroes, both real and mythical. These stories were related to a mute and attentive circle of round young eyes and ears more familiar with interminable catechisms of do's and don't's and the dry-as-dust religious instructions of their elders and betters.

Titles such as these, selected from hundreds of others, the pedlar kept in string-tied bundles in his sail-cloth pack. The chapbooks had to compete for space against a colourful assortment of silks and ribbons, combs and pennywhistles, pencils and writing slates, wooden dolls and spinning-tops, and the rest of the juvenile lures. These vied for attention with the pots and pans, kettles and kitchen ware, that swung from his belt and announced his arrival with their clangs and clatter long before he reached the door.

He was competing in a restricted and specialised market, for chapbooks, ballad sheets, and the rest of the unbound and unsewn pamphlets were beneath the dignity of respectable booksellers. Young people of the day, especially those in the country districts,

devoured the stories like a modern child his comics. For the poorer children in towns and villages alike, they provided a means of escape from the often grim reality of everyday life. With their simple plots and the characters they created, young people could relive their dreams, fighting their playground battles dubbed with the names of the indigenous heroes of a Britain otherwise forgotten.

These mythical tales and legends, eighteenth century adventure stories, were printed on the cheapest and coarsest of untrimmed paper, the sheet roughly folded to make its eight, sixteen or twenty four page gathering. The leaf edges were left unopened, to await the knife or ruler edge of its first owner. There was invariably a large woodcut illustration to top the tale, and the more dramatic and blood-thirsty this was, the better the work would sell. These lurid pictures, badly drawn and crudely printed, often seemed to have little or no connection with the accompanying text. But they were studied with eager eyes by the largely illiterate circle gathered around the one fortunate enough to be able to act as reader of the verses or story the chapbook contained.

By the end of the eighteenth century an empire of cheap journeyman printers thrived in the Seven Dials area of St. Giles-in-the-Fields, London, They depended for their prosperity almost solely on the demand of chapmen and colporteurs for ballad sheets, religious tracts, last-dying-speeches, fairy stories, and the legends and historical tales marked as being 'Printed for the Company of Walking Stationers'. The ones that sold for an old-fashioned penny apiece, they purchased in bulk at '4s. 6d. per 100', about half the ultimate selling price. Despite the horrific tales that many of them told, there was often a little homily in verse beneath the woodcut picture depicting a fight to the death, or the disembowelling of a stunned and prostrate giant. Those I have before me now advise their young readers that:

> Truth, under Fiction I impart,
> To weed out Folly from the heart,
> And choak the paths that lead astray,
> The wandring Youth from virtue's way.

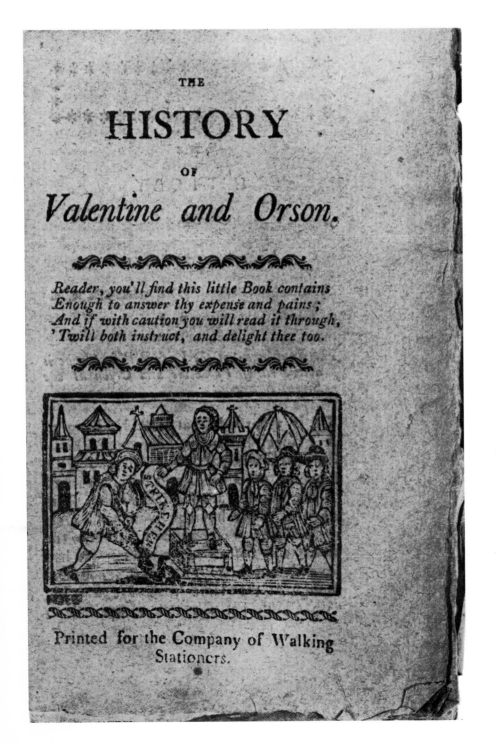

THE

HISTORY

OF

Valentine and Orson.

Reader, you'll find this little Book contains
Enough to answer thy expense and pains;
And if with caution you will read it through,
'Twill both instruct, and delight thee too.

Printed for the Company of Walking
Stationers.

left
An eighteenth-century
chapbook for children

right
The first edition of Daniel
Defoe's classic; a work which
has had an immediate and
permanent success and gave
the English language words
and phrases still in everyday
use. The first volume, dated
1719, was quickly followed
by two others: *The Further
Adventures of Robinson Crusoe,
1719*; and *The Serious
Reflections . . . of Robinson
Crusoe, 1720.* A set of these
three first editions would
now be worth up to £4,000
(nearly $10,000)

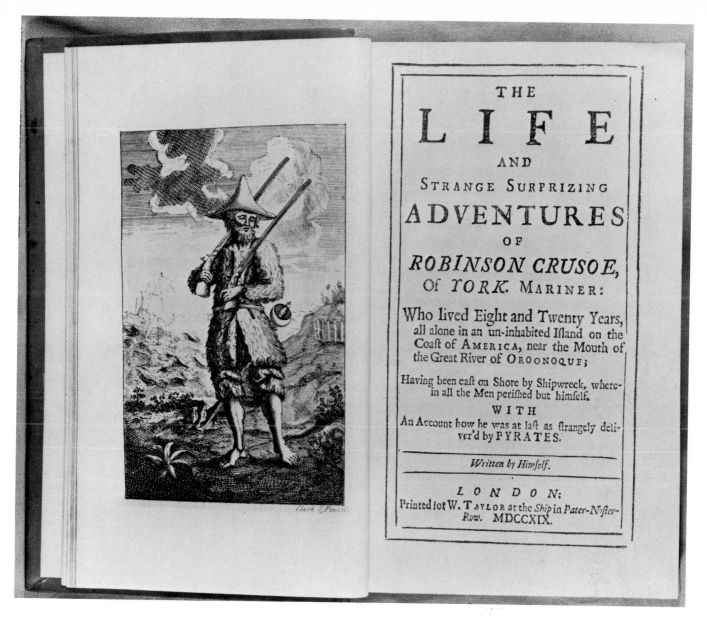

And on the title-page of a late eighteenth century chapbook version of *The History of Valentine and Orson*, an early French romance that achieved immense popularity in English translation, we find the anonymous editor telling his audience:

> Reader, you'll find this little Book contains
> Enough to answer thy expense and pains;
> And if with caution you will read it through,
> 'Twill both instruct, and delight thee too.

The plot of this particular historical romance was used, with variations, in a number of other tales for youth and had been a firm favourite since the middle of the sixteenth century. It appeared in English about 1550 as *The History of two Valyannte Brethren, Valentyne and Orson*, by Henry Watson, and told how Bellisant, sister of King Pepin, is married to Alexander, emperor of Constantinople. She is banished from the land due to the treachery of the chief priest who manages to arouse her husband's suspicions against her. During her wanderings a bear steals one of her children

(Orson), who is reared to become a wild savage of the woods. The other child (Valentine) is found by King Pepin and brought up as a knight. The inevitable happens, when Valentine meets Orson, defeats him, and then brings him to court where he is gradually tamed. From then adventures follow thick and fast, until finally Valentine and Orson and their mother are imprisoned in a castle belonging to Clerimond, sister of the giant Ferragus. But they are rescued by Pacolet, a dwarf, who possesses a little magic horse of wood which conveys him instantly wherever he wishes. A happy ending after chapters of trials and tribulations, and generations of youthful readers read the final pages content that they had received their money's worth of stirring adventure and galloping action.

Many of the publishers and printers of these ephemeral little pamphlets we know only through their names printed on the title-pages; but others prospered to an extent that ensured them a niche in the annals of literary biography. William Dicey succeeded to a degree that enabled him to found the

THE CHILDREN IN THE WOOD.

MANY years since, there lived in the county of Norfolk, a gentleman of family and fortune, who had married a lady of equal rank and property. Having a particular regard for

great wholesale houses in Bow Church Yard and Aldermary Church Yard, London. His firms issued lists containing over twenty different versions of Robin Hood's adventures. Robert Powell, of Stonecutter Street, was one of his rivals in trade; as was John Marshall, who expanded his business in the 1780's and issued hardback versions of many hundreds of children's books. John Pitts (1765–1844), and the great James Catnach (1792–1841), are two names that will always be associated with the ballad sheet and chapbook market that for over two centuries provided exciting reading matter for the poor people of Britain, young and old alike.

But it was to John Newbery (1713–67) that young readers of the day had the most cause to be grateful. His name will ever be remembered as the first bookseller (a term at that time synonymous with publisher) to appreciate the desire of children and teenagers for well-written books of an amusing and entertaining nature, rather than the didactic and morally uplifting works they had been forced to yawn their way through in the past. Newbery had started in business on his own account in Reading in 1740, moving to London four years later to establish a thriving book publishing business. He soon branched out, widening his commercial activities to include several newspapers and magazine enterprises, and even took to manufacturing patent medicines on a large scale, including the famous 'Dr. James's Fever Powder'. One of his earliest, and most famous, titles, introduced Margery Meanwell, alias Goody Two-Shoes, a tale written by Oliver Goldsmith, whose dry humour is evident in the reference he makes to his employer's patent medicine in the opening paragraph of the story:

Care and discontent shortened the days of Margery's father. He was forced from his Family, and seized with a violent fever in a place where Dr. James's Powder was not to be had, and where he died miserably.

The History of Little Goody Two-Shoes, 1765, is now familiar to modern children only through the name of

JACK THE GIANT-KILLER.

giants, who could not defend themselves; and, drawing his own sword, he slew them both, and so delivered himself from their intended cruelty. Then taking the bunch of keys, he entered the castle, where he found three ladies tied up by the hair of their heads, and almost starved to death, who told Jack that their husbands had been slain by the giant, and who had been kept many days without food, in order to force

A rare two-volume edition of
Gulliver's Travels, specially
abridged for children

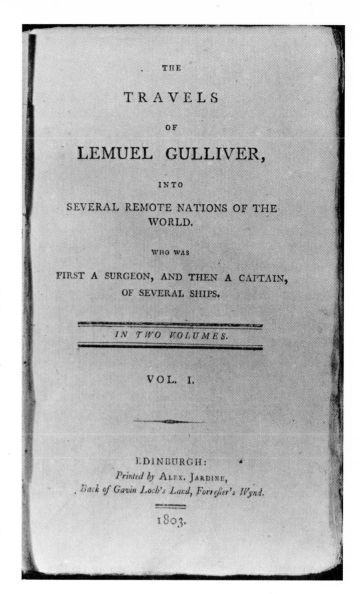

the heroine, but late in the eighteenth century it was a well-loved best-seller amongst the young. Where Newbery led, his rivals were quick to follow, and by the 1790's the trade in books for juveniles had increased to a degree that had at least six other publishing houses specialising in the production of children's books in England alone. Many of the works they produced in abbreviated form were based on classics of English literature originally intended for adult reading. Numerous versions of *The Life, and Strange Surprizing Adventures of Robinson Crusoe; of York, Mariner*, by Daniel Defoe (1661?–1731), appeared, drastically abridged but invitingly 'embellished with cuts', for the use of children. It was a work that almost immediately established itself as a firm favourite with young people of all ages, and one that has never ceased to be in print since its first appearance in 1719. (See plate page 13.) Another title that made an instant appeal to the young was *Travels into Several Remote Nations of the World, by Lemuel Gulliver*, 2 vols, 1726, by Jonathan Swift (1667–1745). Children who had been captivated by the realism and cliff-hanging expectancy of *Robinson Crusoe* were almost equally fascinated with the sustained logic of Swift's satirical fable of *Gulliver's Travels*, its familiar abbreviated title matching the drastic shortening of the text in the juvenile versions.

The themes of these two books have served as plots for a multitude of adventure stories and romances ever since, by no means all of which have been primarily intended for the juvenile market. Teenage children were also quick to discover other prose tales that their authors had never intended for young eyes, and the illustrated versions of scores of adult novels served as illicit but entertaining reading for a widening community of literate youth. Later editions of *The History of Sir Charles Grandison*, by Samuel Richardson (a work that first appeared in seven volumes in 1754), were issued by Harrison & Co., London, in 1782–83, with a series of action-filled copperplate engravings that children loved to examine. Some of the best were engraved by the poet William Blake (1757–1827), after designs by Thomas Stothard (1755–1834), as illustrated on page 18. *Chrysal; or the Adventures of a*

Guinea, 4 vols, 1760–65, by Charles Johnstone (1719?–1800), in which a golden guinea is made to describe its eventful career in the hands of its many owners, made an instant appeal to older children when the first illustrated edition appeared in 3 vols, in 1821. The dramatic hand-coloured copperplate engravings, and the intriguing description, extending over several chapters, of the notorious 'Hell-fire Club', ensured an attentive audience of all age groups. (See colour plate, page 36.)

Although the novel as a form of literary expression was well established by the middle of the eighteenth century it had little in common with the adventure story type of romance. Even with the advent of the 'Gothic novels' as they came to be called, a class of spine-chilling fiction wreathed with the ghosts of murdered noblemen and the pale wraiths of walled-up nuns, it is difficult to discern any affinity with the adventure story as such, although their influence on the many historical novels set in the Middle Ages was noticeable in the early part of the nineteenth century. Their sequence of improbabilities and far-fetched coincidences may perhaps have been mirrored to some

Published as the Act directs, by Harrison & C?.Dec.7.1782.

GRANDISON

Stothard del.

Blake sculp.

Plate VI.

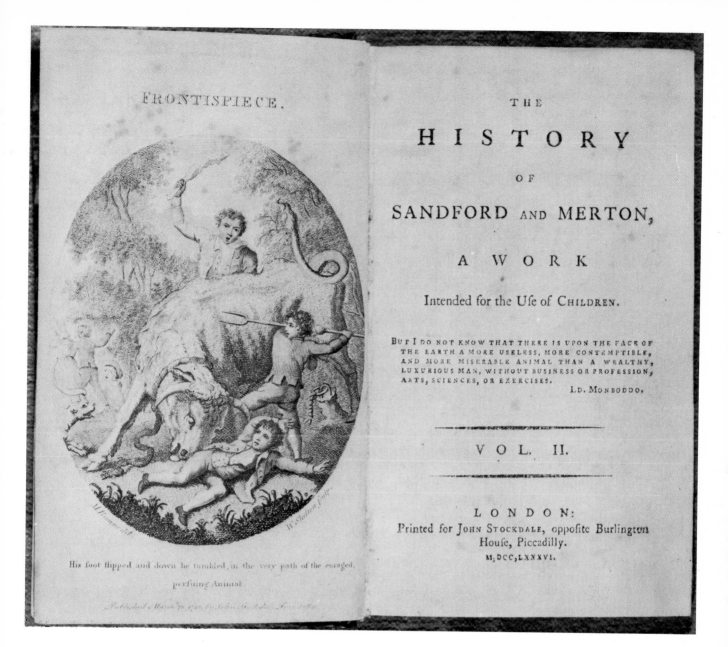

FRONTISPIECE.

His foot slipped and down he tumbled, in the very path of the enraged, purfuing Animal.

Published March 30 1786, by John Stockdale, Piccadilly.

THE

HISTORY

OF

SANDFORD AND MERTON,

A WORK

Intended for the Ufe of CHILDREN.

BUT I DO NOT KNOW THAT THERE IS UPON THE FACE OF THE EARTH A MORE USELESS, MORE CONTEMPTIBLE, AND MORE MISERABLE ANIMAL THAN A WEALTHY, LUXURIOUS MAN, WITHOUT BUSINESS OR PROFESSION, ARTS, SCIENCES, OR EXERCISES.
LD. MONBODDO.

VOL. II.

LONDON:
Printed for JOHN STOCKDALE, oppofite Burlington
Houfe, Piccadilly.
M,DCC,LXXXVI.

One of the most famous eighteenth-century juvenile novels, represented here in a volume of the first edition, dated 1786. Written by Thomas Day (1748–89), in a manner completely devoid of humour, it nevertheless established itself as one of the most widely read storybooks of its age

left
An engraving by the poet William Blake for *The History of Sir Charles Grandison*, 7 vols, 1783, published by Harrison & Co. London

extent in the often creaking plots of juvenile fiction of a later age, but there any similarity ends. One cannot imagine that any eighteenth century parent or governess would have permitted her young charges access to any of the 'horrid mystery novels' described with such relish by Jane Austen's characters in *Northanger Abbey and Persuasion*, 4 vols, 1818; but this veto no doubt made them irresistible to any teenager who managed to get them into his hands.

The ones that provided the most excitement had a blood-and-thunder element about them that later contributed to the success of the penny-dreadfuls of the Victorian era. The most blood-thirsty passages of such titles as *The Mysteries of Udolpho*, 4 vols, 1794, by Ann Radcliffe (1764–1823); or *Frankenstein; or, the modern Prometheus*, 3 vols, 1818, by Mary Wollstonecraft Shelley (1797–1851); were marked and used for regaling in secret the teenager's equally youthful friends. A particular favourite was *The Monk*, 3 vols,

THE LIFE
AND ADVENTURES
OF
DICK TURPIN.

RICHARD TURPIN was born at Hempstead, in Essex, where his father kept the sign of the Bell; and after being the usual time at school, he was bound apprentice to a butcher in Whitechapel, but did not serve out his time, for

JACK SHEPPARD.

An early nineteenth-century chapbook version of one of the most popular boys' stories

below
One of the heroes of eighteenth-century youth

opposite
After his death Jack Sheppard's adventures, in ever-expanding form, became the subject of dozens of fictional romances and supposedly historical biographies. This collection of tales was published in 1860, with the hero's name incorrectly spelled

1796, by Matthew Gregory Lewis (1775–1818), passages of which might still be awarded an 'X' certificate in the present day, although later editions were toned down considerably. *Melmoth the Wanderer*, 4 vols, 1820, by Charles Robert Maturin (1782–1824), was another title banned from youthful hands, but its more shocking and adventurous passages circulated in manuscript beneath the desks at school.

The Gothic novelists relied to some extent for their background material on details of infamous crimes, usually murders of particular violence, set out in *The Annals of Newgate; or, Malefactor's Register*, 4 vols, 1776, by Rev. John Villette, Ordinary of Newgate Prison, London. Early in the eighteenth century a prison chaplain was included in the official staff of Newgate, being given the title of 'The Ordinary Chaplain', soon shortened to 'The Ordinary'. One of his most lucrative perquisites was the publication of confessions, last-dying-speeches, and dramatic personal biographies allegedly taken from the lips of the most notorious criminals in the gaol. These were usually first published as broadsheets and sold to the crowds of sightseers that thronged the scaffold at the frequent public executions that took place at Tyburn. It was John Villette who conceived the idea of augmenting his income still further by issuing the most dramatic of the lives and subsequent trials and confessions of these malefactors in the series of four volumes quoted above. The work appeared complete with thirty seven full-page copperplate engravings which depicted distinguished members of the convicted fraternity in the act of perpetrating their more heinous crimes.

It was from information gleaned from *The Annals of Newgate* that the chapbook printers gave children their first glimpse of one of their real-life heroes, the notorious criminal Dick Turpin, whose romanticised adventures on his legendary horse Black Bess fill pages of juvenile fiction even today. His enduring fame probably owes more to the literary skill of William Harrison Ainsworth (1805–82), whose *Rookwood*, 3 vols, 1834, portrayed Turpin as a gentleman-highwayman whose brave and courageous deeds were prompted by a selfless altruism, in the manner of

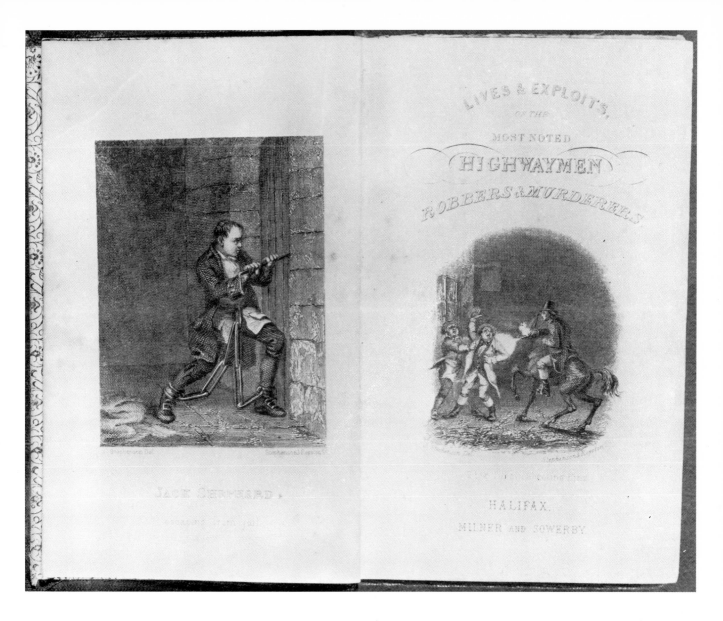

Robin Hood. As with so many other childhood heroes, the real Richard Turpin, 1706–39, bore little resemblance to the dashing cavalier of the story books. He spent much of his career as leader of a gang who specialised in robbing lonely farmhouses while their male occupants were away, torturing their womenfolk to make them disclose the whereabouts of money and other valuables. His many daring escapes, and the fact that he died bravely on the gallows at York, made him a hero with the mob. They rescued his body from the clutches of the surgeons and hurried it away for burial. From that day a legend was born which Ainsworth's novel stimulated to a degree that caused the publishers of juvenile literature to issue story after story in which Turpin figured as hero. Mounted on his horse Black Bess, he acted as the fearless protector of the poor and innocent, robbing the rich only to relieve the distress of the needy, and young people took him to their hearts as an earlier age had taken Robin Hood.

Turpin was only one of many characters to rise, purged and cleansed, from the pages of *The Annals of Newgate*, and take his place as a folk-hero of Victorian

youth. In *Jack Sheppard*, 3 vols, 1839, Ainsworth again used a one-time inmate of the London prison as the central figure of his tale, and Sheppard's audacious escapes from jail gave George Cruickshank an opportunity to display his skill as an illustrator of scenes of low-life. Young people were fascinated by the exploits of the man that no prison could hold for long, and by those of his henchman and faithful companion Blueskin, to whom the author gave every opportunity to appear in the nick of time to save his friend from certain death. Sheppard's arch-enemy was the corrupt and ruthless thief-taker Jonathan Wild, and Ainsworth brought them face to face, with swords flashing and pistols spitting smoke and flame, in every other chapter. The plot's furious bursts of bloodthirsty activity delighted his juvenile readers even more than it did their adult counterparts, for whom the tale had originally been written. The encounter where Sheppard reveals that he is the nephew of the wealthy Sir Rowland Trenchard is typical, and shows why teenagers demanded more in similar vein from authors who later established reputations as writers of juvenile adventure stories.

'I've been robbed, maltreated, and nearly murdered by Jack Sheppard,' sputtered the jailor.

'By Jack Sheppard!' exclaimed the thief-taker.

'Yes; and I hope you'll take ample vengeance upon him,' said Quilt.

'I will, when I catch him, rely on it,' rejoined Wild.

'You needn't go far to do that,' returned Quilt; 'there he stands.'

'Ay, here I am,' said Jack, throwing off his hat and wig, and marching towards the group, amongst whom there was a general movement of surprise at his audacity. 'Sir Rowland, I salute you as your nephew.'

'Back, villain!' said the knight, haughtily. 'I disown you. The whole story of your relationship is a fabrication.'

'Time will show,' replied Jack, with equal haughtiness. 'But, however it may turn out, I disown *you*.'

'Well, Jack,' said Jonathan, who had looked at him with surprise not unmixed with admiration, 'you are a bold and clever fellow, I must allow. Were I not Jonathan Wild, I'd be Jack Sheppard. I'm almost sorry I've sworn to hang you. But, it can't be helped. I'm a slave to my word. Were I to let you go, you'd say I feared you. Besides, you've secrets which must not be disclosed. Nab and Quilt to the door! Jack, you are my prisoner.'

'And you flatter yourself you can detain me?' laughed Jack.

'At least I'll try,' replied Jonathan, sarcastically. 'You must be a cleverer lad than *I* take you for, if you get out of this place.'

'What ho! Blueskin!' shouted Jack.

'Here I am, captain,' cried a voice from without. And the door was suddenly thrown open, and the two janizaries felled to the ground by the strong arm of the stalwart robber.

'Your boast, you see, was a little premature, Mr. Wild,' said Sheppard. 'Adieu, my worthy uncle. Fortunately, I've secured the proof of my birth.'

'Confusion!' thundered Wild. 'Close the doors below! Loose the dogs! Curses! they don't hear me!

I'll ring the alarm-bell.' And he raised his arm with the intention of executing his purpose, when a ball from Jack's pistol passed through the back of his hand, shattering the limb. 'Aha! my lad!' he cried, without appearing to regard the pain of the wound; 'now I'll show you no quarter.' And, with the uninjured hand he drew a pistol, which he fired, but without effect, at Jack.

'Fly, captain, fly!' vociferated Blueskin; 'I shan't be able to keep these devils down. Fly! They shall knock me on the head – curse 'em! – before they shall touch you.'

'Come along!' cried Jack, darting through the door. 'The key's on the outside – quick! quick!'

Instantly alive to his chance, Blueskin broke away. Two shots were fired at him by Jonathan; one of which passed through his hat, the other through the fleshy part of his arm; but he made good his retreat. The door was closed – locked, – and the pair were heard descending the stairs.

'Hell's curses!' roared Jonathan. 'They'll escape. Not a moment to be lost.'

So saying, he took hold of a ring in the floor, and disclosed a flight of steps, down which he hurried, followed by the janizaries.

The excitement of this stirring quick-fire action appealed equally to men and boys, and Ainsworth's vivid though unpolished style of narration, complemented by pleasingly horrible pictures depicting the most dramatic incidents, exactly suited the long list of historical novels that came from his pen. His literary career extended well over forty five years, and gave the youth of his day titles they adopted as their own. These included *The Tower of London*, first issued in a series of thirteen monthly parts, 1840, and in volume form the same year; *Guy Fawkes; or, The Gunpowder Treason*, 3 vols, 1841; *Old Saint Paul's: A Tale of the Plague and the Fire*, 3 vols, 1841; *Windsor Castle: An Historical Romance*, 3 vols, 1843; and *The Lancashire Witches*, privately printed 1849, and issued as a three-volume novel dated the same year.

It was to Sir Walter Scott (1771?–1832), that Ainsworth and the historical novelists of the nine-

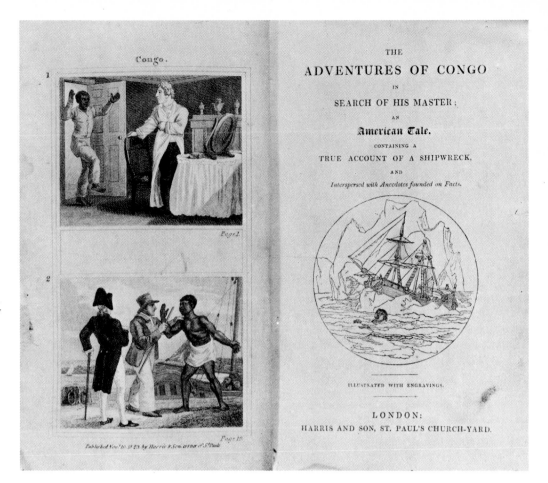

The first appearance (1823) of a tale that passed through numerous editions. The story was founded on fact, and tells of the adventures of a slave whose kind-hearted master lived in Philadelphia. The author was William Gardiner, headmaster of Lydney Academy

THE
ADVENTURES OF CONGO
IN
SEARCH OF HIS MASTER;
AN
American Tale.
CONTAINING A
TRUE ACCOUNT OF A SHIPWRECK,
AND
Interspersed with Anecdotes founded on Facts.

ILLUSTRATED WITH ENGRAVINGS.

LONDON:
HARRIS AND SON, ST. PAUL'S CHURCH-YARD.

Two of George Cruikshank's copperplate illustrations for *Guy Fawkes; or The Gunpowder Treason*, 3 vols, 1841, by William Harrison Ainsworth

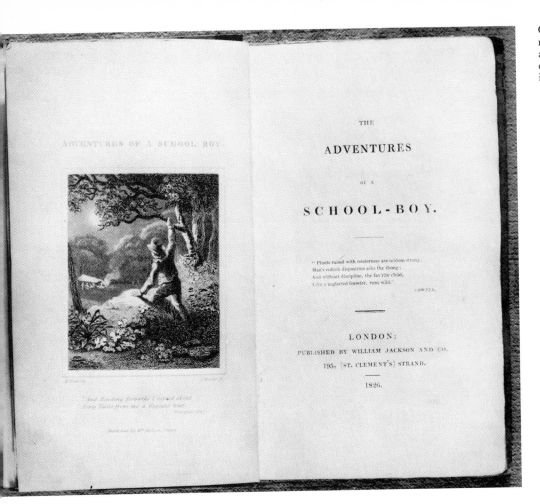

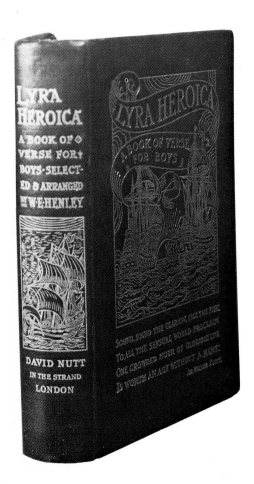

teenth century were most deeply indebted, and it was to the writings of the Wizard of the North that the adventure story for boys owed much of its initial stimulus. Long before Scott had published his first novel, boys of all ages had enjoyed having the more exciting passages from his poetical romances and ballads read to them. From the time of the publication of *The Lay of the Last Minstrel*, 1805, they must have thrilled with anticipation at the opening lines of the introduction with its hints of adventures and deeds of daring to unfold:

> The way was long, the wind was cold,
> The Minstrel was infirm and old;
> His withered cheek and tresses gray,
> Seemed to have known a better day;
> The harp, his sole remaining joy,
> Was carried by an orphan boy.
> The last of all the Bards was he,
> Who sung of Border chivalry. . . .

Yet very few young people in their early and mid-teens would have accomplished the daunting task of reading the whole of this poetical sequence of Border scenes, antique lore, clan rivalries and enthusiasms, and descriptive passages that today seem interminably long, for their own pleasure and amusement. The

George Cruikshank

A novel that fascinated
teenagers as much as adult
readers. A George
Cruikshank illustration for
The Miser's Daughter, 3
vols, 1842, by William
Harrison Ainsworth

thirty two stanzas extended to some hundred and ninety four quarto pages backed by another hundred and twenty pages of explanatory notes, so for the younger members of the family there was a case for having the more exciting and adventurous passages marked in a way which compressed the action and riveted the attention during the readings that took place on weekday evenings. Scott's *Marmion; A Tale of Flodden Field*, 1808, was another favourite that was submitted to much the same treatment, and selected verses were recited by heart as playground battles raged and youthful knights fell beneath the wooden swords of their adversaries. Scott's poems kindled a physical ardour and it mattered little to the young if their limited range left the profounder emotions untouched.

Before Scott commenced his career as a novelist he had reached his forty third year and already had a wealth of literary scholarship behind him. The success of his first novel, and the twenty or more that were to follow during the next eighteen years, can only be described as sensational, and there were many among them that soon established themselves as firm favourites, in abridged form, with the teenaged youth of the nineteenth century. *Waverley; or, 'Tis Sixty Years Since*, 3 vols, 1814, has long since been acknowledged as the archetype of the host of imitators cast in much the same mould, for, without being aware of the fact, Scott had established a new literary art form by writing the first historical novel. By setting the characters of the tale against a factual background of well-recognised historical events, he lent an authenticity to the plot that his readers found a refreshing change from the improbabilities of the Gothic novels of the period. The titles that were soon to follow numbered many that young people adopted as their own, and on which a concourse of specialist writers for the juvenile market modelled their own tales of suspense and adventure during the remainder of the nineteenth century. *Guy Mannering*, 3 vols, 1815, and *The Antiquary*, 3 vols, 1816, were both tales of contemporary life; but *Ivanhoe*, 3 vols, 1820, *Kenilworth*, 3 vols, 1821, and *Quentin Durward*, 3 vols, 1823, were triumphant historical romances on which authors

such as G. A. Henty based so much of their later work. *Rob Roy*, 3 vols, 1818, tells of dashing Highland adventure and the warring Scottish past, stories which Scott himself had heard from the lips of the elderly survivors of the troubles of '15 and '45. And in America, young James Cooper – who was later to insert the 'Fenimore' from his mother's maiden name – was listening eagerly to tales of the Indian braves while sitting at the feet of pioneer backwoodsmen who had fought and struggled to establish the white man's rule in the immediate past. It was to him that the hero of Victorian youth, the prolific R. M. Ballantyne, was to turn, in the way that Henty and his contemporaries made literary acknowledgement to their own guide and mentor Sir Walter Scott. Between them, Cooper and Scott established the criterion of factually accurate geographical and historical backgrounds, against which their fictional characters stood larger than life. It is on this basis that the writers of adventure stories for young people of all ages have ever since woven their most successful tales.

Redskins and Pioneers

It was the second half of the nineteenth century before novels and adventure stories specially written to appeal to a juvenile audience gained the respectability that comes with success. Within a generation they came to be recognised as a new and exciting form of literature, forming a stylistic niche of their own.

The 1840's witnessed the first pioneering efforts in this direction by a handful of authors; but we may use the year 1850 as a convenient if arbitrary dividing line separating the end of the old regime and the beginning of the new. The years of soul-saving didacticism that had done much to stifle the interest of teenagers in juvenile literature were coming to an end, and what may be termed the modern book, for boys in particular and young people in general was at last making its appearance. The middle years of the nineteenth century serve as a starting point of a genre that was to absorb the talents of writers whose names were to become internationally famous through their contributions to the rapidly expanding market for books for teenagers. In both Britain and America there were authors whose entire writing career was to be devoted to this cause.

A number of earlier writers were to discover their reputations established in this field, although they had concentrated their ambitions of literary success with an appreciative adult readership by writing what they believed to be books of lasting worth. It was in 1850, near the end of a writing career spanning some thirty years, and nearly fifty full-length books, that James Fenimore Cooper ruefully penned his own epitaph. 'If anything from the pen of this writer is at all to outlive himself,' he wrote, 'it is unquestionably the series of *Leather-Stocking Tales*.' This turned out to be an accurate prophesy, for this series of adventure stories in which the legend of the Redskin and the Paleface was first created has far outlived what Cooper believed to be his more important contribution to the literary history of the United States of America. Set in the prairies and backwoods of a young and largely unexplored country, the tales he wove have since expanded into the apparently immortal saga known affectionately as 'Cowboys and Indians'. Even today, some hundred and fifty years later, this theme of never-ending conflict is constantly thrust upon us through the medium of children's games, the prolific output of 'Western' novels and films, and by the reiterated dust-filled epics that thunder and ricochet daily from several million TV screens.

James Cooper (1789–1851), spent much of his early life in Otsego Hall, the mansion his father, William Cooper, erected out of the profits he made from land and property speculation. This imposing family home stood in Cooperstown, a rapidly-expanding settlement named for William Cooper, in that part of the state of New York that fronted a wilderness of backwoods and prairie that had not yet felt the civilizing influence of progress American style. The town's location provided the boy with contrasting ways of life: on the one side the pioneering hardships of the trappers and traders, on the other the manorial overlordship and genteel social round at Otsego Hall.

As a young man he listened to the tales of the Indian wars as told by his father, with much the same fervour that kept an equally young Walter Scott silent and attentive while grey-bearded uncles recounted their personal escapes and adventures in the bloody troubles of 1745. As Scott used his first-hand knowledge of the Highlands and Borders of Scotland when writing the first historical novels, so Cooper added life and authentic colour to his father's tales by his own exploring expeditions through the forests and down the rivers of untamed America in the early 1800's.

He attended Yale University for three years, then decided to explore a wider frontier by shipping before the mast prior to entering the Navy and serving on the quarter-deck of a man-of-war. He was to draw freely on his five years of seafaring in some of his later novels, but by the age of thirty he had still not written a book. It was in 1820 that his first novel, issued in two volumes, made its appearance in New York. He had titled it *Precaution*, but it is a work that need not detain us here, having rightly been condemned by critics as a pallid imitation of Jane Austen's *Pride and Prejudice*. It was in *The Spy*, 3 vols, 1822, his second novel, that Cooper for the first time revealed his intimate knowledge of the American countryside. The result was the appearance of a first-class story of romantic adventure and suspenseful excitement set against the background of the American Revolution. The book was a great success, and with it he evolved a formula that was soon to be characteristic: vigorous narrative and staccato action woven into a plot of flight, pursuit and hair's-breadth escapes.

But it was with his next book, and the appearance of one of fiction's most endearing characters, that Cooper first achieved international fame. *The Pioneers*, 2 vols, 1823, issued under a New York imprint, introduced the world to his homespun philosopher from the backwoods, Natty Bumppo, known familiarly as 'Leather-Stocking', 'Deerslayer', or 'Hawk-eye'. Dressed in the fringed leather coat and coon-skin hat of the trapper, he was a character based on the rough-hewn originals that Cooper had known in his boyhood days – one of the pioneers who had gradually carried the frontier of the United States further and further westwards. With the appearance of Natty Bumppo came the tomahawks and war-paint, the adventure stories based on the conflict between the Red Indians fighting desperately for their homeland and the Palefaces determined to push westwards to the Pacific. The tales Cooper told of the Indian Wars proved equally fascinating to young and old alike, and it was from this series of stories that many of the mid-nineteenth century adventure novels written for teenagers directly stemmed.

In all, Cooper wrote five directly linked stories, each of which featured Natty Bumppo at various periods of his life. They came to be known as the *Leather-Stocking Tales*, and included *The Pioneers; The Last of the Mohicans*, 2 vols, 1826, soon to become his most famous work; *The Prairie*, 2 vols, 1827; *The Pathfinder*, 2 vols, 1840; and *The Deerslayer*, 2 vols, 1841. All were issued under a Philadelphia imprint, the first London editions usually appearing within a few weeks, dated the same year. Within less than a decade they had been translated into nearly every European language, and editions were issued in Persian and Turkish.

The books were not specially written for the young,

yet they undoubtedly comprise the first American juvenile classics. They were later joined by a distinguished company of equally famous works from the pens of Mark Twain, Joel Chandler Harris, Jack London, and writers whose magic still conjures memories from boyhoods long ago. Yet Cooper had never imagined, when he first wrote his *Leather-Stocking Tales*, that versions of each of them would become best-selling titles among a juvenile readership that could soon be numbered in hundreds of thousands. They gained acceptance and remained favourites because of the flavour of authenticity he instilled into each of them by what at that period was accepted as a well-researched historical background, coupled with an intimate personal knowledge of the

THE

ENGLISH BOY

AT

THE CAPE:

AN ANGLO-AFRICAN STORY.

BY THE

AUTHOR OF KEEPER'S TRAVELS.

" The world my country, and my friend mankind!"

IN THREE VOLUMES.

VOL. I.

LONDON:

PRINTED FOR WHITTAKER & Co.

AVE MARIA LANE.

1835.

"He caught hold of the child from the arms
of his transported father....and immediately
swam his horse to the shore."

VOL.1 page 146.

LONDON.
PUBLISHED BY WHITTAKER & Co AVE MARIA LANE.
1835.

left
The caricature etchings of
Robert Seymour, with text
by Alfred Crowquill,
published in 1841, were
collected by teenagers for
colouring with paints and
crayons

above
A three-volume novel for
young people by Edward
Augustus Kendall (1776–
1842), whose earliest
children's books were
published by E. Newbery in
the late eighteenth century

right
An omnibus volume of
Fenimore Cooper's best-
known tales

geographical location in which the tale was set. He drew on his own memories of the terrain, and of the flora and fauna, but for his historical facts he relied on the works of contemporaries who had lived among the Indian tribes. He gleaned much material from the works of John Gottlieb Heckewelder (1743–1823), a missionary-historian who had spent years with the Indians of Ohio, and whose *Narrative of the Mission among Delaware & Mohegan Indians, 1740–1808*, published in 1820, was an invaluable source of information.

Cooper was now the literary idol of teenagers on both sides of the Atlantic, yet despite his obvious success with the young, and the vast new market his novels had revealed, publishers were slow in appreciating the extent of the demand. Those responsible for producing books for young people had yet to differentiate between the literary needs of teenagers and the mass of younger children. It should have been obvious to the more progressively minded amongst them that the reign of the straight-laced Calvinistic moralisers, dominated by those eminently 'good' women Mrs Sarah Trimmer and Mrs Martha Sherwood, was rapidly ending. Now that juvenile fiction was shaking itself free from the didacticism of the past and the tedium of out-worn moral platitudes which had continually plagued it, a new and refreshing class of literature could be expected to fulfil young people's demands for books to read and enjoy. By the early 1840's, a tentative start had been made. It was the period which saw the appearance of the first boys' books. These juvenile novels were not to be confused with boyish books or boys' story-books: they were tales specially written to appeal to the teenage group that would soon be young men. It was a period in the annals of juvenile fiction, as Harvey Darton pointed out in his *Children's Books in England*, 1932, that witnessed the start of 'the whole synoptic literary composition, the basis of which is fictitious romance'.

The laurels went to Frederick Marryat (1792–1848), sea captain and adventurer. He was the first writer intentionally to create plots and characters woven into adventure novels for young men in their teens. A dare-devil of a naval officer, who had risked his neck on numerous occasions since he had first run away to sea, Marryat had been in the thick of the fighting during the final years of Napoleon's domination. Even Conrad, on whom he exerted a great influence, lacked his experience in naval warfare, and until the former's rise to fame some fifty years later, Marryat was the most talented writer of seafaring stories that English literature had produced. He was the successor to Smollett as a novelist of the picaresque, and a man to whom a generation of later writers in the field of juvenile literature owed a debt of gratitude.

His first tentative excursions into print attracted little attention, but his earliest titles, such as *A Code of Signals for the use of vessels employed in the Merchant Service*, 1817, and *A suggestion for the abolition of impressment in the Naval Service*, 1822, have long been sought after by collectors determined to have his first editions complete. Neither title will be easy to discover, and some indication of their present day market value is given by a London antiquarian bookseller cataloguing the first item at £550 ($1,320). This happened to be a fine copy in its original boarded binding, inscribed by the author to a distinguished member of the British aristocracy, but even without the inscription a copy of Marryat's first work would hardly be likely to be offered for sale at less than £300 ($720).

Seven years were to elapse before Marryat took the plunge and published his first novel. Like many of his later works in maritime settings, the story he told was largely autobiographical and revealed some of his trials and tribulations as a young cadet in the frigate *Impérieuse* under the command of the irascible Lord Cochrane. The hardships and privations he endured were mirrored in the tale told by the young hero in *The Naval Officer; or, Scenes and Adventures in the life of Frank Mildmay*, 3 vols, 1829, and in several of his later novels. *The King's Own*, 3 vols, 1830; and *Newton Forster; or, The Merchant Service*, 3 vols, 1832, appeared under London imprints, as had his previous titles, but the next work from his pen, generally considered to be his masterpiece, was submitted to the American publishers Carey & Hart and made its appearance in

COOPER'S

LEATHER-STOCKING TALES

FOR BOYS AND GIRLS

WITH ILLUSTRATIONS

LONDON
GEORGE ROUTLEDGE & SONS, Limited
Broadway, Ludgate Hill
Manchester and New York
1892

Boys soon adopted Fenimore
Cooper's stories as their
own, and abridged versions
were issued by specialist
juvenile publishers on both
sides of the Atlantic

below
Poor Jack in the process of
self-education. An illustration
from the book of that name
by Frederick Marryat

JACK IN NANNY'S ROOM

Philadelphia. *Peter Simple*, 3 vols (Vols I and II dated 1833, Vol III dated 1834), was an immediate and enduring success, a further three London editions, all dated 1834, being issued within a few months of the work's original publication in the U.S.A.

Peter Simple was written in the first person singular, and has a strong autobiographical flavour in many of its scenes and narratives. Within a year or two it had established itself as a firm favourite, not least with younger readers, who doubtless had little difficulty in identifying themselves with the likeable but blundering hero of the tale. The author starts by telling of 'the great advantage in being the fool of the family and being made a present of to the country at the age of fourteen', at which age he is sent to sea. Peter Simple's supposed stupidity at first exposes him to several hilarious adventures, but he soon shows himself to be a gallant and courageous officer, is in the thick of several naval actions (as was the author himself), is taken prisoner and escapes, and the tale is rounded by his later promotion and the winning of an attractive and much sought-after wife. It was the sort of exciting adventure story, finishing with a predictably happy ending, that teenagers found as satisfying as the adult readership for which the work had been intended. In 1837, Saunders and Otley, publishers of the London issues, produced a three-volume edition of *Peter Simple* with illustrations by R. W. Buss, a limited number being offered with hand-coloured plates. The first (American) edition is now extremely rare, and any of the three-volume London editions dated 1834 would be priced at over £100 ($240) if in their original paper-labelled cloth bindings.

Mr Midshipman Easy appeared as a three-volume novel dated 1836. It was 'a real boys' book' as Harvey Darton called it, although once again the author had intended its appeal to be to an adult audience. Marryat had made Jack Easy, the hero of the tale, the son of a rich country gentleman of liberal ideals; and when Jack goes to sea as a midshipman he attempts to inculcate his belief that all men are equal into the minds of officers and ratings with disastrous results. But, due to the efforts of a captain of kindly disposition, and to the fact that Jack is the heir to

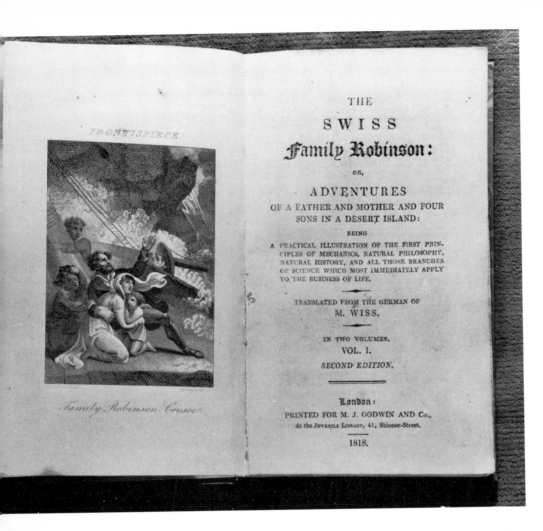

FRONTISPIECE.

Family Robinson Crusoe

THE
SWISS
Family Robinson:

OR,

ADVENTURES

OF A FATHER AND MOTHER AND FOUR
SONS IN A DESERT ISLAND:

BEING

A PRACTICAL ILLUSTRATION OF THE FIRST PRIN-
CIPLES OF MECHANICS, NATURAL PHILOSOPHY,
NATURAL HISTORY, AND ALL THOSE BRANCHES
OF SCIENCE WHICH MOST IMMEDIATELY APPLY
TO THE BUSINESS OF LIFE.

TRANSLATED FROM THE GERMAN OF
M. WISS.

IN TWO VOLUMES.
VOL. I.
SECOND EDITION.

London:
PRINTED FOR M. J. GODWIN AND Co.,
At the Juvenile Library, 41, Skinner-Street.
1818.

Early editions of this famous series of desert island adventures now command high prices at auction

eight thousand a year, he escapes most misfortunes, and with his fellow midshipman, Edward Gascoigne, lives through a series of hair's-breadth escapes from seemingly certain death. Many of the naval characters in the book, such as the bellicose chaplain, Hawkins; Mr Biggs, the boatswain, with his reiterated maxim of 'duty before decency'; and Lieutenant Pottyfar, who finally kills himself with his own universal medicine, are thinly-disguised real-life counterparts whom Marryat had known in his days at sea.

Snarleyyow, or The Dog Fiend, 3 vols, 1837; and *The Phantom Ship*, 3 vols, 1839, followed; but it was not until the appearance of *Masterman Ready, or the Wreck of the Pacific*, 3 vols (Vol I, 1841; Vols II and III, 1842), that the magic words 'Written for Young People' made their first appearance on the title-page of any of Marryat's books. In his preface, the author reveals his intentions:

I promised my children to write a book for them. It was a hasty promise, for I never considered whether I was capable of so doing. On my requesting to know what kind of a book they would prefer, they said that they wished me to continue a work called the "Swiss Family Robinson," which had never been completed, and which appeared peculiarly to interest them. I sent for the work and read it: it was originally written in German,

translated into French, and from French into English, – a very fair evidence of its merits as amusing to children . . . I have said that it is very amusing; but the fault which I find in it is, that it does not adhere to the probable, or even the possible, which should ever be the case in a book, even if fictitious, when written for children.
I pass over the seamanship, or rather the want of it, which occasions impossibilities to be performed on board the wreck, as that is not a matter of any consequence . . . but much ignorance, or carelessness, had been displayed in describing the vegetable and animal productions of the island on which the family had been wrecked. The island is supposed to be far to the southward, near to Van Diemen's Land; yet, in these temperate latitudes, we have not only plants, but animals, introduced which could only be found in the interior of Africa or the torrid zone, mixed up with those really indigenous to the climate. This was an error I could not persuade myself to follow up. It is true that it is a child's book; but I consider, for that very reason, it is necessary that the author should be particular in what may appear to be trifles, but which really are not, when it is remembered how strong the impressions are upon the juvenile mind. Fiction, when written for young people, *should*, at all events, be *based* upon truth; and I could not continue a

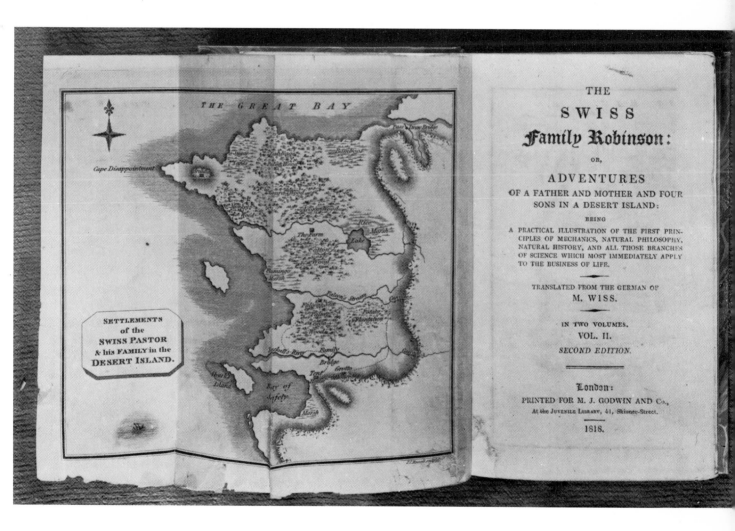

THE
SWISS
Family Robinson:
OR,
ADVENTURES
OF A FATHER AND MOTHER AND FOUR
SONS IN A DESERT ISLAND:
BEING
A PRACTICAL ILLUSTRATION OF THE FIRST PRIN-
CIPLES OF MECHANICS, NATURAL PHILOSOPHY,
NATURAL HISTORY, AND ALL THOSE BRANCHES
OF SCIENCE WHICH MOST IMMEDIATELY APPLY
TO THE BUSINESS OF LIFE.

TRANSLATED FROM THE GERMAN OF
M. WISS.

IN TWO VOLUMES.
VOL. II.
SECOND EDITION.

London:
PRINTED FOR M. J. GODWIN AND Co.,
At the Juvenile Library, 41, Skinner-Street.
1818.

narrative under the objections which I have stated. Whether I have succeeded or not in the construction of my own, is another question.

Masterman Ready appeared in the adult format of a three-volume novel, but, as we have seen, was specifically aimed at the juvenile market. Marryat's long seafaring experience as a naval officer, and his intimate knowledge of so many foreign parts of the world, were to prove invaluable in enabling him to instil a sense of technical accuracy into the scenes of storm and shipwreck and his descriptions of the tropical islands in which the plot of the book was laid. His own career at sea had started in September 1806, and from the beginning he had been plunged into the thick of the continual skirmishing that characterised the fiery Lord Cochrane's adventurous excursions in the frigate *Impérieuse*. His service under this captain was one of continual activity, not only in its almost daily battles while engaged in cutting out enemy coastal vessels or privateers, storming batteries on the French coast and destroying telegraph stations, but also in the defence of the castle of Trinidad in November, 1808, and in the attack on

the French fleet in Aix Roads in April, 1809. At the
end of 1812, Marryat was promoted lieutenant,
before sailing for the West Indies, and in the following
year he assisted in the capture of several American
merchant ships and privateers. Promoted commander,
he joined the sloop *Beaver* on the St. Helena station,
where he remained until the death of Napoleon.
1823 saw him in the East Indies taking an active part
in the first Burmese War. The following year he was
senior naval officer in Rangoon. Returning to England
in 1826, he was appointed to the *Ariadne*, which he
commanded in the Atlantic until November 1830,
when he finally resigned from the Navy in order to
devote himself to literature. With such a career
behind him, he had no difficulty whatsoever in
describing accurately, and in the most vivid terms,
life aboard ship and on the tropical island where
Masterman Ready and the rest of the survivors found
themselves after the storm. Not only was the novel
textually accurate, but Marryat went to considerable
trouble supplying detailed sketches from which the
young artist William Dickes made the illustrations.
The wood-engraver Robert Branston, under whom
Dickes had served his apprenticeship, cut the wood-
blocks for the printer.

Masterman Ready is closely modelled on *The Swiss
Family Robinson*, by Johann David Wyss (1743–1818),
a Swiss army chaplain who wrote the story for the
amusement of his four sons in 1792. Wyss left the work
in manuscript, and the first edition of the German
text appeared in book form in two parts in Zurich in
1812–13, the author's son, Johann Rudolf Wyss
(1781–1830), having prepared the work for the press.
The first English edition appeared as *The Family
Robinson Crusoe; or, Journal of a father shipwrecked with
his wife and children, on an uninhabited Island*, 1814, and
was translated by William Godwin (1756–1836), the
father of the wife of the poet Shelley. The first French
edition, *Le Robinson Suisse*, 1814, was published in
Paris with a set of twelve engraved plates, and by the
1830's there were numerous editions in several
European languages. It was one of these that Marryat
had read at the behest of his children and from which
he had derived many of his ideas that formed the plot

Captain Frederick Marryat,
a painting by J. Simpson, *c.*
1835 (Reproduced by
permission of the National
Portrait Gallery, London)

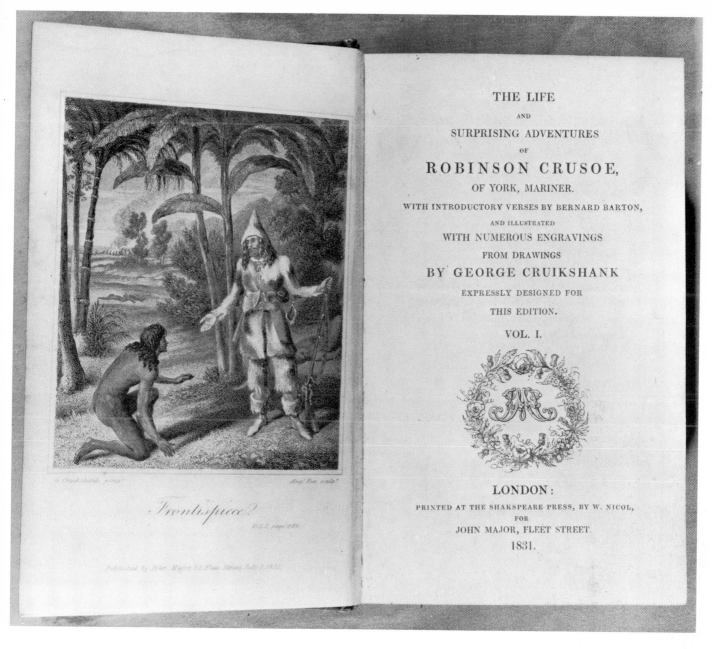

THE LIFE

AND

SURPRISING ADVENTURES

OF

ROBINSON CRUSOE,

OF YORK, MARINER.

WITH INTRODUCTORY VERSES BY BERNARD BARTON,

AND ILLUSTRATED

WITH NUMEROUS ENGRAVINGS

FROM DRAWINGS

BY GEORGE CRUIKSHANK

EXPRESSLY DESIGNED FOR

THIS EDITION.

VOL. I.

LONDON:

PRINTED AT THE SHAKSPEARE PRESS, BY W. NICOL,

FOR

JOHN MAJOR, FLEET STREET.

1831.

Frontispiece

of *Masterman Ready*. Basic differences occur in the structure of the characters in the two books: Wyss has a Swiss father and mother and their four sons shipwrecked on a voyage from England to Otaheite (Tahiti); while Marryat has Mr and Mrs Seagrave, their three sons aged twelve, six and eleven months, their daughter Caroline, aged seven, Juno, their coloured female servant, and the 'old, grey-haired seafaring man Ready', wrecked on an island while sailing from England to Sydney, New South Wales. Both families save their dogs and other domestic animals, and both immediately set about building homes on their remote coral strands. The grizzled old sea-dog, Ready, is the hero of Marryat's tale, finally giving his life in order to save the Seagrave family when their wooden fort is attacked by savages.

Marryat's debt to Johann Wyss was equalled by the latter's indebtedness to Daniel Defoe (1661?–1731), for the use he had made of *The Life, and Strange Surprizing Adventures of Robinson Crusoe; of*

York, Mariner, 1719. This the Swiss writer fully acknowledged in his preface, telling his readers that:

There is no book that has been more universally read and approved for the opening of the infant mind, than *The Adventures of Robinson Crusoe*. Every child is impressed with the conception of this solitary and forlorn individual, existing with no aids but those of his own industry, and carrying on, single-handed, the tremendous battle which man, wherever he lives alone, must have to fight with nature. Robinson Crusoe shows us human nature in its origin and in its weakness, and proves to us what reflection and labour are capable of effecting in the most trying and perilous situations. The persuasion of this truth determined the author to give his little family fiction the form under which it now appears, and to entitle it *The Swiss Family Robinson*.

Versions of *Robinson Crusoe*, 'embellished with cuts',

35

A hand-coloured wood engraving by J. W. Whymper (1813–1903) for a series of folio-sized sheets issued under the title *Natural Phenomena*, 1846, by the S.P.C.K. at 'three farthings plain; twopence coloured'. Most of his early woodcuts are signed 'Whimper', but he later changed the spelling of his name to that shown above

right
Written by J. H. Campe, this edition of *Robinson the Younger* is dated 1856. The translation was by R. Hick

One of a series of original watercolour drawings by J. Burney for the hand-coloured engravings used to illustrate *Chrysal: or the Adventures of a Guinea*, 3 vols, 1821, by Charles Johnstone

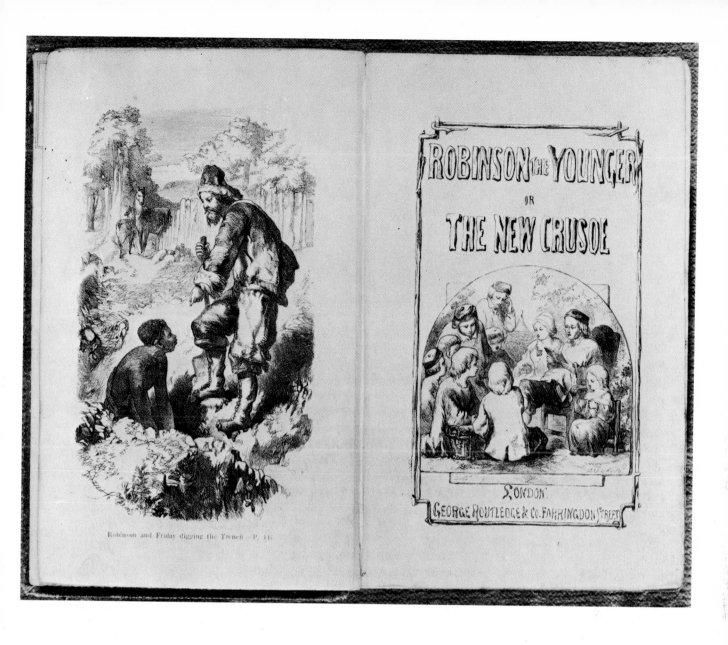

Robinson and Friday digging the Trench — P. 14

and printed in abbreviated form for the use of young people, had been appearing since the middle of the eighteenth century, and in chapbook form long before that. The work is a classic that has never been out of print since its original appearance and has remained a firm favourite with children of all ages. Defoe gave substance to the dreams of overcrowded humanity by offering an escape. He told of little patches of the earth's territory, unsullied and unexplored, where man was refreshed by the challenge of having to fend for himself. Behind the stockade of isolation he was temporarily safe from the competition of the rest of the ant-hill. Defoe gave birth to the Crusoe syndrome, a longing that lurks within most of us, young and old alike. It is the desire to be an individual, free from the mob and escaping the common herd. It is symbolised by the egotistical longing for a place in the country, a clearing in the jungle, or a panting survival on some remote coral island. The reader identification is strong in a book like *Robinson Crusoe*, and this accounts for the appeal of *The Swiss Family Robinson*, *Masterman Ready*, and a host of similar works that

will find a place in later chapters.

The immediate and continuing popularity of Defoe's masterpiece ensured a host of imitations, the first of which appeared from the pen of J. H. Campe (1746–1818), a German author. *Robinson Crusoe der Jüngere* was first published in two volumes in Hamburg in 1779, the author translating it into French the same year and into English in 1781 as *Robinson the Younger*. The most popular edition of Campe's original text was issued by John Stockdale in four volumes in 1788, complete with a total of thirty two woodcut illustrations, all by John Bewick, the younger brother of the famous Thomas Bewick. But any early edition, in any language, is now sought avidly by collectors, as are early versions of the many similar works that were specially produced for young people. One of the most attractive early nineteenth century editions of Defoe's text was published by Cadell & Davies, London. Charles Heath supplied the engravings from the original designs made by Thomas Stothard (1755–1834), a harmonious combination of talents that ensured a wide sale for the work. It was

A selection of early
nineteenth-century annuals
in their original publishers'
cloth and leather bindings

issued in two volumes in paper-covered boards (and reissued ten years later in a cloth binding), but at two guineas (approx. $4·90) a copy it was a fortunate child who was given a set as a birthday, Christmas or New Year's present. It was an edition meant for the adult market, but young people no doubt helped themselves from their father's shelves.

Rivalling *Robinson Crusoe* in popular esteem among young people were the drastically abridged versions of *Gulliver's Travels*. The first issue of the first edition appeared as *Travels into Several Remote Nations of the World, by Lemuel Gulliver*, 1726, and ten thousand copies of the work are said to have been sold in three weeks. This first (and now very valuable) edition was issued by Benjamin Motte, London, in two volumes. The author was the satirist Jonathan Swift (1667–1745), Dean of St Patrick's, Dublin, who managed to combine in the book an extraordinary combination of qualities, incidents and characters which made it a favourite tale (in shortened form) with young people. In essence, the work was a biting condemnation of the lustful ambitions of mankind. Children, while unable to appreciate the satirical qualities of the work to any degree, relished the fairy-tale atmosphere of fantasy and the logical construction of the escapes and adventures of the hero of the story. It was natural to imagine oneself as a giant towering high over the Lilliputians, and a minikin crouching amongst the massive feet of the Brobdignagians. As a novel of adventure, and as a believable tale of fantastical travels in far distant unexplored lands, it made an instant appeal to teenage boys in the way that planetary tales of science-fiction absorb the interest of present-day youth.

This was the background of fictional tales with desert island and nautical settings that Marryat could draw on when constructing the plot of *Masterman Ready*. It was with this book that he had deliberately crossed the border dividing adult and juvenile fiction. The work's immediate success with young people (within twelve months of its original appearance editions in French and German were called for, as well as English reprints) convinced him that he had discovered a new field of literary endeavour, and

one by which he could considerably supplement his earnings. *Masterman Ready* was the pioneer in a series of boys' books that the author later affectionately referred to as his 'little income'.

The critics were enthusiastic in their praise of the books. *The Era* even went so far as to say that 'Captain Marryat will look back at these works as those which have yielded him most pleasure and profit; and we believe they will outlast all else he has written'. John Forster, critic and biographer, said of *Masterman Ready*: 'Children don't read it once, but a dozen times, and that is the true test'; while Charles Dickens wrote a personal letter to Marryat, saying that 'the book is famous: I have been chuckling and grinning and clenching my fists and becoming warlike for three whole days'.

Two adult novels immediately followed *Masterman Ready* however: *Joseph Rushbrook; or, The Poacher*, 3 vols, 1841; and *Percival Keene*, 3 vols, 1842. Soon after this Marryat left London for good and settled at a small country house and farm he had bought some years before at Langham, in Norfolk. It was here, in the heart of the countryside, that he began seriously to devote himself to the task of writing books for older children. The first title he completed at his new home was *Narrative of the Travels and Adventures of Monsieur Violet in California, Sonora, and Western Texas*, 3 vols, 1843, an ungainly title that his publishers, Longmans, London, issued in an unattractive binding of grey paper-covered boards, the cloth spines bearing the name on paper labels. This was hardly the format to catch the eyes of teenagers. Within a few weeks the work was re-issued, again as a three-volume novel, but this time bound in bright scarlet cloth, with the sides and spine pictorially blocked in blind-stamping and in gold. The title on the spines had been changed to read *Adventures of Monsr Violet among the Snake Indians*, the title-pages again being dated 1843. The new title, plus the smarter appearance of the book, proved much more attractive to young people. By the time the Christmas book buying spree was under way Longmans had re-issued the work again, this time with the title-pages altered to read *The Travels and Romantic Adventures of Monsieur*

Violet, among the Snake Indians and Wild Tribes of the Great Western Prairies. Beyond this they could not go, and it was in this style and format that the work continued to be published for many years. As a gift-book for boys, it sold moderately well in its bright new suit, but the work never attained anything like the popularity of most of Marryat's other juvenile tales.

The Settlers in Canada, 2 vols, 1844, proved itself a winner from the first day of issue. The original idea for the book had occurred to Marryat while he was on a visit to America. Modelled to some extent on Fenimore Cooper's earlier tales, he based his plot on the struggles of eighteenth century pioneer settlers to find new homes in the Indian lands. The Campbell family, of Wexford Hall in Cumberland, are disinherited and decide to emigrate to the New World. They sail for Quebec, and the ensuing story tells of the years they spend by the shores of Lake Ontario on land bought for a dollar an acre. The Campbells' four sons and two daughters are involved in a variety of adventures, including capture by the Indians, before the book ends happily with the family fortunes restored. And in chapter eight the author created a phrase that has been quoted ever since, by making one of his characters say: 'I think it much better that . . . every man paddle his own canoe.' He did much the same in some of his other works: *The King's Own* gave us 'As savage as a bear with a sore head'; *Japhet in Search of a Father* has: 'There's no getting blood out of a turnip', usually misquoted; while 'It's just six of one and half-a-dozen of the other', as applied to children, first occurred in print in *The Pirate*. And one cannot forget the disarming plea of the nurse in *Mr Midshipman Easy* as she sought to mitigate the shocking news that she had given birth to an illegitimate baby with the words: 'If you please, Ma'am, it was a very little one'. With such happy turns of speech did Marryat enrich the English language.

The Mission; or, Scenes in Africa, in which the author sought to transfer interest to equally exciting territory, could not be counted amongst his successes, and has been described as Marryat's single fiasco in the field of juvenile writing. Published as a two-volume work, dated 1845, it told the story of a search for survivors from the East Indiaman *Grosvenor* by Alexander Wilmot and friends – Alexander being described as 'the best rower *and* the best cricketer at Oxford'. Marryat's knowledge of conditions in Southern Africa did not match up to his knowledge of most other parts of the inhabited world, with the result that the descriptive passages in the tale lacked life and interest. But he was already working on the outline of what proved to be his best-known book for the young, a title that quickly erased memories of the disappointment many teenagers had experienced after reading *The Mission*.

In the early summer of 1847 the first volume of *The Children of the New Forest* was published under the imprint of H. Hurst, Charing Cross, London, the second (and final) volume being advertised as ready in October the same year. Marryat had once again gone to considerable trouble to make the book attractive to young readers. The title-pages were printed in glowing greens and reds in specially-designed ornamental lettering, and the author's son, Frank, had supplied a series of full-page wood-cut illustrations depicting the most exciting incidents in the tale. Hurst had originally envisaged issuing this and other stories from the same pen in paper-wrappered parts under the general heading of *The Juvenile Library*, but Marryat's failing health caused him to abandon the project after only one part had appeared. So the work was published as a two-volume juvenile novel, in a binding of green morocco-grain cloth, blocked in blind and gilt, with a delay of several months between the appearance of the first and final volumes.

Marryat had set his historical adventure novel in the days of Charles I and the troubles of the Commonwealth period, and he had obviously gone to considerable lengths to make sure that the work was as near historically correct as possible. It has been said that the popularity of the book ensured that children of the period were taught more of the history of the Civil War and the events that followed than any of their text-books could convey. Games of Royalists and

Roundheads became immediately popular in school playgrounds, even ousting for a time Redskins and Palefaces and the perennial Robin Hood. The author told how Colonel Beverley, a close friend of Prince Rupert, was killed at the Battle of Naseby. His four motherless children have to be left in the care of an elderly retainer, Jacob Armitage, and shortly afterwards their imposing home, Arnwood, in the New Forest, is occupied by Cromwell's Roundheads. The soldiers wantonly fire the building and it is believed that all the Royalist's children have perished in the flames. But Edward, Humphrey, Alice and Edith, have already been safely hidden by old Jacob in his own cottage, and it is there that he starts to bring them up to the life of young foresters. The children's delightful rural existence, and their many adventures in the heart of the forest, are described in intimate detail by Marryat in a way that completely captured the imagination of his young readers. It was they who had to fend for themselves under the greenwood trees, with always the possibility of capture by the soldiers of the dreaded Cromwell. And as a final sigh of appreciation as the book was closed, there was the inevitable happy ending when Charles II returned in triumph to England and the family fortunes were once more restored.

The Children of the New Forest is a work that can still be read today with a deal of enjoyment. Its vitality seems only slightly dimmed by time and it comes close to being awarded classical status as a key book of juvenile literature. It was destined to be the last of the author's works published during his lifetime for Marryat had been increasingly unwell as the year progressed. He died at his home in Langham on 9th August, 1848, at the age of fifty six, leaving a half completed manuscript that was to have been another adventure story for boys. The unfinished book was taken up by his son, Frank, who completed the tale so skilfully that it is difficult to discern where his father laid down his pen and the younger writer took it up. It appeared as *The Little Savage*, another story of shipwreck and desert island adventure at which Marryat excelled. Issued in two volumes, marked Part I and Part II, and dated respectively 1848–49, the book was bound with the words 'The Juvenile Library' blocked in gold on its front covers. The work had a ready sale, several editions appearing during the course of the next few years, but it did not reach the heights of popularity attained by many of his previous titles.

The Juvenile Library was to have heralded the start of new style juvenile novels that could hold their own against the chattering rows of adult three-deckers that crowded the booksellers' shelves. But there were other stars rising on the horizon of juvenile fiction. Marryat's last book for boys was published in the year that saw the appearance of the first work by an author who was later to earn the title of 'the hero of Victorian youth'. A new and exciting vista was about to open that would ultimately bring into being publishing houses whose entire output would be devoted to satisfying the growing appetite of young male teenagers for stories of romance and adventure set far from their everyday world.

Ballantyne the Brave

When the news of the death of R. M. Ballantyne reached Britain from Rome in 1894, it was received first with incredulity, and then with heartfelt dismay by his tens of thousands of young readers. The immense popularity of the scores of books he had written for the young men of his day had created a legend regarding their author that made them eager to subscribe to what they hoped would be a lasting monument to perpetuate his name.

Led by the boys of Harrow School, a movement started almost immediately the news of his death reached England. They voted to raise funds to erect a marble edifice so that later generations would remember the name of the man who had brought them so many hours of excitement and pleasure. Within a few months, over six hundred pounds ($1,440) had been collected in schools throughout the country, mostly in hard-won pennies and sixpences from the pockets of teenage boys. Such a spontaneous gesture by the impecunious schoolboys of Victoria's Britain is without precedent and nothing of a similar nature has ever occurred from that day onwards.

As a writer, Ballantyne was held in the highest esteem by his widespread juvenile readership. As their bearded idol, a figure looking as brave and romantic as the most dashing of the fictional heroes he created, he was a man whose name they revered. During a career spanning forty years he had never let them down: each new title from his pen projected into lives that were often drab and humdrum a realistically-coloured adventure image. He had pioneered the trick of mirroring his young readers in the figures of his heroes, leaving them tantalised by the knowledge that they, too, could equally have overcome the fearful odds against which Ralph, Jack and Peterkin battled so bravely. By the death of their hero they knew they had lost a close friend.

Robert Michael Ballantyne was born at Ann Street, Edinburgh, 24th April, 1825, the son of Alexander and Randall Ballantyne. He was the eighth of a family of nine children, and the early years of his boyhood were clouded by the continual atmosphere of financial crisis that his parents had to endure. 'Sandy', as his father was always known, was the

brother of the two men who were respectively printer and publisher to the great Sir Walter Scott, the unfortunate James and John Ballantyne. Sandy's own money was invested in the business, and when the disastrous financial crash of 1826 plunged Scott himself, and all the lesser men associated with his literary and commercial ventures, into ruin, Sandy was dragged down with the rest. Within a few months, he and all the Ballantynes were reduced to the most straitened financial circumstances, and all thoughts of giving his growing children expensive educations had to be abandoned.

Apart from two years spent at the Edinburgh Academy School, which he left at the age of twelve, the only instruction Robert Michael received was from his mother and elder sisters. All the youngsters

HUDSON'S BAY;

OR

EVERY-DAY LIFE IN THE WILDS

OF

NORTH AMERICA,

DURING SIX YEARS' RESIDENCE IN THE TERRITORIES OF
THE HONOURABLE HUDSON'S BAY COMPANY.

With Illustrations.

BY

ROBERT M. BALLANTYNE.

EDINBURGH:
FOR PRIVATE CIRCULATION, AND COPIES TO BE HAD OF
WILLIAM BLACKWOOD & SONS, 45 GEORGE STREET.
M.DCCC.XLVIII.

The privately printed first edition of R. M. Ballantyne's first book, a notorious rarity in the field of juvenilia. Published in 1848, it is an autobiographical account of the young author's adventures in Rupert's Land while in the service of the Hudson's Bay Company

R. M. Ballantyne at the age of 45

had to be sent out into the world to earn their own livings at the earliest possible opportunity, but 'Bob', as his family and friends called him, was sixteen before a suitable post could be found. The position had been sought eagerly, for it meant one less mouth to feed. So in May, 1841, Mr R. M. Ballantyne was signed on as a clerk by 'The Governor and Company of the Adventurers of England, Trading into Hudson's Bay', at a starting salary of twenty pounds ($48) a year. A month later, suffering horribly from sea-sickness, the lad was aboard the *Prince Rupert* on his way to a new life at a remote trading post on the shores of Hudson's Bay.

His first letter home told how he recovered sufficiently to face the food of the ship; but a week later he and the other young apprentices were once again thoroughly enjoying life. Ballantyne was undergoing seafaring experiences that he would one day make good use of in the pages of his books, and he regaled his family with some of the highlights of the voyage:

Within a few weeks I had become a sailor, and

43

could ascend and descend easily to the truck
without creeping through the 'lubber's hole'.
I shall not forget the first time I attempted this:
our youngest apprentice had challenged me to try
it, so up we went together – he on the fore and I on
the main mast. The tops were gained easily, and we
even made two or three steps up the top-mast
shrouds with affected indifference; but alas! our
courage was failing – at least mine was – very fast.
However, we gained the cross-trees pretty well, and
then sat down for a little to recover breath. The
top-gallant-mast still reared its taper form high
above me, and the worst was yet to come. The
top-gallant shrouds had no rattlins on them, so I
was obliged to shin up; and as I worked my way up
the two small ropes, the tenacity with which I
gripped them was fearful. At last I reached the top,
and with my feet on the small collar which fastens
the ropes to the mast, and my arms circling the
mast itself – for nothing but a bare pole, crossed by
the royal-yard, now rose above me – I glanced
upwards.

After taking a long breath, and screwing up my
courage, I slowly shinned up the slender pole, and,
standing on the royal-yard, laid my hands on the
truck. After a time I became accustomed to it, and
thought nothing of taking an airing on the royal-
yard after breakfast.

During the six long years that Ballantyne spent
adventuring in the wilds of Rupert's Land, often
longing to be home again in his native Scotland, he
wrote nearly every month to his family telling of his
life in the backwoods of Canada. Sometimes it was
half a year before his letters left on their long journey
back to Edinburgh, but his mother carefully preserved
the bundles of thumbed and well-read sheets after
they had finished their wide circulation amongst
family and friends. He set out in intimate detail his
day-to-day life in the service of the Company, telling
of his long canoe trips, sometimes lasting months,
when he was transferred to remote outposts, and
finally of his lone command of Seven Islands trading
post on the Gulf of St Lawrence. Trading with the

Ballantyne had the first copy
of *Hudson's Bay* specially
bound in red morocco, and
inscribed it to his mother
who then lived at Portobello
near Edinburgh

Tales of hunting and
exploration made fascinating
reading for nineteenth-
century youth. This
illustration is from *The Old
Forest Ranger*, 1842, by
Captain Walter Campbell

fur-trapping Indians sometimes had its dangers, and his own hunting and fishing trips in territory that was largely unexplored made exciting reading for his anxious folks back home. Mrs Ballantyne kept her favourite son's growing pile of letters in a bulky silk-embroidered wallet, not knowing that one day these were to form the basis of the first of his many books.

In July 1847, Bob Ballantyne, now twenty two years old, was back in his native Scotland, and soon found himself a job in the office of the Edinburgh, Portobello & District Railway Company. One of the friends of the family who had read and enjoyed his letters was an elderly spinster, Miss Greig, and at her first meeting with the young man, whose Canadian adventures she knew by heart, she offered to pay for their publication. The delighted author-to-be now devoted every spare moment to the work of re-writing and editing the mass of material that had accumulated over the years, and by the autumn he had persuaded William Blackwood & Sons to give the volume the honour of their imprint. A thousand copies were privately printed and paid for by Miss Greig, who had agreed, on the Ballantynes insisting, that the sum she was out of pocket should be treated as a loan.

In mid-December, 1847, Robert M. Ballantyne's name appeared for the first time on the title-page of a book. One can well imagine his pride at seeing in print the magic words, and in handling the cloth-bound volumes with their gold-lettered spines and exciting smell of printer's ink. So it was that *Hudson's Bay; or, Every-Day Life in the Wilds of North America*, 1848, was given to the world. It was the year that saw the publication of a diversity of titles to tempt a languid public appetite: Ainsworth's *Lancashire Witches*; Anne Brontë's *Tenant of Wildfell Hall*; Dickens' *Haunted Man*; Gaskell's *Mary Barton*; Leigh Hunt's *Jar of Honey*; and, for the more seriously minded, John Stuart Mill's *Principles of Political Economy*, together with a host of others by names long-since buried and forgotten. But Ballantyne's story of his adventures in the Far North was heavily subscribed for and continued to sell very well. By late January, 1848, the last copies of the limited edition, privately printed at the author's expense, had all been sold, and the sum owing to the kind-hearted Miss Greig was gratefully repaid. On a final reckoning the young author found himself in pocket to the tune of over twenty pounds 'to his most entire satisfaction'.

One of the subscribers who had read and enjoyed the book was John Blackwood, the editor of *Blackwood's Magazine* and a partner in the publishing firm of the same name. He wrote to Ballantyne offering to have printed one thousand copies for public sale, any profit from the transaction (or loss!) to be divided equally between the author and the publishers, William Blackwood & Sons, Edinburgh. This was an offer which Ballantyne accepted with alacrity, rejoicing in his new-found professional status as a writer. On the 7th March, 1848, this second (or first published) edition of 1040 copies appeared for sale in the bookshops at nine shillings each, bound in a similar style to the previous issue, but this time with the publisher's imprint in gold on the spine. The whole text had been completely reset and all the errata corrected, and Bob awaited the news of the first month's sales with expectant heart. He was soon to learn that there is a world of difference between disposing of a newly issued book with a limited printing amongst one's own relations and friends, and their own friends and relations, and in having the second thousand volumes of the same work of a new and untried author appear for sale on the counters of London and the provinces. He was unknown to the reading public: a few hundred copies were disposed of and then sales diminished to a trickle. This first published edition proved a financial failure, and it was not until the end of 1853 that his publishers were finally able to remainder the balance and clear their shelves of the stock of *Hudson's Bay*.

Blackwoods themselves were partly at fault in not making the exterior of the volume more attractive to a juvenile readership, having chosen to issue it in a style similar to that selected for the first, privately published, edition by the inexperienced Mr Ballantyne. The austere, plain grey cloth cover, unrelieved by any exciting inducements in the form of gold-blocked pictures, was far too dignified a format to attract the young. The exterior of the book appeared

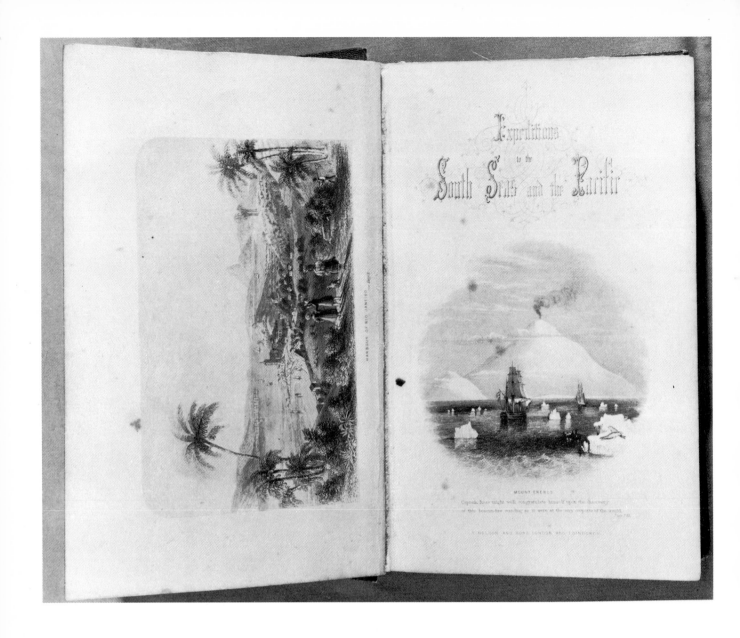

so uninteresting that it is most unlikely that it persuaded boys to take it down from the bookseller's shelf or entreat parents to purchase it on their behalf. And in the adult market it was swamped by a glut of travel books, written, it seemed, by practically every titled lady and gentleman who had completed the Grand Tour. *Hudson's Bay* stayed glumly on the shelves, and, far from this time sharing in the division of any profits, the author finished by owing the publishers money. The episode had a depressing effect on the hopes of a young man who had found himself a writer largely by accident. Any ambitions Ballantyne might have had of earning his living by the pen were dashed. It was to be many years before he wrote again for publication.

The episode has been recounted in detail to explain the long gap that ensued before the appearance of his next full-length book. Copies of *Hudson's Bay* had been in circulation for over five years before he ventured to try his hand for a second time, but the number of enthusiastic letters he had received during this period from readers in Britain, Canada and the U.S.A.,

restored his self-confidence. This was not misplaced, for *Hudson's Bay* can still be read today with a great deal of pleasure. It has stood the test of time, and is certainly one of the most readable and interesting accounts we have of the life of the fur-traders in the Canada of the 1840's.

Ballantyne's knowledge of the Far North, and his interest in travel and exploration, led him to edit and largely rewrite *A View of the Progress and Discovery of the Northern Coasts of America*, 1832, by Patrick Fraser Tytler. He rewrote the whole of Tytler's text to make it more attractive to juvenile readers, then added three chapters of his own at the end of the book to bring it up to date. The finished manuscript was offered to Thomas Nelson & Sons, the Edinburgh and London publishing house, who were sufficiently impressed to offer Ballantyne twenty five pounds for its outright purchase. Illustrations were supplied by the artist Birket Foster after sketches by Ballantyne, and the work was published as *The Northern Coasts of America, and the Hudson's Bay Territories – A Narrative of Discovery and Adventure*, 1853. A second issue appeared a

46

The source-book for many of R. M. Ballantyne's most famous tales, including *The Coral Island*, 1858. *Recent Exploring Expeditions to the Pacific, and the South Seas*, 1853, by J. S. Jenkins, supplied the background material for many of his desert island books

few months later, dated 1854.

By this time Ballantyne had changed his job and was working in the office of Thomas Constable & Company, designated as Her Majesty's Printer and Publisher in Edinburgh. He was ambitious to establish himself as a writer, and the success of *The Northern Coasts of America*, which was reprinted several times within two years, convinced him that there was a good chance he might succeed. The publisher William Nelson had been attracted by the treatment the unknown writer had given Tytler's original text, and he borrowed a copy of his first book in order to gain a clearer knowledge of his style. Reading Ballantyne's autobiographical account of his adventures in Rupert's Land impressed him that here was an author who could write a quick-moving adventure story, sufficiently exciting to retain his readers' interest and have them asking for more. Without more ado he wrote offering the sum of fifty pounds ($120) for the outright purchase of a fictional adventure story for boys set in the Frozen North. This letter marked the start of the career of R. M. Ballantyne as a writer of juvenile fiction, a career that was to continue for nearly forty years and which had a profound influence on his contemporaries, and on those writers who were to follow in his footsteps.

Snowflakes and Sunbeams; or, The Young Fur Traders, 1856, was his first full-length book for teenage boys, purposely written to appeal only to a juvenile audience and with no thought of attracting an adult readership. The book was designed as an adventure novel for boys, for Nelsons were already gaining a reputation for eye-catching bindings that made an instant appeal to this special market. Later, they were to concentrate most of their output into this restricted but everexpanding field of juvenile teenage fiction, experimenting with pictorial binding styles, and being one of the first publishing houses to incorporate colourprinted full-page illustrations in their children's books.

Ballantyne's publishers had set the trend with *The Northern Coasts of America*, clothing it in any one of a variety of brightly-coloured ripple-grain cloths, while below the wording on the spine they incorporated an action picture of a hunter in snow-shoes, blocked in gold. They issued *The Young Fur Traders*, as the work soon came to be known (the first part of the title was quietly dropped after three editions), in almost exactly the same format: diagonal ripple-grain cloth, with the same gun-carrying figure of a fur-clad hunter ploughing his way purposefully through the snow. Later, when his name was well known, they allowed Ballantyne to choose his own cloth colours. His letters, quoted in *Ballantyne the Brave*, 1967 (Rupert Hart-Davis, London), reveal that he usually selected three or four bright and contrasting colours, and these bolts of cloth the binders used as they came to hand, taking down a fresh and perhaps different colour as earlier bolts were used up. This point is mentioned as a reminder that priority of issue cannot be claimed for a volume merely on the grounds that it is bound in a particular colour of cloth, providing that the format and internal make-up of the book equates with other copies of the same edition. This observation applies to much of the juvenile fiction issued in the latter half of the nineteenth century, and includes the works of Ballantyne, W. H. G. Kingston, G. A. Henty, and a host of similar writers in the same field.

The enduring success of *The Young Fur Traders* can be judged by the fact that the work has seldom been out of print since the date of its original issue. It appeared in November, 1856, as a five-shilling adventure book for boys and its sales that Christmas far exceeded the expectations of both publisher and author. Within a few weeks repeat orders from booksellers up and down the country began to flow into the publisher's office as the recommendations of the critics and those who had already read and enjoyed the book began to take effect. Most of the newspapers and periodicals that noticed the work gave it a warm welcome, a typical review being that of the influential *Athenaeum*:

This book will be the delight of high-spirited boys. It is full of fun and adventure. The description of hunter-life in the backwoods, and the society and manners of the trading-stations of the Hudson's Bay Company, are excellent, and have unmistakeable signs of having been drawn from life. The adventures and escapes are very exciting, and are told with great freedom and spirit. It is one of the most fascinating books of the kind; and fortunate will those youngsters be who find it hanging on their branch of the Christmas-tree.

Could any aspiring writer ask for more! Reading the book, one is not long in gaining the impression that young Charley Kennedy's adventures display, in a highly-coloured and romanticised form, the type of life Ballantyne himself would dearly have wished to lead while acting as store-keeper and clerk at the Company's log-built trading stations. The action takes place in the snow-covered wilderness of Rupert's Land, and there is a strong autobiographical flavour throughout the tale. This understandable desire on Ballantyne's part to play the hero is also evident in many of the illustrations that accompanied his works. He supplied pictures for nearly all the books he wrote, and obvious self-portraits, showing the heroes of the tales as bearded stalwarts who stand fearlessly grasping outsize Colt revolvers, or muzzle-loading rifles, while facing fearful odds, appear in many of them. An example is given on page 63 which can be compared with the author's own portrait. He was in the habit of conducting the many lectures he gave on life in the wilds dressed in trappers' hunting kit – leather jerkin, coon-skin hat, bowie-knife, and long-barrelled gun, – an outfit to stir the heart of any boy and which exactly equated with his young readers' image of how their author/hero ought to appear.

Throughout his life, Ballantyne sought situations where he could court danger and adventure, leaving his wife and growing family at home for months at a time while he disappeared in search of background material for his next book. He had landed at Hudson's Bay as a lad of sixteen hoping for high adventure and a life as romantically exciting as those he later fashioned for the young heroes of his tales. Although many of his dreams came true, and there were weeks of canoeing and snow-shoe tracking down the trails and rivers of the Canadian wilderness, there were also many long months chained to the office desk in the Company's stores, tallying furs and writing ledger accounts as junior book-keeper of the trading post. As he told his readers in *Hudson's Bay*, he rebelled against the life of clerk and ledger keeper:

It is needless to describe the agonies I endured while sitting, hour after hour, on a long-legged stool, my limbs quivering for want of their accustomed exercise, while the twittering of birds, barking of dogs, lowing of cows, and neighing of horses, seemed to invite me to join them in the woods; and anon, as my weary pen scratched the paper, their voices seemed to change to hoarse derisive laughter . . . for their proud masters, who coop themselves up in smoky houses during the live-long day, and call themselves free. . . .

Much of the plot of *The Young Fur Traders* mirrors his own frustrated hopes of one day becoming a real-life hero while manning the stockade of a lonely trading post against the onslaught of Redskins on the warpath. In the opening chapter, we are told how Charles Kennedy, a young man about his own age at the time Ballantyne first landed at Hudson's Bay, is determined to seek adventure rather than life on an office stool. Charles lives with his parents and a surviving sister near to Red River Settlement, at that time in the heart of the fur-trading empire built up by the Hudson's Bay Company. It was here that the writer of the tale had passed the long months of a frozen winter as an office boy, and he was determined that his young hero would seek a more romantic fate. Charley refuses to let himself be sacrificed on the family altar of security and a distant pension. The more his father tries to convince him of the social advantages of a settled, if pedestrian, existence, the more resolutely young Kennedy shakes his head. The tranquillity of an ordered existence is anathema to our virile young marksman, and in desperation the exasperated Mr Kennedy attempts to chill his blood by painting a lurid picture of the dangers of life in the backwoods:

'You'll have to rough it, as I did,' he threatened,

'when I went up the Mackenzie River district, where I was sent to establish a new post, and had to travel for weeks and weeks through a wild country, where none of us had ever been before – where we shot our own meat, caught our own fish, and built our own house – and were very near being murdered by Indians. Ay, lad, you'll repent your obstinacy when you come to hunt your own dinner, as I've done many a day up the Saskatchewan, where I've had to fight the Redskins and grizzly bears, and to chase the buffaloes over miles and miles of prairie on rough-going nags till my bones ached and I scarce knew whether I sat on –'

'Oh!', exclaimed Charley, starting to his feet, while his eyes flashed and his chest heaved with emotion – 'That's the place for me, father!'

'And me, too!', echoed the author's teenage readers. It was a formula that Ballantyne used with success on numerous occasions during the course of his literary career and one that ensured reader identification with the hero of the tale through an identity of romantic, if frustrated, interests.

The year 1857 saw the publication of what soon proved to be two of the most popular stories Ballantyne ever wrote. The success of *The Young Fur Traders* made Nelson press their promising young author for another tale of the Far North. This time he set it amongst the Esquimaux of Ungava Bay, and by the early summer of that year the manuscript was completed. *Ungava: A Tale of Esquimaux-Land*, was in the bookshops by November, 1857, dated forward to 1858; but by this time Ballantyne had an adventure novel in the press that was to make his name internationally famous amongst his juvenile audience.

In June, 1857, he had received from Nelsons the sum of thirty golden sovereigns ($72) on his handing over the completed manuscript of *Ungava*. The final payment of a similar sum was made on publication of the book. Ballantyne had once again been forced to accept an offer for the outright purchase of the copyright of the book, and the sixty pounds in cash was only to be handed over on his agreeing to relinquish any claim to a financial interest in any subsequent editions of the title. On the strength of this happy windfall, as he then called it, he packed his bags, said goodbye to the relatives he was living with, and, with brushes and paints, notebooks and pencils, set off on a month's holiday at the seaside.

He was still a bachelor, with few responsibilities, but had been urged by his still impoverished family to spend at least part of each day writing, and had given a promise to return from holiday with at least three chapters of his next book completed. He took lodgings at Burntisland, just across the Firth of Forth opposite Edinburgh, but, as he later wrote in *The Idler Magazine*, he had no idea of any plot for his book, and both the subject and the setting of the tale eluded him. He believed that he had written out all he knew of the Frozen North, and 'felt compelled to seek new fields of adventure in the books of travellers'.

From his bedroom window in the lodging-house he was able to look across the Forth to the island of Inchkeith about four miles away. It was while sitting at his table before the window, idly chewing his pen and gazing out to sea, that the sight of the little island shimmering in the distant sunlight brought suddenly to his mind the idea of making the characters of his next tale castaways on just such a place. With Defoe in mind, he had no hesitation in making it a tropical island, wild and crowded with snarling dangers through which his youthful heroes would have to fight their way to a happy ending.

Next day, or so he told his wife in later years, he caught the morning ferry back to Edinburgh, and borrowed from amongst Nelson's file copies several works of reference and travel books dealing with the islands of the Pacific Ocean. Amongst their recent publications he must have noticed a book which had appeared in 1852, entitled *The Island Home; or, The Young Cast-Aways*, written by an American author, James F. Bowman, who used the pseudonym of 'Christopher Romaunt'. *The Island Home*, Bowman's only novel, was first published by D. Lothrop & Company, Boston, dated 1851, and Nelsons had issued the first English edition the following year.

With this and other works at his elbow, Ballantyne

What a pleasant scene it is out beneath those grand old trees, and how beautiful in the freshness of youth is the merry little band collected here.— Page 11.

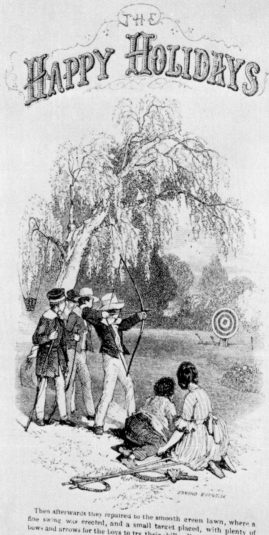

THE HAPPY HOLIDAYS

Then afterwards they repaired to the smooth green lawn, where a fine swing was erected, and a small target placed, with plenty of bows and arrows for the boys to try their skill.— Page 89.

T. NELSON AND SONS, LONDON AND EDINBURGH.

settled down to write the book with which his name will always be first associated. A few days later he had completed the first chapter, and had decided to title the work *The Coral Island*, a name that has since found a secure niche in the annals of juvenile literature. His three young heroes he named Ralph Rover, Jack Martin, and Peterkin Gay, and before long he had them shipwrecked on his remote tropical island, battling for their lives against cannibals and braving dangers in manly fashion with true British pluck.

Reading Bowman's *Island Home*, one can have little doubt that Ballantyne used many of the incidents described by the American author as background material for his own book. There is little plot in either story, but the sequence of events portrayed by Ballantyne is duplicated in large measure in Bowman's earlier work. Bowman told how five young Americans

above
An anonymous collection of short stories for teenagers. Dated 1852, it appeared as *Woodleigh House: or, The Happy Holidays* in T. Nelson & Sons' *Royal Juvenile Library*

right
Four much sought-after first editions by R. M. Ballantyne

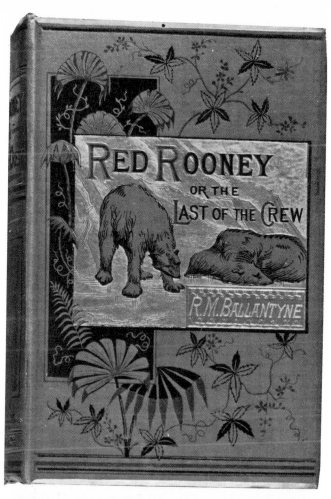

and a Scot were marooned on a coral island in the Pacific by mutineers; while Ballantyne chose a similar setting but had his three young men shipwrecked. In the course of their adventures the boys in both stories scramble up palm trees to drink the 'lemonade' from the coconuts, rub sticks together to make fire, are scared to death by a mysterious noise which they later believe to be made by a species of penguin, and witness a ferocious club fight between rival parties of cannibals in which they themselves become involved. Even the celebrated attack on the boys by a man-eating shark appears in both stories, so there is no doubt that Ballantyne helped himself liberally from the work of his obscure American rival.

The Island Home may now be accorded a greater measure of recognition by students of juvenile literature, for as the source from which came many of the incidents portrayed in *The Coral Island* (itself a book, as we shall see later, which exercised a considerable influence over the boyhood imagination of Robert Louis Stevenson), it helped nineteenth century youth to develop a taste for the romance of the Southern Seas and the mystery and excitement of those far-off coral strands. With *Recent Exploring Expeditions to the Pacific, and the South Seas*, 1853, by J. S. Jenkins, it constituted Ballantyne's most important source book for the several tales of adventure set in the southern oceans that were later to come from his pen.

The Coral Island proved to be an immediate and lasting success, and its enduring qualities are shown by the fact that it has been translated into over thirty different languages, and has never been out of print since its first day of issue. It was in the bookshops in December, 1857, just in time for the Christmas shopping spree, selling at six shillings a copy by virtue of its coloured plates, while *Ungava*, with its illustrations printed in black-and-white, cost a shilling less. For the copyright of each of these two tremendously popular books, the author received only sixty pounds, plus *ex gratia* payments amounting to a further thirty. Due to the holes that could be punched in the Copyright Act in the mid-Victorian era, he was paid not a penny more for the many subsequent issues of these two titles, deriving no extra benefit whatsoever from the many thousands of volumes which were printed after the first editions were exhausted. A like fate awaited many of his contemporaries in the same field of literary endeavour.

During 1858, his publishers put a number of easy hackwork tasks in his hands, and Ballantyne's name was soon appearing on the title-pages of such diverse subjects as *Handbook to the New Gold Fields of the Fraser and Thompson Rivers*, 1858; *Environs and Vicinity of Edinburgh*, 1859; *Ships – The Great Eastern and Lesser Craft*, 1859; *The Lakes of Killarney*, 1859; etc., for all of which the necessary information was fed to him by their own researchers. *How Not to Do It – A Manual for the Awkward Squad*, 1859, reflected his interest in the Edinburgh Volunteer Corps, the nineteenth century equivalent of our present day Territorial Army, in which Ballantyne held the rank of captain. These ephemeral little booklets constitute some of the most difficult of his first editions to discover in their original format, but are of concern to those bibliophiles who make a point of seeking out every title of the authors whose works they collect. A complete list is given in *R. M. Ballantyne – A Bibliography of First Editions* (Dawsons of Pall Mall).

Reviews of *Ungava* and *The Coral Island* were even better than the author's most optimistic hopes, *The Scotsman* telling its readers that Ballantyne was now the clear favourite amongst writers for juveniles – 'for not content with introducing them to far distant lands – ranging from the cold and cheerless regions of North America to the beautiful islands of the Pacific – he makes young boys the heroes of all his stories, endowing them with wonderful fortitude and perseverance'. The reviewer had perceived the quality, almost unique in those days, which above all others was making Ballantyne's books so popular with young people. They were able personally to identify with the heroes of the tale they were reading, for nearly all of his principal characters were teenagers very similar to themselves. So it was his readers who rescued helpless natives from a cruel death at the hands of cannibals, or dashed through smoke and flames to the side of the swooning heroine, or plunged

First editions of the works of R. M. Ballantyne, showing the evolution of publishers' binding styles during the period 1848–93, spanned by the appearance of his first book, *Hudson's Bay*, and his last, *The Walrus Hunters*

R. M. Ballantyne supplied nearly all the illustrations for his many books himself. His designs for the frontispiece and engraved title page of the first edition of *The Coral Island*, 1858, are shown here

Given as a bonus with the Christmas number of the magazine *Young England*, 1895, this illustration was later used as a frontispiece for the annual volume issued under the same name

without a moment's hesitation into shark-infested waters for the sake of an injured friend. And, at the end of their courageous display of selfless devotion to duty, they modestly refused to accept any thanks from the victim of the drama other than perhaps a firm shake of the gratefully outstretched hand of one who had been snatched from the jaws of a fearful death. It was during 1858, within a few months of the two books being published, that Ballantyne first experienced the agreeable but embarrassing sensation of being followed through the streets of Edinburgh by admiring youngsters, and his autograph became the prized possession of many a keen Scots lad.

During much of this year Ballantyne was working on the manuscript of a title which proved to be yet another best-seller. *Martin Rattler; or, A Boy's Adventures in the Forests of Brazil*, 1858, appeared in the bookshops in November of that year, and set the seal on his success as a writer of juvenile fiction. He had woven the threads of his narrative into much the same design as those of his previous adventure tales, but this time choosing as his setting the steaming forests and snake-infested swamps of South America. He prefaced the work by telling his readers that 'all the important points and anecdotes are true; only the minor and unimportant ones being mingled with fiction'. This was the foundation on which he was to base nearly every adventure story he wrote, imitating Fenimore Cooper by setting his fictional characters against a background of accurate factual descriptions of the lands and peoples amongst which the tale was made to unfold. He had been badly caught out when writing *The Coral Island*, describing coconuts hanging in bunches in the tree-tops in the same shape and form that he had seen them in his native Scotland in the fair-grounds and green-grocers' shops. Letters arrived by the dozens over the course of the next few years, gleefully pointing out his mistake. He ruefully admitted his error in his autobiographical *Personal Reminiscences in Book-Making*, 1893:

... despite the utmost care of which I was capable, while studying up for the *Coral Island*, I fell into ... a blunder through ignorance in regard to a familiar fruit. I was under the impression that cocoa-nuts grew on their trees in the same form as that in which they are usually presented to us in grocers' windows – namely, about the size of a large fist with three spots, suggestive of a monkey's face, at one end. I sent one of my heroes up a tree for a nut, through the shell of which he bored a hole with a penknife and drank the "lemonade" ... but in fact that cocoa-nut is nearly as large as a man's head, and its outer husk over an inch thick, so that no ordinary penknife could bore into its interior!

The error he made in *The Coral Island*, later reinforced by the discovery of other inaccuracies that had somehow crept into his earlier books, persuaded Ballantyne that he must not only read up his subject thoroughly before starting to write, but he must also do his best to gain first-hand experience of the locality in which he proposed to set his tale. This was certainly not possible with *Martin Rattler*, but it was a story built on a solid sub-stratum of factual information gleaned from a small library of travel books he now used as a reference background. This was a new and refreshing departure in the juvenile novel of mid-Victorian days, and helped to impart to nearly everything Ballantyne wrote a ring of authenticity which masked the improbabilities of most of his plots. It also meant that his young readers had sometimes to wade through several pages of instructional dialogue, in which the fauna and flora were often minutely described, together with a potted history of whatever country or locality they happened to find themselves in. But he was always careful to sandwich these didactic passages between joints of red-blooded action and nail-biting suspense. There was certainly nothing pastel-shaded about his dramatic scenes of action and violent conflict. The savage ferocity of the natives towards the white men they find trespassing on their preserves is only equalled by the cold-blooded slaughter by the white men and their young companions of any creature they see moving in their sights, human or animal, young or old.

The story of *Martin Rattler* is still one of Ballantyne's most readable tales, and is typical of many others he

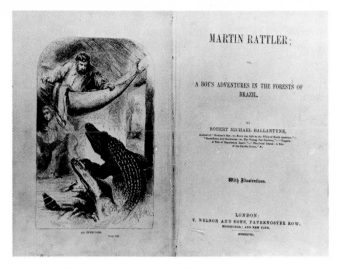

The first edition of one of Ballantyne's most famous books for boys. Dated 1858, the work was later reprinted several times

wrote. The young hero after whom the book is named has been reared by an old and crochety aunt, Dorothy Grumbit. At school he is forced to fight a bully older and heavier than himself in a desperate attempt to save his aunt's white kitten from being slowly drowned before an interested group of the bully's cronies. After a gory battle, Martin knocks the heavier boy unconscious, and is congratulated by an Irish sailor, Barney O'Flannagan by name, who has witnessed the fight. The tales Barney tells the boy about his adventures afloat inflame the lad's imagination with a determination to go to sea, but his aunt tearfully refuses to part with her darling boy. Martin, like the good lad he is, respects her wishes, but is later accidentally swept out to sea in a small punt when boating, only to find himself saved from drowning by the providential appearance of a ship bound for Brazil. One of the salty tars on deck dives overboard to his rescue, and by one of the happy coincidences of fiction Martin's saviour turns out to be none other than his old friend and future shipmate Barney O'Flannagan!

The young man becomes one of the crew, later slipping overboard with Barney when their ship is attacked and overrun by pirates near the coast of South America. They swim ashore and find themselves in Brazil, in whose dense tropical forests they quickly become lost – luckily stumbling on the hut of a hermit just when things seem blackest. After passing a fitful night's sleep in the hut, Martin awakes pale and weak, having been attacked by a vampire bat. He is nursed back to health by the old hermit, who appears to know whole chapters of the Bible off by heart, and later they leave on a hunting expedition. Game abounds, and in the course of a few hours they have succeeded in dashing out the brains of a large iguana by swinging it around by its tail until its head comes in violent contact with a conveniently situated tree; have ruthlessly speared a magnificent jaguar to death; and have built a fire over a hole into which the hermit had observed an armadillo scuttle, thus driving the hapless creature into the open where it is quickly despatched.

A little breathless after this scene of variegated slaughter, Martin and Barney bid goodbye to their pious guide and set off for the Amazon River, where they are befriended by a plantation owner. An invitation to take part in an alligator hunt results in a massacre of every reptile within half a mile of their camp, but shortly afterwards the two friends are taken prisoner by a party of Indians armed with blow-pipes and poisoned arrows. They are separated and taken as prizes to different villages. Martin is made a slave by his Indian hosts, learns a smattering of their language and quickly becomes an expert with the blow-pipe. On being forced to witness a scene of native festivity, in which some of the participants become tipsy and one or two more than a little drunk, Martin leaves the revels 'with a feeling of pity for the poor savages', recalling the soulful cry of his erstwhile friend the hermit – 'They want the Bible in Brazil!'

After months of slavery, Martin escapes from his captors by plunging over a steep precipice into the swirling waters of a rock-bound pool some hundreds of feet below. He spends weeks fending for himself and wandering in the dense jungle before luckily meeting with a party of Brazilians who allow him to accompany them to the diamond mines. Here he is at first ignored and later confined for several hours in a dark and cheerless room by Baron Fagoni, the overseer. Just as Martin is beginning to wonder what next a cruel fate has in store, the door is opened and a dozen slaves enter with flaming candelabra and trays loaded with steaming dishes of mouth-watering food. They are followed by the now smiling Baron Fagoni, who doffs his disguise and reveals himself to be none other than Martin's old friend Barney O'Flannagan. After yet further adventures, the two leave the mine together, and return safe and sound to England, each with about four hundred pounds in his pockets, the proceeds from the sale of gold-dust and diamonds. Arriving once more at his boyhood home, Martin discovers that his old aunt has disappeared from the rustic surroundings of her native village, but he manages to trace her to a cold and dreary garret in Liverpool where she lies dying. The sight of her long-lost nephew has a miraculous effect and quickly restores the old woman to health, and she proudly returns to her ivy-covered cottage. The story rolls on to a happy end, telling how Martin Rattler prospers and eventually becomes a wealthy man, spending his leisure hours visiting the poor and reading a Bible to the sick and bed-ridden, while himself leading a God-fearing and upright life.

It is difficult to imagine our own sophisticated youth accepting as genuine traits of character the evangelical fervour displayed so openly by the heroes Ballantyne created. The boys of today would not be terribly impressed by the priggish attitude of the mid-nineteenth century Martin Rattler, and his obvious pride in the indiscriminate and senseless slaughter of any animal, timid or wild, which happened to stray across his path, would certainly be condemned out of hand. But in the period when his tales appeared, Ballantyne expressed the public mood. Boys thoroughly enjoyed reading about the bloody suppression of native uprisings, the spearing of elephants and the shooting down of row after row of birds and monkeys with poisoned darts or muzzle-loading rifles. Bone-cracking violence is still a best-seller amongst the young and older generations of the present-day, with the emphasis shifted from the animal kingdom to that of civilized man. The right to condemn the sadistic pleasures that have bloodied the pages of juvenile fiction from the days of the eighteenth century chapbooks cannot be the sole prerogative of this, or any other, age. Victorian youth relished reading about the destruction of their imaginary enemies, be they human or animal, in much the same fashion that readers do today. The only variable element in the continuing saga seems the choice of victims.

The World of Ice, 1860, translated Ballantyne's readers back to the Arctic regions; while *The Dog Crusoe*, 1861, he sub-titled 'A Tale of the Western Prairies'; but neither title proved as popular as *The Gorilla Hunters – A Tale of the Wilds of Africa*, 1861. In the early spring of that year, Paul du Chaillu had published *Exploration in Equatorial Africa*, containing some of the first accurate accounts of the gorilla, a species of animal about which little was then known. His tales of the 'ferocious wild men of the forest', as he termed the great anthropoid apes, so engrossed the public's imagination that the Nelson brothers wrote immediately to Ballantyne asking him to prepare a fictional adventure novel on the subject. The controversy surrounding the publication of *On the Origin of Species*, 1859, by Charles Darwin, was raging unabated, and apes and monkeys, big and small, were of intense topical interest. In the publishers' letter was a firm offer to Ballantyne of eighty pounds in cash for the outright purchase of the copyright of the book provided he could complete the tale in time for Christmas publication.

Nelsons' sense of timing and business acumen paid dividends, for the publicity given to Darwin's and du Chaillu's works ensured *The Gorilla Hunters* a very wide sale. The title appealed to the adult imagination as well as to juveniles, so parents, uncles and aunts bought the book in their hundreds as a most acceptable Christmas present for their young charges. Ralph Rover, Jack Martin and Peterkin Gay, all of whom Ballantyne's readers had met and liked in the pages of *The Coral Island*, were once again introduced. They were a little older now, and Ballantyne had transferred the venue to the heart of darkest Africa, where the three young heroes appear intent on killing the maximum number of gorillas in the minimum possible time, plus any other of the continent's fauna which might inadvertently stray within range of their guns.

The principal characters of this plot to wage war on the animal kingdom consist of the narrator, Ralph Rover, an unflappable sober-sided individual cast in the youth-leader image; Jack Martin, 'a tall, strapping, broad-shouldered youth of eighteen, with a handsome, good-humoured, firm face', and Peterkin Gay, 'little, quick, funny, decidedly mischievous, and about fourteen years old'. Viewed from the standpoint of an author, this is a very malleable and interesting trio to work with, the contrasting idiosyncrasies of its members making each easy to identify in the mind of the reader without talented inflexions of emphasis. With Ralph Rover, the narrator of the story, Ballantyne employed quite a modern, sophisticated technique, standing back from the character to derive full benefit from the part he has to play, not merely using him as commentator of events.

In *The Gorilla Hunters*, the author once again plays on the deep-seated fears of the young by confronting them with forces they believe will overwhelm them if not ruthlessly destroyed. Even if one takes the view that most boys are bloodthirsty little savages beneath the veneer which civilised society is supposed to impart (and *The Lord of the Flies*, 1954, by William Golding, lent emphasis to this viewpoint), the immense popularity of *The Gorilla Hunters*, surely one of the most vicious juvenile novels in its treatment of wild animals, must have been stimulated by other qualities besides its cruel hunting scenes. Few copies of the first edition seem to have survived the eager embrace of generations of teenage fingers, and the book appears to have been literally read to death. This scarcity of surviving copies is a measure of the popularity of this widely-read cloth-bound edition, and the very few that have come down to us today in their original pictorial binding show that most must have finished their first few years of existence dog-eared and tattered, finally to be consigned to the dust-bin at the next spring clean.

It was in *The Gorilla Hunters* that Ballantyne revealed his thoughts on the type of life a teenage boy should endeavour to lead by allowing Ralph Rover to soliloquise as he rests exhausted after a series of kills:

Boys should be inured from childhood to trifling risks and slight dangers of every possible description, such as tumbling into ponds and off trees, etc., in order to strengthen their nervous system. . . . They ought to practise leaping off heights into deep water. They ought never to hesitate to cross a stream over a narrow unsafe plank for fear of a ducking. They ought never to decline to climb a tree to pull off fruit, merely because there is a possibility of their falling off and breaking their necks. I firmly believe that boys were intended to encounter all kinds of risks in order to prepare them to meet and grapple with the risks and dangers incident to a man's career with cool, cautious self-possession, a self-possession founded on

PETERKIN TOSSED BY A BUFFALO BULL — Page 114.

NATIVE TOSSED BY A WILD BULL.

R. M. Ballantyne based his book *The Gorilla Hunters*, 1861, on Paul du Chaillu's book *Exploration in Equatorial Africa*, 1861. He also used du Chaillu's illustrations as guides to his own drawings for his boys' adventure novel, as a comparison of these two pictures shows. Du Chaillu's original illustration is below

experimental knowledge of the character and powers of their own spirits and muscles.

The muff is a boy who from natural disposition, or early training, or both, is mild, diffident and gentle. So far he is an estimable character. Were this all, he were not a muff. In order to deserve that title he must be timid and unenthusiastic. He must refuse to venture anything that will subject him to danger, however slight. He must be afraid of a shower of rain; afraid of dogs in general, good and bad alike; disinclined to try bold things; indifferent about learning how to swim. He must object to the game called 'dumps', because the blows from the ball are sometimes severe, and be a sworn enemy to single-stick, because the whacks are uncommonly painful. So feeling and acting, he will, when he becomes a man, find himself unable to act in the common emergencies of life; to protect a lady from insolence; to guard his home from robbery; or to save his own child should it chance to fall into the water.

Let muffs, therefore, learn to swim, to leap, and to run. Let them wrestle with boys bigger than themselves, regardless of being thrown. Let them practise 'jinking' with their companions, so that if ever they be chased by a mad bull, they will, if unable to get out of the way by running, escape perhaps by jinking. Let them learn to leap off considerable heights into deep water, so that, if ever called on to leap off the end of a pier or the side of a ship to save a fellow creature, they may do so with confidence and promptitude. Let them even put on 'the gloves', and become regardless of a swelled nose, in order that they may be able to defend themselves or others from sudden assault. So doing they will become sensible fellows, whose character I have thus, to some extent, described.

The next few chapters are littered with the carcases of the lions, elephants, zebra and other denizens of the jungle which they encountered, while the unfortunate gorillas are shot down with machine-gun-like rapidity:

'It seems to me.' said Jack, 'that notwithstanding

the short time we stayed in the gorilla country, we have been pretty successful. Haven't we bagged thirty-three altogether?'

'Thirty-six, if you count the babies in arms,' responded Peterkin.

'Of course we are entitled to count those.'

'I think you are both out in your reckoning,' said I, drawing out my note-book; 'the last baby that I shot was our thirty-seventh.'

'What!' cried Peterkin, 'the one with the desperately black face and the horrible squint, that nearly tore all the hair out of Jack's head before he managed to strangle it? That wasn't a baby; it was a big boy, and I have no doubt a big rascal besides.'

'That may be so,' I rejoined; 'but whatever he was, I have put him down as number thirty-seven in my list'.

'Pity we didn't make up the forty,' observed Jack.

Whatever a more enlightened age may think of such an enthusiastic tally of kills, there can be little doubt that both the author and publisher were more than satisfied with the reception the book received in the 1860's. During the succeeding years it passed through numerous editions, but Ballantyne had to be content with the single lump sum payment of eighty pounds his publishers allowed. This was the last book he wrote for Thomas Nelson and Sons: they resolutely refused to allow him a proper scale of royalties against the continuing sales of his earlier titles, and he became determined to submit no further manuscripts to their care.

As far as the eldest partner of Thomas Nelson & Sons was concerned, there might not have been a Copyright Act, 1842. His stubborn refusal to negotiate royalty agreements with new and comparatively unknown authors lost the firm many of the most profitable writers in their stable of novelists. The rights of a title, he insisted, had to be sold for a lump sum, and he was astute enough to make this just large enough to prove well nigh irresistible to the impecunious hopefuls who submitted their manuscripts. Had Ballantyne been a married man with a family to

A DESPERATE STRUGGLE FOR LIFE

A SPILL.—*Frontispiece.*—PAGE 88.

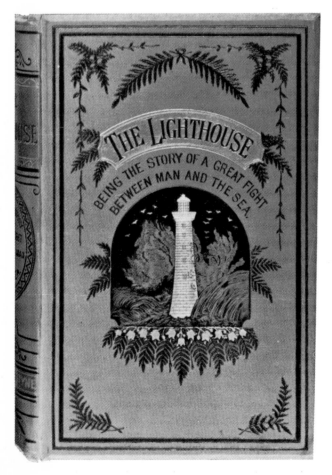

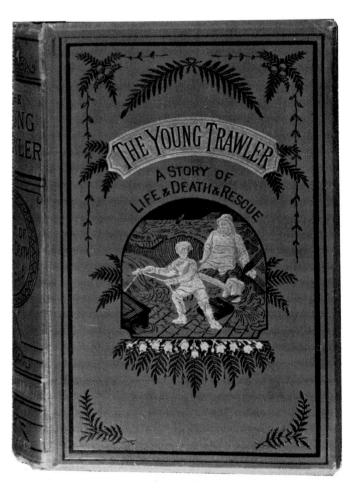

Two original drawings by
R. M. Ballantyne for his
book *Freaks on the Fells*, 1865

Uncle Bob meets with an accident.

After which he feels peculiarly uncomfortable.

support, it is extremely doubtful if he would have had the courage to sever his relationship with the firm; but he was now determined that if he was ever to earn an adequate living by his pen he had to find a publishing house willing to give him his fair share of the profits his books earned.

The Golden Dream; or, Adventures in the Far West, 1861, appeared under the imprint of John F. Shaw & Co; while *The Red Eric; or, The Whaler's Last Cruise*, 1861, and *The Wild Man of the West*, 1863, were published by Routledge, Warne and Routledge; but Ballantyne had still not formed a satisfactory relationship with a publishing house he could trust to guard his interests. He submitted the manuscript of *Gascoyne, The Sandal-Wood Trader*, 1864, to James Nisbet & Co., Berners Street, London, who immediately accepted the book and sent him a cheque for £80 ($192) on account of royalties expected to accrue from the first edition of two thousand copies. 'I never got more from Nelson for any book,' he told his sister, and this despite the fact that as many as twenty five thousand copies of some of his early titles had now been printed and sold. From that time onwards all Ballantyne's annual volumes bore the James Nisbet imprint, only the occasional work that appeared in serial form in magazines going elsewhere. The company treated him well, all his books earning him regular royalty payments commensurate with the number of copies sold, and for the first time Ballantyne was in receipt of a substantial income from his literary work.

The Lifeboat, A Tale of our Coast Heroes, 1864, was published in November of that year as his Christmas book. It marked the beginning of the author's long series of boyish escapes from everyday life in search of adventure images. In the following years we find him marooned for weeks on a lighthouse, finding background material for *The Lighthouse*, 1865; dashing through the London streets on a swaying fire-engine, for *Fighting the Flames*, 1867; in a granite mine-gallery thousands of feet underground, for *Deep Down – A Tale of the Cornish Mines*, 1868; drenched to the skin in the North Sea, for *The Floating Light of the Goodwin Sands*, 1870; speeding as driver of an express train, for

The Iron Horse, or Life on the Line, 1871; disguised as an Arab in the native quarter of Algiers, for *The Pirate City – an Algerine Tale*, 1874; disappearing beneath the sea as a diver, for *Under the Waves, or Diving in Deep Waters*, 1876; detecting crime in the Post Office, for *Post Haste, a Tale of Her Majesty's Mails*, 1880; and hauling the nets of a deep-sea trawler, for *The Young Trawler, a Story of Life and Death and Rescue on the North Sea*, 1884. This lists only a few of his documentary adventure novels for young people. Before writing any one of them, he lived the part of his characters for a few weeks, ensuring that his background material was as factual as actual experience of the conditions of the tale could make it.

Prior to commencing the story of *The Lifeboat* he lived for several weeks at Deal, in Kent, eagerly donning a sou'wester and oilskin coat to join the crew of the rescue boat whenever a storm threatened shipwreck and disaster. He had no sooner seen the book through the press, than he set out to walk the distance of 'some four hundred and twenty six miles, by the route I pursued' that separated London from Edinburgh, hoping to sell the story of his journey as a serial to one of the fashionable London magazines. He arrived at his destination, footsore and weary, at the end of May, 1864, but within a day or two was writing to the Commissioners of the Northern Lighthouses asking their permission to spend a fortnight in the Bell Rock Lighthouse, twelve miles off the coast of Forfarshire, Scotland. When it appeared the following Christmas, *The Lighthouse* was even more successful than *The Lifeboat* had been, yet no fewer than four editions of fifteen hundred copies each of the latter title had been issued before the end of 1865.

Ballantyne was easily the most successful of the

many authors whose talents were wholly engaged in writing adventure novels for teenagers. Despite his generous treatment of several members of his immediate family, most of whom appeared to be continuously in 'straitened circumstances', he had managed to save sufficient capital from his literary earnings to enable him to think about taking a wife of his choice and shouldering the responsibilities of raising a family. When he was forty one, he and Miss Jane Grant, an Edinburgh girl some twenty years his junior, were married at Park Place in her native city. It was here, at Millerfield Place, that they lived for many years; later moving to Harrow-on-the-Hill, London, with what finally proved to be a family of six healthy children.

Shifting Winds – A Tough Yarn, 1866, was the first book Ballantyne completed after his marriage, inscribing it, in loving terms, to Jeannie, his wife. With a family to support, books came thick and fast – *Silver Lake; or, Lost in the Snow*, 1867; *Erling the Bold*, 1869; *The Norsemen in the West*, 1872; *The Pioneers, A Tale of the Western Wilderness*, 1872; *Life in the Red Brigade* (1873); *Black Ivory*, 1873; these being interspersed with the previous titles cited, several remunerative hackwork items, and a selection of stories in his *Tales of Adventure* series. *The Ocean and its Wonders*, 1874; and *Rivers of Ice*, 1875, for which he spent several months in Switzerland; were followed by *The Settler and the Savage*, 1877, and *In the Track of the Troops*, 1878. The following year he made a journey to Cape Town, writing *Six Months at the Cape*, 1879, and *The Red Man's Revenge*, 1880. The story of *Philosopher Jack*, 1880; *Post Haste*, 1880; and *The Lonely Island, or The Refuge of the Mutineers*, 1880; all appeared within a few months of one another.

Until the year of his death in Rome, Ballantyne always turned out at least two full-length books for boys each year, the best of his later titles being: *The Giant of the North*, 1882; *The Battery and the Boiler*, 1883, an adventure story describing the hazardous laying of submarine electric cables; *The Madman and the Pirate*, 1883; *Dusty Diamonds Cut and Polished*, 1884; *Twice Bought, A Tale of the Oregon Gold Fields*, 1885; *The Rover of the Andes*, 1885; *The Prairie Chief*, 1886;

The Big Otter, 1887; *Blue Lights, or Hot Work in the Soudan*, 1888; *The Eagle Cliff* (1889); *Charlie to the Rescue*, 1890; and *The Buffalo Runners*, 1891.

By this time Ballantyne's health was rapidly failing. He was suffering from Ménière's Disease, a chronic complaint causing attacks of intense giddiness lasting a few minutes to many hours, and a large part of his savings were spent in paying the fees of doctors and specialists, none of whom did him the slightest good. Finally, accompanied by his daughter, Jean, he left England for Italy in October, 1893, bound for a nature-cure clinic at San Antonio, Tivoli. It was a last attempt to effect some sort of a partial cure. Several months of hard Italian winter, during which the disease became progressively worse, at last caused him to lose heart. It was on his way home to England that he collapsed and died in Rome on 8th February, 1894. He was buried in the Protestant Cemetery there, his grave being within a few yards of the casket containing the heart of Shelley and close to the spot where the body of the poet Keats lies.

The amount of space devoted to this one Victorian author is a measure of the influence his works exerted over his contemporaries and the writers who later followed in his footsteps. He was a particular hero to young Robert Louis Stevenson, who dogged his steps for a whole morning back in May, 1866, sitting a few rows behind him when Ballantyne and his wife-to-be attended St Cuthbert's parish church, Leith. As Bob and his fiancée left the church arm-in-arm to walk home, they were stopped within a few yards of the lych-gate by the fifteen years old Stevenson, who apologised sincerely for his intrusion, but begged to inform Mr Ballantyne how much he enjoyed reading his books. On being asked which of his books Stevenson had like best, Ballantyne was informed that the young man thought *The Coral Island* a wonderfully exciting story and that he had already read it twice and hoped to read it twice more. After they had said goodbye to the thin and delicate-looking lad and commenced walking home, Ballantyne turned and saw the future author of *Treasure Island* still gazing after him in rapt admiration.

The story of their meeting is related in full in

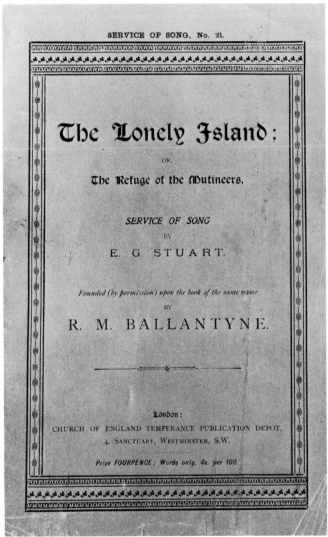

Ballantyne the Brave, but the incident detailed above lends weight to the supposition that Stevenson's passionate love of the romantic islands of the South Seas, to one of which he eventually retired and died, may first have been kindled by his reading of the adventures of Ralph, Jack and Peterkin as they fought the cannibals and braved the dangers of shipwreck and desert sand. When, in 1883, the first edition of *Treasure Island* appeared in the bookshops, Stevenson remembered his boyhood hero in the lines which preceded the text:

> If sailor tales to sailor tunes,
> Storm and adventure, heat and cold,
> If schooners, islands, and maroons
> And Buccaneers and buried Gold,
> And all the old romance, retold
> Exactly in the ancient way,
> Can please, as me they pleased of old,
> The wiser youngsters of today:
>
> – So be it, and fall on! If not,
> If studious youth no longer crave,
> His ancient appetites forgot,
> Kingston, or Ballantyne the Brave,
> Or Cooper of the wood and wave:
> So be it, also! And may I
> And all my pirates share the grave
> Where these and their creations lie!

In his last years as a writer Ballantyne produced *The*

Coxswain's Bride, 1891; *Hunted and Harried* (1892); *The Hot Swamp*, 1892; and *The Walrus Hunters*, 1893. His autobiographical *Personal Reminiscences in Book-Making* (1893), an unfortunate title that was later re-issued as *An Author's Adventures*, was followed by a posthumous work that ranks as the most difficult of his first editions to discover in any form of binding. *Reuben's Luck – A Tale of the Wild North* (1896), was issued by the S.P.C.K., London, in coloured pictorial paper wrappers, in their series *The Penny Library of Fiction*, and seems to have disintegrated in the intervening years. Only two copies have been located.

Despite his too-good-to-be-true heroes and often threadbare plots, Ballantyne has earned a place far above the lowly in the annals of English juvenile literature. As one of the first authors to allow his youthful characters to wander far from home, unrestrained by the curbing hands and stifling platitudes of accompanying adults; and as a pioneer of the straightforward adventure story woven into a well-researched factual background, he deserves a measure of literary immortality. His weakness lay in his being straitjacketed by his puritanical Scottish upbringing, so that the action in his stories may well suddenly be braked by a pious outburst from one of the blood-thirsty young characters he made his heroes. He was considerably less didactic and self-righteous than writers who had gone before, and his excellent qualities as a story-teller held the attention of his readers from one volume to the next. And after a little evangelistic soliloquising his teenager characters quickly resumed their lighthearted slaughter of the fauna and the nearest available natives, before once again falling on their knees to thank God for a very successful day's sport. Notwithstanding his manifest faults, and the fact that he was never able to write a book that was completely free of moralising and unashamedly earthy – as Stevenson did when he produced his immortal *Treasure Island* – the boys of Victoria's Britain purchased his annual Christmas tales in their thousands.

He portrayed a world in which the good were terribly good, and the bad were terribly bad, and the British were terribly British – and worth ten of any foreigners alive, by Jingo! For any writer to have dared to suggest otherwise would have been considered the blackest heresy by the young men of his day. His readers were the boys who were to become the explorers and trail-blazers, the missionaries and merchant adventurers, the soldiers and sailors, the Word-Spreaders, the successes and failures of the great British Empire on which the sun would never set.

The Treasure Seekers

The lucrative market that was opening up in the early 1850's to satisfy the appetite of young teenagers for novels and adventure stories of their own, soon attracted a wide variety of writers whose talents were as diverse as the plots they created. Many graduated into the school by way of the three-decker novel or travel book written for an increasingly sophisticated adult readership, an ever-expanding class whose critical demands caused many of the less talented writers either to fall by the wayside or to find a thankful haven in the realms of juvenile fiction. Amongst those who set out to seek their fortune on the high seas of boys' adventure tales was a man whose earliest juvenile novels preceded those of Ballantyne by several years, and who later became both his most serious literary rival and one of his closest friends.

William Henry Giles Kingston (1814–80) was born in Harley Street, London, the eldest son of Lucy Henry Kingston, and grandson on his mother's side of Sir Giles Rooke. His father conducted a successful business in Oporto, and it was there, for many years, that young Kingston lived, his frequent voyages between Portugal and England instilling a love of the sea that was later reflected in the many seafaring adventure stories he wrote. Unlike Ballantyne, who never attempted any fictional work for the adult market, Kingston commenced his literary career with the publication of several three volume novels that soon found their way into the circulating and subscription libraries. They included *The Circassian Chief*, 3 vols, 1843; *The Prime Minister*, 3 vols, 1845; *The Albatross*, 3 vols, 1849; as well as several books of travel, such as *Lusitanian Sketches*, 2 vols, 1845; and *Western Wanderings; or, a Pleasure Tour in the Canadas*, 2 vols, 1856.

None of these works created any considerable stir in literary circles, but the fact that he could now call himself a fully-fledged author proved of great help when he decided to make journalism his career. He was appointed editor of several periodicals, notably *The Colonist* and *The Colonial Magazine and East India Revue*. He became sought after as a lecturer and took a particular interest in the ever-growing army of unemployed and poverty-stricken workers and their families that crowded into the ports and larger cities throughout the land. He even devised a scheme for their resettlement abroad, and articles setting out the supposed advantages of emigration to the far-flung shores of the British Empire, or into the still welcoming arms of the United States and Canada, came frequently from his pen. *How to Emigrate; or, The British Colonists*, 1850, enjoyed a considerable sale, and Kingston fast became an acknowledged authority on the subject of shipping the unwanted influx of Irish emigrants and unemployed 'lower-orders' to the sparsely-populated ends of the earth. Ridding Britain of the surplus work-force created by the Hungry Forties in Ireland and the drift from the land at home became a political dogma he advocated with increasing vigour for the rest of his life.

The most important turning point in Kingston's career came when he was thirty seven years old. It was the year 1850, at a time when he was still a bachelor working hard to make a living solely by his pen. He had recently completed *The Pirate of the Mediterranean – A Tale of the Sea*, a three-volume novel, issued early in 1850, but dated forward on the title-pages to 1851, a common practice with Victorian publishing houses. Several of his friends had told him of the interest young people had taken in the work, the teenagers of the household commandeering the book as their own, then disappearing for hours at a time while they devoured the story in private. Kingston needed little persuading that a tale of adventure, specially written for young people, would almost certainly find a ready sale, and he put the proposition to Grant & Griffiths, his London publishers. The result was the appearance, in November 1850, of the book by which he is most often remembered today, a work that almost instantly brought him to the notice of a wide public as the author of an enduring best-seller.

Peter the Whaler, 1851, was published in an attractive binding of red straight-grained cloth, blocked on the sides in blind-stamping and on the spine pictorially in gold. The four full-page illustrations by the landscape painter Edward Duncan (1804–82) captured the spirit of the story in a way that must have pleased

The last picture of W. H. G.
Kingston, taken shortly
before he wrote his farewell
letter to his young readers of
the *Boy's Own Paper*

THE INGENA.

PAGE 208.

below
Believed to be the first
printed picture of a gorilla
to appear in any book, this
illustration is taken from
The African Wanderers, 1847,
by Mrs R. Lee. The name
'gorilla' was coined that
same year by the explorer
Dr. T. S. Savage

the author's heart (see illustration page 68). At 6s. a copy (also obtainable at 6/6d. 'with gilt edges'), it sold so well in the bookshops at Christmas that Kingston's publishers immediately commissioned a series of similar titles from his pen.

The book vividly describes the adventures of young Peter Lefroy, the fifteen year old son of an Irish Protestant clergyman; a boy whose passion for shooting over his neighbour's estates leads to his arrest by Lord Fetherston's gamekeepers. Despite his tender years, the noble lord insists on keeping the lad in solitary confinement for several days, and then orders his father to have him sent to sea for at least a year as a punishment for his misdeeds. Without more ado, Peter is taken to Liverpool, and it is there that he signs on as one of the crew of the *Black Swan*, under the command of the rascally Capt. Swales. The ship sails for North America heavily loaded with several hundred Irish emigrants, and no sooner are they on the high seas that a long series of trials and tribulations begin. The *Black Swan* navigates too far north and is trapped in floes and icebergs; fire breaks out below decks and the steerage passengers riot and plunder the vessel's stores of food and drink. Worse still! their only supplies of drinking-water are broached in a desperate attempt to quell the flames. Before long crew and passengers are dying like flies of disease and the extremities of thirst; the fire being held partly in check as the vessel ships increasing amounts of sea-water. Capt. Swales deserts the slowly sinking ship, while young Peter bravely stays behind to assist what are left of the unfortunate emigrants. In the nick of time, he and those still living are rescued by the crew of the ship *Mary*, named after Mary Dean, the captain's daughter, with whom Peter falls winsomely in love.

After a series of storms and fearsome gales, they reached Quebec, where Peter disappears for a few week's shooting and trapping with his new-found friend Silas Flint. When he returns he learns that the *Mary* has sailed for New Orleans without him, taking the captain's daughter with her; but Peter is soon in hot pursuit. At New Orleans, he ships on board *The Foam*, a suspiciously rakish schooner captained by

A boys' book of 1856

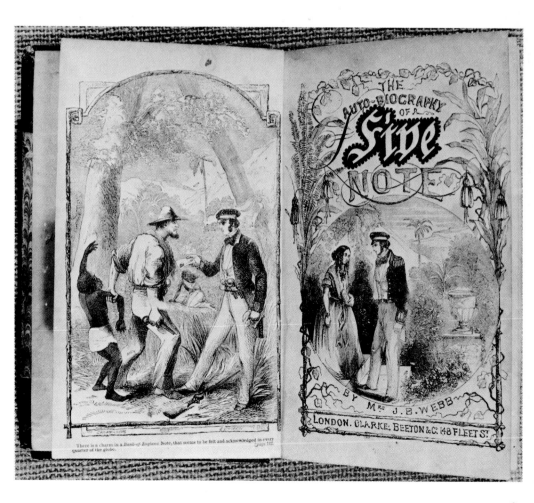

Frontispiece and title page
of a popular boys' adventure
story, 1853

CAPTURING OUR FIRST WHALE

PAGE 245.

John Hawk, and the lad soon discovers that he is a member of the crew of a slaver and pirate. Kingston's knowledge of the sea is now displayed to the full in the descriptions he gives his readers of the manning and working of the pirate schooner, and of the fights and storms that follow in quick succession throughout the chapters of the book. Cruising off the Bahamas, they sight a sail on the horizon and are soon crowding on the canvas to give chase:

I thought, when I went on deck, that nothing would tempt me to take any part in the acts of the pirates, even so far as in assisting to navigate the vessel; but there is something so exciting in the chase of a vessel, that it is difficult not to wish to come up with her. At first I stood merely looking on, but the breeze freshened, and rather headed us; and Hawk issued an order to flatten in the fore-and-aft sails, and to brace up the yards. I flew instinctively to the sheets, and found myself pulling and hauling with the rest.

The captain made no remark; nor did he appear even to notice what I had done. The wind was about south, and the chase was to the eastward, standing us on a bowline. She was a brig of some size; and at first glance I thought she was a man-of-war; but Hawk pronounced her to be a Spaniard, and homeward bound from Cuba.

Hawk, who was usually so calm and almost apathetic, walked the deck full of energy and excitement. Every order he gave was uttered in a sharp quick tone, which demanded instant obedience. . . . We rapidly came up with the chase, and were within about three miles of her, when she began, it seemed, to suspect that all was not right, for sail after sail was set on her, till she could carry no more, while she edged a little from her course, so as to allow every one of them to draw properly. This threw us soon completely to windward, for we held on the same course as before; and she appeared at first to be recovering her lost ground. In a short time we also kept away with the wind almost a-beam, a point on which *The Foam* sailed her best.

The brig once more hauled her wind, and this brought us soon nearer again to her. Hawk thought it was because the captain saw indications of a shift of wind, and hoped to be placed well to windward. He was scrutinising her narrowly through a telescope. 'She does not shew any guns,' he remarked; 'but it is no reason that she has not got them. Get all ready for action, in case she should prove a Tartar.'

I scarcely knew what I was about; but I confess that I not only assisted to hand up the powder and shot, but to load and run out the guns.

Neither of us made any further variation in our course; but the chase was, it appeared, a very slow sailer, for we so rapidly came up with her, that five hours after she was seen, she was within range of our guns. She did not fire, nor did we; for supposing her to be unarmed, Hawk was anxious to capture her without in any way injuring her hull or cargo.

An illustration by E. Duncan
for *Peter the Whaler*, 1851, by
W. H. G. Kingston

We sailed on, therefore, as if we were engaged in a friendly race; and no one, by looking at us, could have supposed that we were deadly enemies.

Still we stood on till the chase was within the distance of half the range of our guns. I was again aft. 'Hoist our bunting to make him shew his colours,' I heard Hawk say; 'and give him a shot from our bow-chaser to hurry him.'

Directly afterwards, a broad red flag, without any device, was run up at our peak, and with a spout of smoke, a shot went flying over the water, and with a crash that made the splinters fly, it struck the dark sides of the brig. The effect was instantaneous, and such as was little expected by the pirates. A flag was run up to the gaff of the brig; but instead of the Spanish ensign, the stars and stripes of the United States was displayed; and the ports were opened as if by magic, eight guns were run out, and luffing up, she let fly her broadside right into our bows. The shot tore up our decks, and knocked away part of our starboard bulwarks, killing two of our people, and wounding three more, but without injuring our rigging. Then I saw the sort of men I was mingling with. I cannot describe the fierce rage which took possession of them; the oaths and execrations to which they gave vent. The bodies of the two men killed, while yet warm, were thrown overboard directly they were found to be dead, and the wounded were dragged below, and left without a surgeon or any one to attend them. Instead of the timid Spanish merchantman we expected to get alongside, we found that this vessel was none other than a United States man-of-war sent to look out for *The Foam*, in fact, we had caught a Tartar. Hawk, to do him justice, stood undaunted, his energies rising with the occasion. Keeping away a little, so as to get our broadside to bear, we fired in return, and the guns being planted high, some of the running rigging was cut away, and her foretop-mast was struck, and must have been badly wounded, for some hands instantly were seen going aloft to fish it.

'About ship, my lads – down with the helm; and while she's in stays, give Uncle Sam our larboard broadside.'

The sails of the schooner were well full; she quickly came round, and before the brig could follow our example, we sent the shot from our whole broadside flying among her rigging. A loud shout of exultation from our pirate crew shewed their satisfaction at the damage they had done; for several spars and sails, with blocks and ropes, were seen coming down by the run on deck.

'Now, my lads, let's up stick and away,' cried Hawk. 'They thought, doubtless, that they were sure of us; but we'll shew them that *The Foam* is not to be caught so easily.'

All hands who could be spared from the guns, and I among the rest, flew to their stations to trim sails; the yards were braced sharp up, and with her head to the south-west, *The Foam* stood away on a bowline from her powerful antagonist. We were not to escape, however, with impunity; for as soon as the brig's crew had somewhat recovered from the confusion into which the damage done by our shot had thrown them, such guns as could be brought to bear were fired at us with no bad aim. One struck our taffrail, and another killed a man on the forecastle; but our rigging escaped. Twice the brig missed stays in attempting to come about, from so much of her head-sail having been cut away, and this, as she all the time was sailing one way and we the other, contributed much to increase our distance. At last, at a third trial, the brig came about, while she continued without cessation firing at us. Not much damage was done, though our sails had daylight made through them several times by her shot, and another man was killed; but this casualty the pirates seemed to make light of: it was the fortune of war, and might happen every instant to any one of us. . . .

We soon found that the brig-of-war, instead of being a slow sailer, was remarkably fast, and that while we were in chase of her, she must, by towing a sail overboard, or by some other manoeuvre, have deadened her way on purpose to allow us to come up with her. We had now, therefore, to put the schooner's best leg foremost to get away from her, even before she had got all her gear aloft again. To try and do her further damage a gun was got over the taffrail, and a constant fire was kept up from it as fast as it could be loaded. . . .

The brig did not fire at us, as to do so she would have had to yaw and thus lose ground, while we continued to ply her with our long gun. Her fore-topsail could not be set while the mast was being fished. An attempt was now made to hoist it; but the breeze at that instant strengthening, away went the mast, rigging and sail together. A loud cheer arose from our decks: a parting shot was given her from our gun, and in two hours darkness hid her from our sight.

Passages like the one quoted above eventually earned Kingston the title of 'the boys' Marryat'. It seems plain that, on his many voyages to Portugal and back to England, he personally took part in the manning and working of the sailing ships in which he travelled. It was an exciting and vigorous experience in which a young man with a love of the sea would revel, and by which the long hours aboard a creaking and yawing three-master could profitably be turned to account. These voyages certainly stood him in good stead in later years. His intimate knowledge of every facet of seamanship, coupled with his seemingly inexhaustible store of exciting incident, meant that the action seldom flagged in the stories he wrote about the sea.

Peter the Whaler was a longer book than the average juvenile novel of the period, and young Peter Lefroy's adventures were still less than half-way through. By his escape from the pirates he landed himself into even deeper trouble. Capt. Hawk had forced him to take the binding oath of the buccaneers, an oath which, Peter says later, effectively prevented him from deserting ship when the opportunity at last arrived. Hidden in a small lagoon in one of the Bahama Keys, the pirates believe themselves quite safe from detection, but the schooner is eventually spotted by the American brig *Neptune*, fiercely engaged, and finally blown sky-high. Peter and a few of the crew escape death, only to be captured and sent as prisoners to stand trial for piracy at Charles-town. All are sentenced to hang from the yard-arm of an American man-of-war; but at this point in the tale Kingston draws his young audience on one side and quells their fears by confiding:

Now the reader will almost be prepared to know how I (Peter) was saved. I must own that I never expected to be hung. I felt I was innocent, and I trusted that some means would be offered for my escape.

This, happily, proves to be the case, witnesses as to his former good conduct arriving in the proverbial nick of time. His sentence is commuted to one of serving before the mast for two years in a ship of war; thus giving the author ample opportunity to continue his adventures through chapter after chapter of death and destruction. In the latter half of the book, Peter finally becomes a whaler, until he is marooned amongst a tribe of Esquimaux who befriend and care for him for several years. Rescued by a French whaler, he is once again shipwrecked, this time on the west coast of Ireland, and returns to his home there half-starving and in rags and tatters:

I set off alone, and a stranger, without shoes, hat or jacket, to beg my way across Ireland. Some disbelieved the tale I told of my disasters, and turned me from their doors; but others gave me bread and meat, and the poorest never refused me a potatoe and a drink of milk, for their eyes, accustomed to real misery, could discern that I spoke the truth.

But all finally ends happily. He is reunited with his parents in Dublin, discovers his beloved Mary and her father in the same city, and henceforth resolves to live a better and more obedient life:

'Well, Peter,' said my father, after I had been washed and clothed, and had put on once more the appearance of a gentleman, 'you have come back, my lad, poorer than you went away, I fear.' He made this remark with the kind intention of filling

Four volumes of *Kingston's Magazine for Boys*, 1860–63, were published and monthly parts (as shown) of the fifth volume were issued. Few copies have survived, and volume 5 was never published in book form

a purse my sisters and Mary had given me.

'No, father,' I answered, 'I have come back infinitely richer. I have learned to fear God, to worship Him in His works, and to trust to His infinite mercy. I have also learned to know myself, and to take advice and counsel from my superiors in wisdom and goodness.'

'Then,' said my father, 'I am indeed content; and I trust others may take a useful lesson from the adventures of PETER THE WHALER.'

Kingston borrowed extensively from the works of other authors in order to write this book. The liberties Ballantyne permitted himself when writing *The Coral Island*, and his unacknowledged debt to Bowman's *Island Home* and Jenkins's *Recent Exploring Expeditions* has already been stated. Most of the technical information for the whaling episodes Kingston appears to have lifted bodily from *The Arctic Regions and the Northern Whale-Fishery*, 2 vols, 1820, by William Scorseby (1789–1857). He also drew on *Memorials of the Sea*, 1833, by the same author, and appears to have been stimulated into writing *Peter the Whaler* by the publication of Scorseby's *The Whaleman's Adventures in the Southern Ocean*, 1850, a boys' adventure book issued about a year before Kingston's work. The only illustration in the former volume, depicting a whaling scene (drawn by Duncan), bears a striking resemblance to one of the eight full-page plates Henry Vizetelly supplied for Scorseby's earlier work. Plagiarization of this description was common practice amongst writers of juvenile novels during most of the

nineteenth century, and Kingston was only as guilty in this respect as his rivals. He escaped uncensored, for this particular piece of literary piracy was not detected by the critics and reviewers of his own day and age.

The success of this tale of the sea made it the archetype of several dozen others that came from Kingston's pen during the ensuing years, and it was only when, as a writer, he ventured too long on to dry land, that his powers of invention seemed to flag and the pace of his stories to slow. He was no match for Ballantyne when in the heart of the Amazonian forests or digging for gold in California, but give him a schooner full of buccaneers scudding before a threatening gale and Kingston was able to hold his own with any writer living. This was undoubtedly his forte, and once having discovered his literary strongpoint he settled down to make full use of his abilities by providing his young readers with a continual stream of adventure novels.

The Ocean Queen and the Spirit of the Storm, 1851, was set in the Southern Seas; but his next considerable success came with *Mark Seaworth; A Tale of the Indian Ocean*, 1852, a story he dedicated to his brother, George Templeman Kingston, M.A., then a tutor at Cambridge University. As the first boys' book to feature the gruesome rites of the head-hunters and Dyak tribes of Borneo, it fascinated its readers to an extent that called for several editions over the next few years. Sea battles and pirates occur in nearly every chapter, interspersed with the occasional political soliloquy in praise of the British Raj:

To what nobler purpose could the power and influence of Great Britain be turned, than by putting a stop to such atrocities [i.e. slavery], and by bringing the blessings of Christianity and civilization among a people so capable of benefiting by them. Until piracy is put down by force, and the piratical tribes are taught, by severe and summary punishment, that these proceedings are against the laws of nations, those blessings cannot be enjoyed by the people of the Eastern islands. I firmly believe that the power we possess

Part of the author's library
of first editions of boys'
adventure stories

The same book over a
period of thirty-five years.
The first edition, issued
under the imprint of F. V.
White & Co., and dated
1896, is shown at top left.
Editions published in
cheaper bindings continued
to appear every few years,
until even the title itself was
updated in 1931 to that
shown at bottom right. The
text remained identical with
that of the first edition

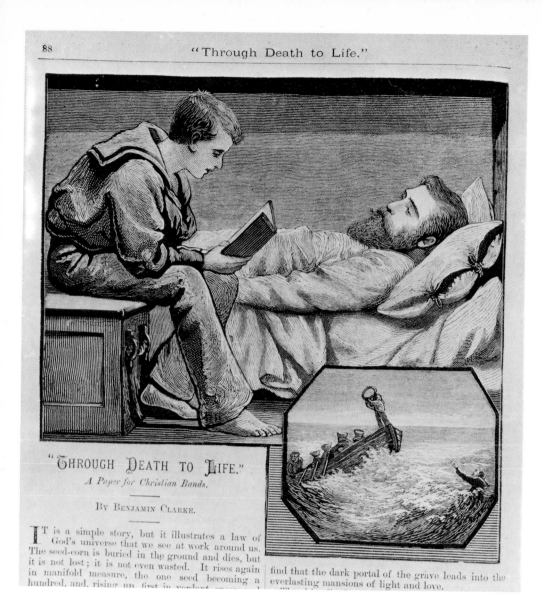

"THROUGH DEATH TO LIFE."

A Paper for Christian Bands.

BY BENJAMIN CLARKE.

IT is a simple story, but it illustrates a law of God's universe that we see at work around us. The seed-corn is buried in the ground and dies, but it is not lost; it is not even wasted. It rises again in manifold measure, the one seed becoming a hundred, and, rising up first in verdant grass and

find that the dark portal of the grave leads into the everlasting mansions of light and love.

A typical death-bed scene from the magazine *Young England.* Many Victorian writers endeavoured to incorporate at least one death-bed conversion or dying repentance in each full-length story

was given us by Providence for that great object – not for war and conquest, but to ensure peace and to repress wrong – and that unless we so employ it, most assuredly it will be taken away from us. I assert, therefore, that this duty, which has been sadly neglected by Holland, and but feebly performed by Spain, has especially devolved on Great Britain.

These were the sentiments that imbued the writings of nearly every adventure novelist of the mid-Victorian era. No sooner had their young heroes landed on a foreign shore than the revolting natives were most forcibly subdued, their tribal customs swept ruthlessly away, and the blessings afforded by Christianity and Western civilization left simmering before them when the adventurers sailed for home. In the age in which the books were written things could hardly have been otherwise.

Kingston saw to it that his readers were not disappointed in this or any other Empire-building aspect by planting the flag of British dominance and God-fearing benevolence in every territory his

characters invaded. Many and bloody were the battles which raged on his pages to bring peace to foreign lands, and many were the struggles to further the commercial interests of the enterprising merchants whose labours ensured British prosperity. These and related interests are reflected in the titles of the juvenile novels that flowed from the pen of this prolific writer in seemingly ever-increasing numbers as he advanced in years. They fill eight closely-printed pages in the British Museum Catalogue, yet the holdings of even that august establishment are far from complete. A cross-section taken from my own shelves lists tales covering a diversity of aspects of boys' adventure stories, many of the earlier titles being now almost impossible to acquire in acceptable condition in their original pictorial-cloth bindings. *Mance, the Peruvian Chief,* 1853, eluded me for years, before being tracked down in the back room of a small Birmingham secondhand bookshop; while *Salt Water; or, The Sea Life and Adventures of Neil D'Arcy,* 1857, was almost as difficult to find. *Fred Markham in Russia; or, The Boy Travellers in the Land of the Czar,* 1858, was issued under the imprint of Griffith &

ADVENTURE WITH CURL-CRESTED TOUCANS.

Frontispiece to Vol. I.

THE

NATURALIST ON THE RIVER AMAZONS,

A RECORD OF ADVENTURES, HABITS OF ANIMALS, SKETCHES OF BRAZILIAN AND INDIAN LIFE, AND ASPECTS OF NATURE UNDER THE EQUATOR, DURING ELEVEN YEARS OF TRAVEL.

By HENRY WALTER BATES.

Saüba Ant.—Female.

IN TWO VOLUMES.—VOL. I.

LONDON:
JOHN MURRAY, ALBEMARLE STREET.
1863.
[The Right of Translation is Reserved.]

Farran, London, who had earlier published his *Blue Jackets; or, Chips off the Old Block*, 1854, at the surprisingly high price of 7/6d a copy. 'A more acceptable testimonial than this to the valour and enterprise of the British Navy has not issued from the press for many years,' wrote the reviewer in the literary periodical *The Critic*; and Kingston returned to the same theme with *The Early Life of Old Jack: A Sea Tale*, 1859. *Round the World: A Tale for Boys*, 1859, is sought as much by collectors of tales of travel, due to its vivid description of San Francisco in the chapter headed 'Californian Experiences', as by collectors of boys' adventure stories, thus forcing up the price of good copies in original pictorial-cloth bindings to around the £20 ($48) mark.

Amongst the best of Kingston's other tales are *Old Jack – A Man-of-War's-Man and South-Sea Whaler*, 1859, a sequel to the similar title mentioned above; *Digby Heathcote: or, The Early Days of a Country Gentleman's Son and Heir*, 1860, with a notable series of illustrations by Harrison Weir; *Ernest Bracebridge; or,*

School Days, 1860; *My First Voyage to Southern Seas*, 1860, published by T. Nelson & Sons with a series of coloured full-page illustrations; and *Adventures of Dick Onslow among the Red Skins*, 1863, with 'by Barrington Beaver, Esq' on the title-page, although Kingston's name also appears as 'editor' of the tale.

From that time onwards titles appeared every few months, but I have space to mention only a handful of favourites, such as *John Deane of Nottingham*, 1870; *Great African Travellers*, 1874, a non-fictional work complete with folding-map and dozens of illustrations to delight the hearts of boys; *The Three Midshipmen*, 1873; *The Three Lieutenants; or, Naval Life in the Nineteenth Century*, 1875, both tales full of wrecks and seafaring disasters; *The Frontier Fort; or, Stirring times in the North-West Territory of British America* (1879), issued undated under the S.P.C.K. imprint; and *In the Wilds of Florida*, 1880. To give some idea of Kingston's prodigious output of boys' adventure stories, one can quote a string of titles all published during a single twelve month period. Here on my shelves I have first

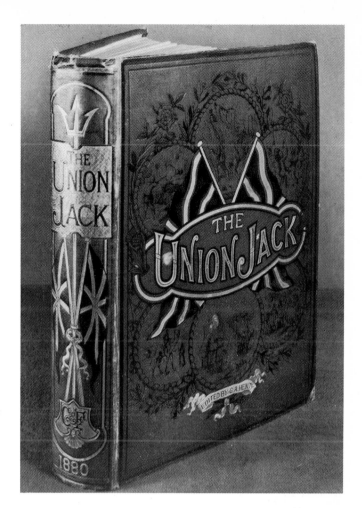

editions of *In the Rocky Mountains*, 1878; *The Three Admirals*, 1878; *With Axe and Rifle; or, The Western Pioneers*, 1878; *The Mate of the 'Lily'; or, Notes from Harry Musgrove's Log Book* (1878); *Ned Garth; or, Made Prisoner in Africa* (1878); and *The Two Super-cargoes; or, Adventures in Savage Africa*, 1878; every one of which, as can be seen by the list, dated or published during the same year. And this was at a time when Kingston was hard at work translating into English a series of half a dozen full-length novels by Jules Verne.

Two years later he founded *The Union Jack*, a penny magazine issued weekly and advertised as containing vigorously-illustrated 'tales for British Boys'. The stories were written by 'the foremost writers of the day', and the first issue was in the bookshops and on the news-stands dated 1st January, 1880. Kingston himself edited the magazine, despite the fact that he had become increasingly unwell during the latter half of the preceding year. It was a story of his that appeared on the front page of the first issue: *Paddy Finn; or, the Exploits and Adventures of an Irish Midshipman, Afloat and Ashore*, a tale that was followed by the first of G. A. Henty's many contributions: *Times of Peril – A Tale of India*. For some months Kingston continued at the helm, but by the spring of the year it became obvious that he was suffering from a progressive disease. In July his doctors told him that he had cancer and that the time had come to put his earthly affairs in order. He resigned the editorship of *The Union Jack* on the completion of issue No. 18, dated 29th April, 1880, vacating the chair in favour of G. A. Henty. He was working on a story to within a few days of his death, and almost his last conscious act was to write a letter wishing goodbye to the thousands of youngsters he had striven so hard to please. He addressed it to them through the pages of *The Boy's Own Paper*:

Stormont Lodge, Willesden,
August 2nd, 1880

My Dear Boys,
I have been engaged, as you know, for a very large portion of my life in writing books for you. This occupation has been a source of the greatest pleasure and satisfaction to me, and, I am willing to believe, to you also.

Our connection with each other in this world must, however, shortly cease. I have for some time been suffering from serious illness, and have been informed by the highest medical authorities that my days are numbered. Of this truth I am convinced by the rapid progress the disease is making. It is my desire, therefore, to wish you all a sincere and hearty farewell! I want you to know that I am leaving this life in unspeakable happiness, because I rest my soul on my Saviour, trusting only and entirely to the merits of the Great Atonement, by which my sins have been put away for ever.

Dear boys, I ask you to give your hearts to Christ, and earnestly pray that all of you may meet me in Heaven.

Yours very sincerely,
W. H. G. Kingston

Three days after he had written this farewell, Kingston breathed his last. His letter touched the hearts, not only of his many thousands of young readers, but of a far wider audience. The fact that, by the time it appeared in print, the writer was already dead, lent it

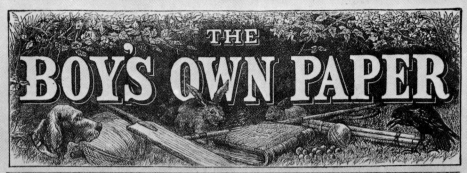

THE BOY'S OWN PAPER

No. 3.—Vol. I.   SATURDAY, FEBRUARY 1, 1879.   Price One Penny.
[ALL RIGHTS RESERVED.]

MY STRUGGLE WITH A TIGER.

By Charles Jamrach,
St. George's-in-the-East.

IT is now a good many years ago, when one morning a van-load of wild beasts, which I had bought the previous day from a captain in the London Docks, who brought them from the East Indies, arrived at my repository in Bett Street, St. George's-in-the-East. I myself superintended the unloading of the animals, and had given directions to my men to place a den containing a very ferocious full-grown Bengal tiger, with its iron-barred front close against the wall.

They were proceeding to take down a den with leopards, when all of a sudden I heard a crash, and to my horror found the big tiger had pushed out the back part of his den with his hind-quarters, and was walking down the yard into the street, which was then full of people watching the arrival of this curious merchandise. The tiger, in putting his forepaws against the iron bars in front of the den, had exerted his full strength to push with his back against the boards behind, and had thus succeeded in gaining his liberty.

As soon as he got into the street, a boy of about nine years of age put out his hand to stroke the beast's back, when the tiger seized him by the shoulder and run down the street with the lad hanging in his jaws. This was done in less time than it takes me to relate; but when I saw the boy being carried off in this manner, and witnessed the panic that had seized hold of the people, without further thought I dashed after the brute, and got hold of him by the loose skin of the back of his neck. I was then of a more vigorous frame than now, and had plenty of pluck and dash in me.

I tried thus to stop his further progress, but he was too strong for me, and dragged

To the Rescue.

76

a dramatic quality that made an instant appeal to Victorian sentiments, and for years afterwards it was quoted from pulpit and evangelistic soap-box as a shining example of 'how a true Christian can compose himself to die'. Kingston was sorely missed by his large concourse of readers and a considerable number found time to follow his funeral *cortège* to the grave. Henty paid him tribute in a long obituary notice printed in *The Union Jack*, naming him as 'the father of the school of writers of healthy stirring tales for boys'. But the magazine itself did not long survive its founder: the last number was dated 25th September, 1883. A total of four cloth-bound annuals were all that challenged the ever-growing popularity of *The Boy's Own Paper*.

By the time of his death competition from other writers in the field had become fierce; but at the commencement of his career as an author of boys' stories Kingston had few serious rivals until Ballantyne issued his challenge. One figure to appear early on his literary horizon and who soon became a firm favourite with the youth of the day was the re-doubtable Captain Mayne Reid (1818–83). He was a writer who proved he could stir the youthful blood of the nation as seldom before, although his stories were most often set as deep inland as Kingston's were far at sea. This battle-scarred veteran of the United States Army and the Mexican Wars mirrored his action-filled career as a soldier in the titles of the books he wrote. Their names were as exciting and as provocative as the after-dinner stories with which he delighted to chill the blood of any lady within earshot. A glance at the titles listed below will reveal why so many of them exerted such an attraction over readers of all ages, while with teenage boys their fascination was strong enough to have them saving for months in order to purchase his latest book.

He was born at Ballyroney, Ireland, being named after his father, the Rev. Thomas Mayne Reid, a presbyterian minister. His mother was a descendant of the 'hot and hasty Rutherford' immortalised by Walter Scott in his poem *Marmion*, and young Mayne Reid (he early discarded the name Thomas) inherited the fiery temper and eruptive personality of his distinguished forbear. Educated with a view to the ministry, he soon kicked over the traces by emigrating to America, arriving in New Orleans in January 1840. He had a dozen jobs in as many months, even trying his hand as an actor, all with scant success. In 1843 he settled for a journalistic career in Philadelphia, where he soon became an intimate friend and drinking partner of Edgar Allan Poe, before joining the *New York Herald* as correspondent. In December 1846 he obtained a commission as second lieutenant in the 1st New York Volunteers, soon afterwards sailing for Vera Cruz to take part in the Mexican War.

From the start of the campaign Mayne Reid was in the thick of the fighting, volunteering for the most hazardous patrol work and eventually leading the final charge of the American infantry storming the walls of Chapultepec. He described the assault in a memoir written later; a narrative displaying the same action-filled prose style he employed in his novels:

When about half-way across the open ground, I saw the parapet crowded with Mexican artillerists in uniforms of dark blue with crimson facings, each with a musket in hand, and all aiming, as I believed, at my own person. On account of the crimson sash I was wearing, they no doubt fancied me as a general at least.

The volley was almost as one sound, and I avoided it by throwing myself flat along the earth, only getting touched on one of the fingers of my sword-hand, another shot passing through the loose cloth of my overalls. Instantly on my feet again, I made for the wall, which I was scaling when a bullet from an escopette went tearing through my thigh, and I fell into the ditch.

He was severely wounded and nearly bled to death; but by the spring of 1848 he was convalescent at the home of his friend Donn Piatt, in the valley of the Mac-o-Chee, Ohio. It was here, while slowly regaining the use of his injured leg, that he wrote the greater part of the first of his many novels, a tale he titled *The Rifle Rangers*. He carried the manuscript with him when he sailed for England in June 1849, hoping to

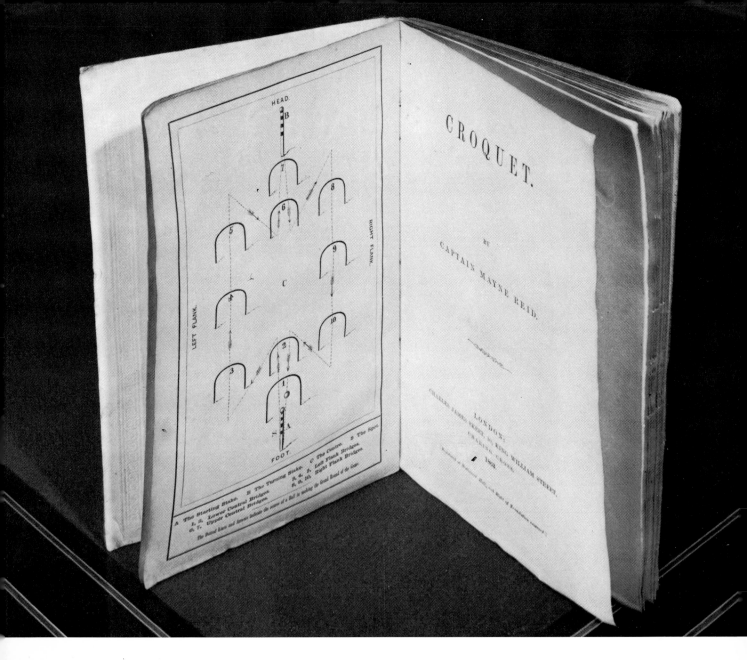

take part as a volunteer in the revolutionary movements that he believed would soon lead to fighting in Bavaria and Hungry. To his intense annoyance, he arrived on the scene too late, and he was forced to settle in London in the hope of a literary career.

The Rifle Rangers; or, The Adventures of an Officer in Southern Mexico, 2 vols, 1850, was published by William Shoberl, London, in a binding of red fine-ribbed cloth, the spine being blocked in gold. Vol I had a lithographed frontispiece; while Vol II contained a frontispiece and two full-page plates, all drawn on stone by the artist R. J. Hamerton. The work is now particularly difficult to find in acceptable condition in its original cloth binding, the majority of copies that do come on the market having been rebound, usually setting the two volumes between a single set of covers. At the time of its publication Mayne Reid was convinced that his partly autobiographical work might well prove to be a best-seller, but to his disappointment, and that of his publishers, the reverse proved to be the case. It was several years before the book was reprinted, and when it did reappear it was under the imprint of Simms and M'Intyre, London, dated 1853. From Chapter II onwards he had given his readers a running commentary on his life in the Americas, and the book contains the first mention in any fictional work of the famous Colt revolver, a weapon on which the author had pinned much of his military faith:

In the 'fall' of 1846, I found myself in the city of New Orleans, filling up one of those pauses that occur between the chapters of an eventful life – doing nothing. I have said an *eventful* life. In the retrospect of ten years, I could not remember as many weeks spent in one place. I had traversed the continent from north to south, and crossed it from sea to sea. My foot had pressed the summits of the Andes, and climbed the Cordilleras of the Sierra Madre. I had steamed it down the Mississippi, and sculled it up the Orinoco. I had hunted buffaloes with the Pawnees of the Platte, and ostriches upon the pampas of the Plata: today shivering in the hut of an Esquimaux – a month after, taking my *siesta* in an aëry couch under the gossamer frondage of the corozo palm. I had eaten raw meat with the trappers of the Rocky Mountains, and roast monkey among the Mosquito Indians; and much more, which might weary the reader, and ought to have made the writer a wiser man.

But I fear the spirit of adventure – its thirst – is within me slakeless. I had just returned from a 'scurry' among the Comanches of Western Texas, and the idea of 'settling down' was as far from my mind as ever.

'What next? what next?' thought I. 'Ha! the war with Mexico.'

The war between the United States and that country had now fairly commenced. My sword – a fine Toledo, taken from a Spanish officer at San Jacinto – hung over the mantle, rusting ingloriously. Near it were my pistols – a pair of Colt's revolvers – pointing at each other in sullen muteness. A warlike ardour seized upon me; and clutching, not the sword, but my pen, I wrote to the War Department for a commission; and, summoning all my patience, awaited the answer.

On his arrival in London in 1849, Mayne Reid had brought with him a large wooden box filled with dozens of massive Colt revolvers, and enough ammunition to supply a whole company of volunteers. With funds running low, he was now forced to sell the collection, keeping only a single pair for his own personal use. These were the first Colts to be seen in Europe, and in later years their owner delighted to show them off in thunderous fashion on the lawn of his house at Gerrard's Cross, Buckinghamshire.

Mayne Reid received only £25 from William Shoberl as his share of the profits of *The Rifle Rangers*, and he returned in straitened circumstances to his old home at Ballyroney, Ireland. It was here that he wrote *The Scalp Hunters; or, Romantic Adventures in Northern Mexico*, 3 vols, 1851, later published by Charles J. Skeet, London. Once again it fell to Simms and M'Intyre to publish the second edition, this time dated 1852, and once again it seemed that literary and financial success had eluded the author. It was

then that he decided, as Kingston had that same year, that greater interest was being taken in his works by the teenagers of the families into which his novels strayed. The many letters of appreciation he received from young people convinced him that his fortune as a writer might well be found amongst the youth of the country. These were not the readers who could afford to purchase multi-volume novels, or could persuade their parents to buy these for them, so Reid set himself the task of writing a boys' adventure story that would sell as a single-volume work in the juvenile market.

The Desert Home; or, The Adventures of a Lost Family in the Wilderness, 1852, was described by the author as the story of an English Family Robinson (in fact, the sub-title was finally changed in 1858 by the then publishers, W. Kent & Co., to read *The Desert Home; or, English Family Robinson*). The book first appeared under the imprint of David Bogue, Fleet Street, with a series of full-page illustrations by the well-known artist William Harvey (1796–1866), who had been taught the art of wood-engraving by the famous Thomas Bewick. It was an immediate and lasting success, five large editions (with a choice of black and white or coloured plates), appearing in the space of the next few years. At last it seemed that Mayne Reid had hit the jack-pot, and he settled down to write a series of companion volumes aimed at an expanding readership of teenage boys.

The Boy Hunters; or, Adventures in Search of a White Buffalo, 1853, was quickly followed by *The Young Voyageurs; or, the Boy Hunters in the North*, 1854 (second edition dated 1855) the same young heroes, Basil, Lucien and François, being the principal characters in both volumes. The author's partnership with David Bogue and William Harvey continued the winning streak, and other titles from his pen were clamoured for by a readership which had now increased to tens of thousands. They were not kept waiting long, Mayne Reid thoroughly enjoying his new-found popularity and welcoming the substantial sums that were now accruing from his literary success. In the meantime his earlier books, such as *The Rifle Rangers* (with its sub-title now changed to read 'or, Adventures in Southern Mexico'), and *The Scalp*

Hunters, both appeared as single-volume works illustrated by William Harvey, being issued under the imprint of J. & C. Brown & Co., London, and helped to swell the writer's increasing income.

The next few years saw the publication of a series of titles calculated to whet the appetite of any boy gifted with a fertile imagination. They included *The Forest Exiles or the Perils of a Peruvian Family amid the Wilds of the Amazon*, 1855, with its famous frontispiece of 'The Monkey's Bridge'; *The Hunter's Feast; or, Conversations around the Camp-fire*, 1855; *The Bush-Boys; or, the History and Adventures of a Cape Farmer and his family in the Wild Karoos of Southern Africa*, 1856, with its cruel picture of an unfortunate lion stuck in the top of a chimney; *The Young Yägers*, 1857, a sequel to *Bush-Boys*; *The Plant Hunters*, 1858 (second edition dated 1859); and *The War Trail*, 1857, a story that made its first appearance in *Chamber's Journal. Ran Away to Sea*, 1859, was published anonymously, although there was no secret about the author for he allowed his name to appear in the pictorial arrangement on the gold-blocked spine of the book; while *The Boy Tar*, 1859, was notable for the unusual series of illustrations by Charles S. Keene.

In 1853, with financial success seemingly assured, Mayne Reid married Elizabeth Hyde, a girl just thirteen years old, later to figure as the heroine in his three-volume novel *The Child Wife*. They lived in an isolated furnished cottage at Stokenchurch, Oxfordshire, later moving to Gerrard's Cross, Buckinghamshire. It was at Stokenchurch that the thirty five years old newly-wedded author completed another of his adult novels, *The White Chief*, 3 vols, 1855; following this by one of his most successful works *The Quadroon; or, A Lover's Adventures in Louisiana*, 3 vols, 1856. This book was later the subject of a furious controversy between Mayne Reid and the dramatist Dion Boucicault, whose play *The Octoroon* was acted before packed houses at the Adelphi Theatre, London, in November, 1861. Reid, in characteristic fashion, alleged that the plot of Boucicault's play had been lifted from his book, and demanded a public apology.

With the completion of *Bruin; or, The Grand Bear Hunt*, 1861, published by Routledge, Warne, & Routledge, London, a most popular tale with the boys of the day, he again attempted circulating library success, writing *The Wild Huntress*, 3 vols, 1861 (Bentley); then *The Maroon*, 3 vols, 1862 (Hurst & Blackett). He was now changing his publishers almost as often as he did his titles, and one of the rarest of his first editions *Croquet*, 1863, a serious treatise on the game, appeared as a slim octavo, bound in limp orange cloth, with the imprint of Charles James Skeet. Books for boys came just as rapidly from his pen, *The Cliff Climbers*, 1864, and *Ocean Waifs*, 1864, appearing within a few months of one another, soon to be followed by *The Boy Slaves*, 1865.

Mayne Reid was now at the zenith of his fame; money was pouring in from royalties and the sale of stories to magazines and periodicals, while offers from American publishing houses were too tempting to be ignored. His ambition to be accepted as one of the landed gentry led him to an extravagant outlay of capital in land and buildings at Gerrard's Cross. Here he erected a massive flat-topped house, built in the style of a Mexican hacienda and named *The Ranche*, a pretentious edifice that soon consumed thousands of hard-earned pounds. He became as infatuated with his *folie de grandeur* as had Sir Walter Scott with his ill-fated Abbotsford, and with almost identical results. Hardly had the workmen finished their three years work than the new owner was declared bankrupt, *The Ranche* and all its expensive furnishings being confiscated to meet the demands of his creditors. The outstanding success of his most famous novel, *The Headless Horseman*, first published in a series of sixpenny, monthly, paper-wrappered parts (twenty in all) commencing in March, 1865, had gone to his head, leading him to commission building on a scale that would have daunted men ten times as wealthy. Publication of *The Headless Horseman* (a title as popular with young people as it was with adults) was shared jointly between Chapman & Hall and the rival publishing house of Richard Bentley. The book was issued as a two-volume novel, dated 1866, with Chapman & Hall's imprint occurring in Vol I, while Bentley's was on the title-page of Vol II. On January 5th, 1867, Bentley published a single-volume edition (dated 1866), with the red cloth-binding blocked in gold, and from that time onwards reprints and new editions continued to appear in Britain and America, the work being translated into nearly every European language. It was a money-spinner that later came to the rescue of the impecunious author on many a thankful occasion, but for the present he was hard-pressed to fend off a lean and hungry pack of unforgiving creditors.

In October, 1867, Mayne Reid and his wife found sanctuary in the U.S.A., living for some time at Newport, Rhode Island, where he became a naturalised American citizen. It was here that he wrote *The Child Wife*, for which the editor of *Frank Leslie's Paper* paid him the unheard of sum of $8,000 for the serial rights. The work later appeared under the Ward, Lock & Tyler, London imprint as a three-volume novel, dated 1868. Part of the money Mayne Reid immediately invested in a magazine for boys which he founded in New York. *The Onward Magazine* continued in circulation for some fourteen months, with the proprietor as editor, the first issue appearing in December, 1868. But the wound that nearly killed him during the Mexican War, and which had never properly healed, became badly infected yet again, and in 1870 he was near to dying in a New York hospital. He was a patient for nearly three months, and his absence spelled out the death of his boys' magazine. In October the same year he sailed with his wife for England, and they finally settled in modest style at Ross, Herefordshire, their home for the remainder of their married life.

Many of Mayne Reid's later works made their first appearance in magazines, and although none attained the popularity of *The Headless Horseman*, he was able to restore the family fortunes to some degree before his death at Ross on 22nd October, 1883. He was buried at Kensall Green Cemetery, his wife surviving him until 30th December, 1904. Of his later titles I have on my shelves a mixture for young and old, including *The White Gauntlet*, 3 vols, 1865; *The Half-Blood*, 1859, a single-volume juvenile version of his three-volume novel *Oceola*, 1858, a work originally issued under a New York imprint (and later by Hurst

& Blackett, London, dated 1859); *No Quarter!*, 3 vols, 1888; and *The Naturalist in Siluria*, 1889.

Reid was one of the very few British authors of the nineteenth century who could claim extensive first-hand knowledge of the United States. Unlike so many of his contemporaries, he was not an imperialist and would-be Empire-builder, but a left-of-centre liberal with radical (perhaps even republican) political views. In his books, America is invariably depicted as the land of promise and endless opportunity, in diametrical opposition to the views Dickens so forcefully expressed in *Martin Chuzzlewit*. The same democratic idealism is evident in many of his books for boys, and his influence can be discerned in the works of many later (and greater), writers of the calibre of Robert Louis Stevenson.

The quest to complete my collection of the works of this interesting but often unpredictable author continues; but his habit of revising a book and then re-issuing it under an entirely different title, plus his method of syndicating a tale for simultaneous publication in a number of London and provincial magazines and newspapers, has made the task of any would-be bibliographer an extremely difficult one. There are many others in hot pursuit, and the price of his earlier books for boys, and of almost all of his three-volume novels, have now risen to such astronomical heights that new additions to my shelves are few and far between. But the search continues, if at a considerably slower tempo.

Ballantyne, Kingston and Mayne Reid, were the triumvirate who dominated the field of teenage juvenile fiction in Britain during the most interesting period of its development from the 1850's to the 1870's. Without exception, their best work, and the books by which they are remembered today, were all written and published within these two decades, although all three continued writing books for boys right up to the year of their deaths.

The works of some of the minor figures of the genre, whose titles appeared during this same twenty year period, are now even more difficult to acquire than the trio of well-known names discussed above. Friedrich Gerstäcker (1816–72), was a German

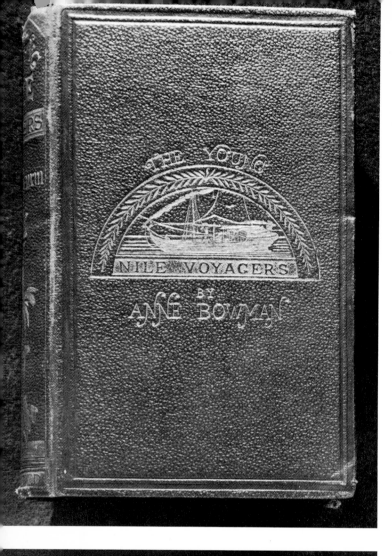

THE YOUNG
NILE VOYAGERS
BY
ANNE BOWMAN

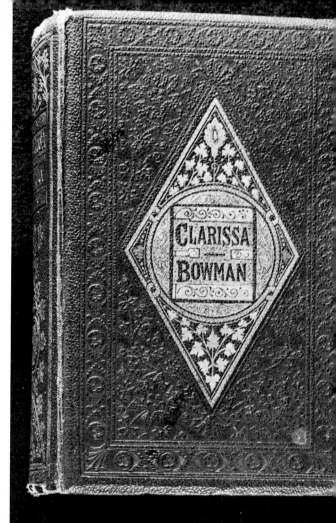

CLARISSA
BOWMAN

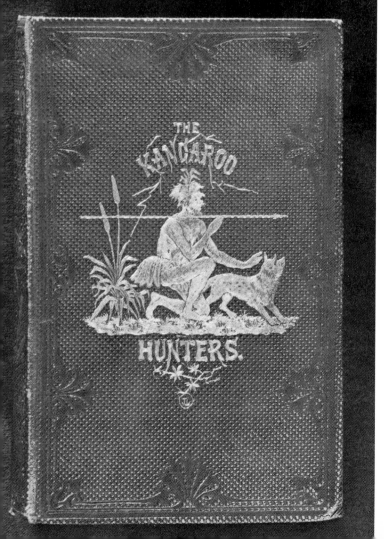

THE
KANGAROO
HUNTERS.

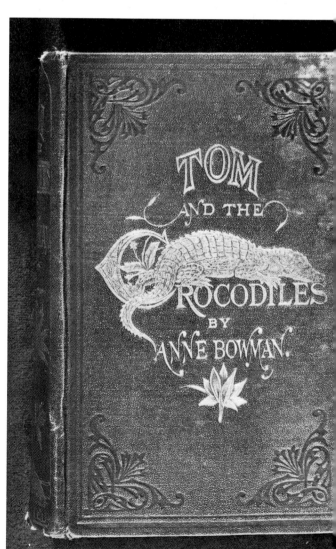

TOM
AND THE
CROCODILES
BY
ANNE BOWMAN.

I EXERTED ALL MY STRENGTH AND RAMMED MY LONG SPEAR
FURTHER UP. *Page 92.*

writer and traveller in both America and Africa, whose subsequent narrative descriptions of his trials and tribulations in the wilds enjoyed considerable popularity. They also acted as source books for many other writers, notably W. H. G. Kingston. One of the most successful translations of his books for boys was *The Little Whaler*, which appeared under a London imprint dated 1857, with eight full-page illustrations by Harrison Weir. Anne Bowman was a rarity amongst writers; a lady novelist who specialised in adventure stories for boys. Most of her books were first issued by George Routledge & Sons, and comprised such titles as *The Castaways*, 1857; *The Kangaroo Hunters*, 1859; *The Boy Voyagers*, 1859; *Among the Tartar Tents*, 1861; *Clarissa*, 1863, one of the few books she wrote for 'the pleasure of young ladies'; *The Young Yachtsmen*, 1865; *Tom and the Crocodiles*, 1867; *The Young Nile-Voyagers*, 1868; and a dozen or more titles in much the same vein. She also wrote several grammar and reading books for younger children; but little else is known about Miss (or Mrs) Bowman, except that she resided at Richmond, Surrey, and produced at least one book a year during the period 1855–75. Some of her best work can be very favourably compared with that of her masculine rivals in the same field. Mary Gillies is another long-forgotten authoress, whose *The Voyage of the Constance – A Tale of the Polar Seas*, 1867, achieved some success.

Collecting in this difficult field sometimes results in the discovery of writers whose titles eventually become favourite volumes on one's shelves, either by reason of their vivid pictorial bindings, the quality of their illustrations, or the enjoyment derived from texts written by names now lost in the mists of time. Who, today, remembers, Alfred Elwes, author of *Frank and Andrea*, 1860; *Paul Blake* (1891); *The Ocean and her Rulers*, 1854; *Ralph Seabrooke*, 1861; and, amongst many other stories, *Guy Rivers; or, A Boy's Struggles in the Great World*, 1862. It was seeking forgotten titles by unknown authors that led to the discovery of that remarkable book for boys, *The Adventures of Seven Four-Footed Foresters – Narrated by Themselves*, 1865, by James Greenwood. An illustration from it is shown above. Greenwood (1832–

1929) wrote an amazing series of books, all of which featured some form of savage cruelty involving animals and/or humans. A glance at his titles reveals that his descriptive powers were heightened as soon as he sank his teeth into a story in which the blood could really be made to gush. *Curiosities of Savage Life*, 1863, regales his young readers with the details of agonising initiation ceremonies that Red Indian braves had to undergo before being admitted to tribal manhood; *King Lion*, 1864, gives highly-coloured descriptions of stalking and kills; *The Hatchet Throwers*, 1866, whistles with sudden death; *Legends of Savage Life*, 1867, repeats his earlier performance with the Red Indians and delves deep into African voodoo; *The Purgatory of Peter the Cruel*, 1868, leaves no rack un-notched; while *The Bear King*, 1868, lightheartedly views hunting from inside the skin of a grizzly.

The Adventures of the Seven Four-Footed Foresters first introduced me to Greenwood's works, but I have still many of his first editions to find in anything like acceptable condition in their original cloth bindings. It was in this story that he told how Timothy Jagel came to possess a fluent knowledge of the language of animals, enabling him to converse with the most savage of them on intimate terms. Gradually this one-time keeper at the Surrey Zoological Gardens finds his appearance changing to that of a werewolf, until the real wolves in his charge recognise a fellow member of the pack:

As I was sweeping out his den, the Siberian wolf
had made a grip at my foot, and, having nothing
handier, I hauled him down by his chain, and
flogged him with the iron rake. My blood was up, I
can tell you . . . I felt my eyes grow quite hot as I
laid on the blows, and I laid them on the harder,
because all the while he was threatening me in the
most shocking manner. At last he gave a wriggle,
and, turning his head suddenly, nipped my ankle so
severely that the blood trickled through the holes
in my boot his teeth had made; at the same time he
looked at me with a grin, and said, as plainly as
ever wolf yet spoke, –

'Thrash away! You can't hurt me as I have hurt
you, if you flog for a week.'

'Can't I?' replied I, bringing the teeth side of
the rake down on his ribs with force enough to
splinter them; 'Anyhow, I'll try.'

Certainly there was nothing in the character of
this reply to astonish a thick-headed wolf; but,
somehow, it seemed to take him all aback, and
turning his face towards me with quite a different
expression to that which it had hitherto worn, and
wincing before my furious gaze, he whined out, –

'That's enough; I give in. How was I to know
that you, too, were a wolf? Why couldn't you speak
before?'

'You know me now, do you?' said I, still with
my foot on his throat, though ceasing from flogging;
'I have known you all along. How is it that we did
not recognise each other earlier?'

'Because,' replied he, 'your man's shape
conceals your wolfish nature so neatly; at the same
time, it is curious that I should have been so long
deceived. After all, it is not so much your voice as
your *eyes* that betrayed you. Your wolf part must
have broken bounds very suddenly.'

And so – another werewolf is born! Greenwood's
anti-hero Jagel commences to tell the story of seven
case-histories related to him in their own language
by the most ferocious animals in the zoo. They growl
descriptions of their bloody struggles against their
arch-enemy Man, and the manner of the deaths of

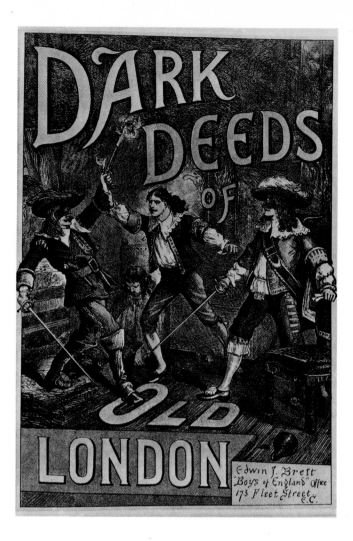

their human victims are proudly set forth, each with a
wealth of gruesome detail. H. S. Melville's illustrations
do full justice to Greenwood's text, and the two
combined must have been calculated to terrify the
more sensitive of his young readers. Perhaps because
of this the book sold well, and Ward & Lock were
soon advertising it as being available 'with gilt
edges for school prizes'.

Greenwood most probably conceived the idea of
writing his bloodthirsty tale after reading *The Book of
Were-Wolves: being an account of a terrible superstition*,
1865, by Sabine Baring-Gould. This work appeared
several months before Greenwood's book was issued
and soon achieved sufficient notoriety to ensure a
series of sensational novels by other writers, all
with vampires and werewolves as their central
characters. Greenwood's book is the only title of the
period with this theme for the plot that was specially
written for the juvenile market.

An end date of 1870 has been set to conclude this
chapter, and space forbids more than a brief mention
of other writers of adventure novels and stories for
boys whose main body of work appeared within this
period. Those who must not be overlooked include
Charles Kingsley (1819–75), whose fairy stories and
other works are discussed in *The Collector's Book of*

An illustration from *The
Story of a City Arab* (1876),
by George Etell Sargent.
Ballantyne's *Dusty Diamonds*,
1884, made use of the same
theme

MY ADVENTURE IN SMITHFIELD.

Children's Books. Two of his novels, *Westward Ho! or,
The Voyages and Adventures of Sir Amyas Leigh*, 3 vols,
1855; and, *Hereward the Wake*, 'Last of the English',
2 vols, 1866; have remained favourites with young
people since the time of their first appearance,
although both were originally intended to appeal to
an adult readership. William Dalton (1821–75),
contributed a number of now extremely difficult to
find adventure stories, among the best of which are

The Wolf-Boy of China, 1857; *The English Boy in Japan;
or, the perils and adventures of Mark Raffles*, 1858; *The
War Tiger; or, Adventures and Wonderful Fortunes of the
young Sea Chief and his lad Chow*, 1859; *The White
Elephant*, 1860; *Lost in Ceylon: the story of a boy's and
girl's adventures in the woods and wilds of the Lion King of
Kandy*, 1861; *The Nest Hunters*, 1863; *The Tiger
Prince; or, Adventures in the wilds of Abyssinia*, 1863;
and *Lost among the Wild Men*, 1868. John George
Edgar (1834–64), wrote a number of books for boys,
notably *The Boy Crusaders*, 1865. George Etell Sargent
(1809–83) I have represented in the collection by
only a handful of titles, including – *Frank Layton: an
Australian Story* (1865), a work that made its first
appearance in the magazine *Leisure Hour*.

Finally, an author who has earned a place in any
bibliography of boys' adventure stories: Percy
Bolingbroke St John (1821–89). Born in Camden
Town, London, he accompanied his father on his
travels in Europe and America. When still in his
'teens he wrote a number of short stories and was
later influenced by the works of the French novelist
Gustave Aimard (1818–83). Aimard had spent over
thirty years roving through North and Central
America, and he turned this to good account when he
began his long series of novels of life among the Red
Indians. The teenage boys of France, as well as their
adult counterparts, devoured his fictional tales,
published under such titles as *Les Trappeurs de
l'Arkansas*, 1858; *Les Pirates de la prairie*, 1858; *La loi de
lynch*, 1859; *Les outlaws du Missouri*, 1868; *L'ami des
blancs*, 1879; and *Les bandits de L'Arizona*, 1882. Many
of these were translated into English by St John, and
found a ready sale as boys' adventure tales. But St
John also wrote a number of books especially for
boys, notably *The Trapper's Bride; and Indian Tales*,
1845; *Quadroona; or, The Slave Mother*, 1861; *The
Backwood Rangers*, 1865; *The Coral Reef*, 1868; and
The Young Buccaneer, 1873. Like most other first
editions of juvenile fiction of the period, all are
difficult to acquire in anything approaching their
original condition. The vast majority appear simply
to have been read to death, a tribute to their popularity amongst the boys of Victoria's England.

85

Mark Twain
and the American West

By the time of Fenimore Cooper's death in 1851, the romantic traditions of the American West were firmly imprinted on the heart of the nation and had secured a place in its literary annals. The frontier wars, and the ceaseless battles that had raged between the white settlers and the Indian tribes endeavouring to protect what was left of their homeland, formed a vivid and exciting background against which to set novels and romances. They spanned an ever-widening horizon in which the adventurous world of boys' books and teenage novels soon gained a prominent position.

The breathless tales of heroism surrounding the names of the early pioneers and frontiersmen, such as Daniel Boone (1734–1820), and David Crockett (1786–1836), became the inexhaustible stock-in-trade of many a grateful writer, and the staple literary diet of thousands of readers of the cheap pulp magazines that flourished during the middle of the nineteenth century. Boone's supposed exploits had been given world-wide celebrity by Byron in his epic satire *Don Juan*; while Crockett had set the seal on his own fame by meeting his death in the siege of the Alamo during the Texan War of Independence. It was not long before both names were indissolubly linked with the expanding saga of pioneer America, and the writing of sensational tales of their prowess, and the adventures of other fearless trackers and scouts, occupied scores of authors of diversified talents.

Amongst the first of these was John Beauchamp Jones (1810–66), whose *Wild Western Scenes*, 1841, has since established itself as a minor classic of frontier life. It became the source book of numerous fictional works; as did his *A Rebel War Clerk's Diary*, 2 vols, 1866, both used extensively by novelists intent on weaving authentic backgrounds against which to set their tales. One writer who made extensive and generous use of Jones' works was the prolific Edward Sylvester Ellis (1840–1916), whose first book, *Seth Jones; or, the captives of the Frontier* (1860), was written when the author was only nineteen years old. The work appeared undated as No. 8 in a paper-wrappered series called *Beadle's Dime Novels*, the production of I. P. Beadle & Co., New York, and was the forerunner

of over three hundred titles from the same pen. *Seth Jones* had become a collector's rarity as early as 1877, in which year it was produced in facsimile form by the original publishers, then known as Beadle & Adams, a facsimile that was itself reproduced in 1946, no copy of the original edition being available. No other fictional writer of the period, whose works appeared in so cheap and ephemeral a format, has ever been accorded a similar honour, and this is a measure of the respect collectors of first editions pay to an author whose sheer weight of output left an indelible imprint on the field of juvenile fiction.

One is quite safe in stating that no complete collection of the first editions of E. S. Ellis exists today, or is ever likely to be assembled at any future date. Merely to compile a check list of his works would be a bibliographer's nightmare, for the number of pseudonyms and aliases he used seem almost to keep pace with the diversity of his titles.

At the beginning of his career as a writer he was employed in compiling sensational biographies of well-known figures in the immediate past, all of which were published under the imprint of *Beadle's Dime Biographical Library*. Issued in pictorial paper-wrappers, they comprised such titles as *The Life and Times of Col. Daniel Boone, the hunter of Kentucky* (1860); *The Life and Times of Christopher Carson, the Rocky Mountain scout and guide* (1861), a work later re-issued as *The Life of Kit Carson*; *The Life of Pontiac, the conspirator, Chief of the Ottawas* (1861); and *The Life and Adventures of Colonel David Crockett* (1862); all with portrait frontispieces, and all published undated. Later Ellis turned to fictional characters for his heroes, and changed to *Munro's Ten Cent Novels* for *The Lion-hearted Hunter; or, the captives of the Wyandotter* (1864); and *Scar-cheek, the wild Half-breed* (1864).

Within a few years he had built up a readership of hundreds of thousands, the vast majority of whom were young men still in their teens. He moved from Geneva, Ohio, where he was born, and established a permanent office in New York, churning out six, eight, or even ten titles in a single twelve month period. He donned and discarded literary disguises by the dozen, and had devoted followers of his contrasting pseudonyms who had no idea that the works of apparent rivals in the field were all written by one and the same man. An alphabetical list of some of his known aliases reads rather like a tally of battle-hardened survivors after an Indian raid; but every title from these pens is known to have been from Ellis's hand:

Capt. J(ames) F(enimore) C(ooper) 'Bruin' Adams; Boynton H. Belknap; J. G. Bethune; Mahan A. Brown; Latham A. Carleton; Edwin Emerson; Col. H. R. Gordon; Oswald A. Gwynne; Capt. R. M. Hawthorne; Capt. Marcy Hunter; Lieut. R. H. Jayne; Charles E. Lasalle; Seward D. Lisle; Capt. H. Millbank; Billex Muller; Geoffrey Randolph; Lieut. J. H. Randolph; Seelin Robins; Emerson Rodman; Capt. Wheeler U.S.A.; Harry Winton.

It took the present writer several months of research to establish the authenticity of this short list of disguises. By taking any name at random, it is possible to give at least a handful of titles for which Ellis used that particular pseudonym. He used 'Edwin Emerson' for a few years in the early 1870's, and gave his young readers *Dusky Darrell, trapper* (1871); *Dingle, the Outlaw; or, the secret slayer* (1871); *The Wood Witch; or, the squatter's secret* (1871); *The Mad Horseman* (1872); and *Red-Knife, the Wyandotte; or, the arrow-maker of the Miamis* (1873). Any other of the names on the list could be cited in similar fashion, and he also turned out more than a hundred titles using his own name. Listing a selection of his stories spanning forty years of his career (published under his own, and several pen-names) perhaps gives a better indication of his literary talent than any published extract from his works. The lurid titles of his books still have a fascination. They immediately conjure up the excitement his young readers must have felt when they managed to secure one of his cheaply-produced but dramatically-illustrated works to hurry off with; later to be passed through the affectionate embrace of similar teenage fingers until the volume finally fell, grubby and imperfect, in dog-eared sheets across the floor. Nearly every Indian tribe fought at least one ferocious battle in the pages of his books, and a list of their tribal names reads like the aboriginal history of the North American continent. He told of the braves of the Apaches, Blackfoot, Cherokee, Chickasaw, Chotoctaws, Comanches, Dakotas, Fox Indians, Hopi, Iroquois, Mohawks, Mohicans, Pawnee, Pueblos, Seminoles, Siouan, and the Wyandots, and recounted their exploits in such titles as: *Nathan Todd; or, the fate of the Sioux' captive* (1860); *Irona; or, Life on the Southwest border* (1861); *Bill Bidden, trapper; or, Life in the North-west* (1862); *Indian Jim: a tale of the Minnesota massacre* (1864); *Comanche Bill; or, Black Wolf's Scalp* (1872); *The Female Trapper; or, Lone-star Lizzie* (1873); *Kit Carson on the War Path* (1873); *The Young Spy; or, Nick Wiffles among the Madocs*, 1873; *Light-house Lige; or, Osceola, the firebrand of the Everglades* (1877); *The Scalp King; or, the human thunderbolt*, 1883; *Hunters of the Ozark*, 1886; *Yankee Josh, the rover*, 1893; *On the trail of Geronimo; or, in the Apache country* (1889); *The Great Cattle Trail* (1894); *Klondyke Nuggets, and how two boys secured them*, 1898; and *Cowmen and Rustlers*, 1898.

Besides his many adventure stories and sensational biographies, Ellis wrote an impressive list of mythologies, grammars, mysteries, histories, bible stories, text books, and even a collection of science-fiction tales. The ephemeral nature of a large proportion of his literary output (nearly all his earliest titles were issued as flimsy paper-wrappered booklets in the *Dime Novels* series), make the successful tracking down of acceptable copies of his early first editions an all-but impossible task. A full set of his texts would make an impressive wall of shelves; but this is the province of the Library of Congress rather than that of a private collector of boys' adventure stories. Yet Ellis has earned a rightful place in every library devoted to the juvenile novel. The attractive format of the cloth-bound volumes, each blocked pictorially on the front and spine, in which most of his first English editions appeared (and those of the American issues of his later works), ensure that he will be remembered by at least a handful of titles in any representative collection devoted to the genre.

Before turning to one of the most important figures

Buffalo Bill's

WILD WEST

Meisenbach

Drawings from life

by

CHARLES HENCKEL.

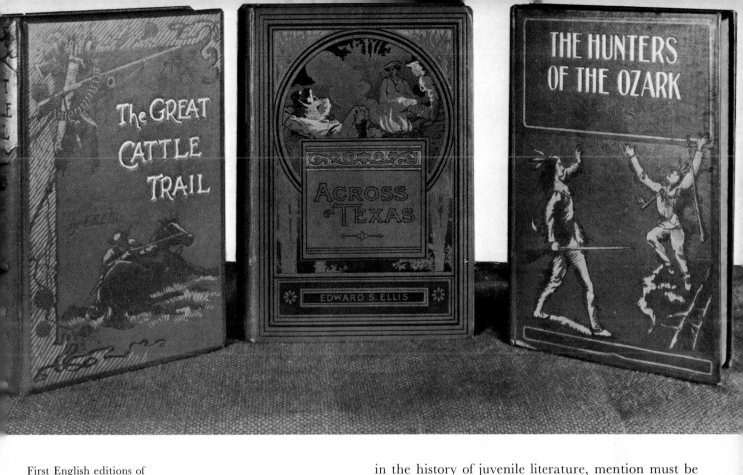

First English editions of some of Edward S. Ellis' best-known works

By the 1890's the fame of Buffalo Bill had resulted in the appearance of hundreds of Wild West adventure stories in the style shown on left

in the history of juvenile literature, mention must be made of an earlier writer whose output of well over two-hundred titles came near to equalling that of E. S. Ellis. Jacob Abbott (1803–79), was born at Hallowell, Maine. He was educated at Bowdoin College, where he graduated in 1820, and at Andover, later entering the church as a congregational minister. His first book, *The Young Christian*, 1832, was the fore-runner of dozens of others in much the same vein, including a large selection of educational works. Today, he is remembered almost solely for his series of 'Rollo' books, a total of twenty eight titles that achieved immense popularity and continued in print almost to the outbreak of World War I. In them, Abbott detailed the adventures of a hero he modelled on his son, a young man destined to become a distinguished minister and editor of periodicals devoted to church affairs. The Revd Layman Abbott never quite lived down the fact that he had once been cast as Rollo, the tough young hero of his fathers adventure tales, leading a select band of juvenile outlaws with Lucy and Jonas as his first lieutenants. *Rollo's Vacation*, 1839, published in Boston, is typical of the rest of Abbott's stories, many of which drew excellent pictures of ordinary life in New York State. Yet his works had little success in Britain, although several titles, including *Rollo in Paris*, 1854, were later reprinted and published in London.

As early as 1843, the poet Ralph Waldo Emerson prophesied in *The Dial* that the ascendancy writers in the eastern states maintained over American literary life would shortly come to an end. 'Our eyes will be turned westward,' he told his readers, 'and a new and stronger tone in literature will be the result.' He praised 'the genuine growth of Kentucky stump-oratory, telling of the exploits of Boone and David Crockett, the journals of the Western pioneers . . .' and, he might have added, the emergence of a distinctive Western humour, later to be epitomised in the Boston weekly *The Carpet Bag*, which in 1852 was to give the American public its first taste of the wit of Artemus Ward and Mark Twain.

Samuel Langhorne Clemens (1835–1910) was born in the little township of Florida, Missouri, but is always associated with the river town of Hannibal, the steamboat stop above St Louis where he spent the formative years of his youth from 1839–53. It was here that he earned his first few cents whitewashing a paling fence or two, fell in love with a bevy of Becky Thatchers, watched a man shot down in a street gun-battle, and time and again heard the cry of the leadsmen on the prow of the river steamers as they edged into shallow waters – 'M-a-r-k twain! . . . M-a-r-k twain!' – yelling to their captains that the mark was now only two fathoms. This was the cry Clemens was later to adopt as his pseudonym, a *nom de plume* that soon came to be loved the world over.

On the death of his father in 1847, young Clemens was apprenticed to a printer, rapidly became an expert at that trade, read widely and began to contribute articles to his brother's newspaper, published in Hannibal. After an abortive plan to seek his fortune in South America, he set out in 1857 for New Orleans, on the way apprenticing himself to a river pilot, thus fulfilling his most fervent boyhood ambition. His four years as a pilot on the Mississippi were his 'university'; they presented him with an epic theme, widened his outlook and experience of human nature, and left him with a wealth of colourful material for later work. The outbreak of the American Civil War in 1861 disrupted the river traffic, and, after a few weeks as a Confederate irregular (during which it rained every day) Clemens deserted and followed his brother to the West.

It was while earning his living as a reporter in Virginia City in 1862 that Clemens first used the pseudonym 'Mark Twain'. This was the turning point in his life and marked the beginning of his true career. Within a few months he adapted himself to frontier journalism in all its boisterous and sometimes burlesque phases; but with the well-publicised arrival in Virginia City of 'Artemus Ward' (Charles Farrar Browne – 1834–67), his literary horizon broadened and he determined to aim a deal higher than mere journalistic hack-work. Ward gave the young man every encouragement, and urged Twain to publish the manuscript of a full-length book he had shown him. *The Celebrated Jumping Frog of Calaveras County and Other Sketches*, 1867, was issued under a New York imprint at the end of a most successful lecture tour, the author soon afterwards leaving on the steamship *Quaker City* for the Holy Land with a party of eager excursionists. His hilarious experiences were detailed in *The Innocents Abroad*, 1869, first published at Hartford, Conn., a book that became an immediate best-seller and brought its author national fame. Through an acquaintance made on this voyage he met and married Olivia Langdon in 1870, his marriage ensuring that his roots were now permanently set in East Coast America.

Twain's intimate knowledge of the Old South and the Far West enabled him to meet a popular demand for information relating to America's romantic past. In *Roughing It*, 1872, he gave a classic account of his days in Nevada; while *The Gilded Age*, 1873, written in collaboration with Charles Dudley Warner, satirized contemporary life but drew on Twain's recollections of his own boyhood on the Mississippi.

But it was his next major work that secured Twain an honoured place amongst writers of juvenile novels and adventure stories for boys; a book destined to be followed some eight years later by the story acclaimed to be his masterpiece. *The Adventures of Tom Sawyer*, 1876, established itself as a classic of the genre and has remained a firm favourite with young people for close on a hundred years. Its plot is familiar through the medium of the countless reprints and new editions that have appeared with regularity since its original publication, and from the many cinema films and dramatic television presentations that occur in the present day. In the book, Tom Sawyer lives with his brother Sid and his Aunt Polly in St Petersburg, Missouri. In the course of one of his many mischievous and high-spirited pranks he sees Injun Joe stab the village doctor to death, and he is later able to absolve Muff Potter of the crime when he is arrested and tried. Tom and his sweetheart Becky Thatcher wander away on a school picnic and become lost in the caves where Injun Joe has also been trapped and has died. Action is fast and furious, and finally leads to the discovery of Joe's treasure, which Tom shares with his companion, the memorable Huck Finn, to close the book with a happy ending.

After his marriage and his settlement in Hartford, Conn., in the early seventies, Twain had written constantly, travelled as a lecturer in Europe and through much of the United States, dabbled with the stage, invested heavily and without success in a mechanical type-setter and other highly speculative ventures, and had finished by losing a small fortune in financing his own publishing business.

It was in the midst of all these diverse activities and trials and tribulations that he wrote an immortal classic of juvenile literature which is today accepted as his masterpiece and acknowledged as one of the greatest works of American fiction. *The Adventures of Huckleberry Finn*, 1884, was admirably told in Twain's inimitable way, carrying on the tradition of the boys' adventure tale in the manner of *Tom Sawyer*, in vividly descriptive and often grippingly exciting passages of vernacular prose. The middle chapters of the book, particularly the brilliantly written episode where Huck and his friend Jim, a runaway slave, drift in thick fog down the Mississippi, ever deeper into hostile Southern territory, are laced with philosophic and moral commentary that bears directly on the nature of the 'American experience' and contemporary way of life. In this respect at least, the work is far more than a mere adventure story for boys, and its deeper meaning is perhaps summed up in the author's comment through the tender-hearted Huck that 'Human beings *can* be awful cruel to one another'.

The young hero, Huck Finn, tells of his adventures after being removed from the care of the Widow Douglas by his drunken father. Huck manages to escape from his father and joins up with Jim. Together they make their way down the Mississippi River on a home-made raft; an adventurous journey that allows the author to introduce characters and situations in picaresque fashion as they drift further and further South. Huck becomes involved in the blood feud that has embittered the Granger and Sheperdson families, and he and Jim are later joined by two villainous confidence tricksters, the 'Duke' and the 'Dauphin'. Before long these crooks sell poor Jim into captivity; but at the end of the book Tom Sawyer reappears in time to help Huck to rescue his friend, neither of them knowing that Jim has earlier been given his freedom.

Copies of *Tom Sawyer* and *Huckleberry Finn* must form two of the cornerstones of any representative collection devoted to the history of the juvenile novel or library of teenage adventure stories. The first American edition of *Tom Sawyer*, 1876, if it is the first issue, printed on wove paper, with the verso of the half-title left blank, complete with its four pages of advertisements, and in its original publisher's binding of blue cloth, could well cost a collector as much as £500 ($1,200); although later issues of this edition can change hands for as little as £25 ($60). The first English edition, also dated 1876, can still be acquired for £10 ($24) to £20 ($48), depending on its condition. The first edition of *Huckleberry Finn*, 1884, was published by Chatto & Windus, London, the earliest issues having publisher's advertisements inserted at the end of the text printed with the date 'October, 1884'. Subsequent issues of the same edition have inserted advertisement leaves bearing later dates. At the time of writing, even fine copies of this first English edition seldom fetch more than about £30 ($72) at auction, and it is a book that can confidently be predicted to appreciate sharply in price in future years. The first edition to bear an American imprint was dated '1885'; but in this instance the values placed on the work by collectors reflect its true importance in the annals of literary endeavour. Those seeking to acquire a copy would do well to consult the relevant bibliography, for the volume is hedged around with the minutia of points of issue so beloved by members of the antiquarian and secondhand book-trade. The most important of these call for the original *blue* cloth binding (later changed to green); the portrait-frontispiece to be in the first or earliest state (it was re-etched on later occasions); page 283 to be of the first state of printing (it was later cancelled and inserted on a stub); and with the uncorrected words *Him & Another Man* listed on page 88. Two other minor points relate to the final figure '5' in the numeral at top of page 155 being missing (later replaced by a slightly larger figure 5); and the word 'was' on page 57 (instead of 'saw'). Much the most important attribute is that the volume should be bound in its original *blue* pictorial cloth, in which case it could well be worth as much as £400 ($960), although much depends on the condition in which it is found. A text as popular with young people as *Huckleberry Finn* seldom comes down to us today in anything but a well-read and much handled state, so a copy in really good or fine condition might well make as much as twice the figure I have quoted above. Copies of the first American edition bound in the later *green* cloth may still be picked up for as little as £45 ($108).

Few of Mark Twain's other books achieved any great popularity with young people, although many turned to his very readable *Life on the Mississippi*, 1883. The first part dealt with life on the river and his own youthful adventures, two subjects about which he was pre-eminently well informed and which allowed his talents for humorous autobiography full scope. *The Prince and the Pauper*, 1881, Twain wrote after reading *The Prince and the Page; a story of the Last Crusade*, 1866, by Charlotte Yonge; and he advertised it as 'a tale for young people of all ages'. His two later juvenile novels were more ambitious ventures, but neither *Tom Sawyer Abroad*, 1894, nor *Tom Sawyer, Detective*, 1895, achieved anything like the success of his earlier works and were only feeble shadows of his classic tales that children throughout the world had come to love.

Following his disastrous venture into the publishing business resulting in his bankruptcy in 1894, Twain set off on a lecture tour around the world. By 1898 he was once again solvent and had paid off all his debts; but he remained a restless traveller, commenting freely on contemporary affairs in his never-ending series of public lectures. During his latter years he received many honours, but he cherished most the degree of Doctor of Literature conferred on him by Oxford University in 1907. Three years later he died at his house, Stormfield, in Redding, Connecticut. More than one obituarist prophesied that Twain would be remembered as the one great literary genius produced by the American West, and there are few who would quarrel with that assumption even in the present day.

One of the few other American writers of the period whose adventure novels achieved international fame, and were read by boys all over the world, was Jack London (1876–1916). Born in San Francisco, he spent most of his youth in acute poverty. He received the major part of his education in the slums and the dockside taverns of the Oakland waterfront; but he read voraciously every book he could lay his hands on and spent days hidden away in public libraries. London was the natural son of a music teacher and a poverty-stricken quack doctor, and as a boy earned the few cents that kept him from semi-starvation by selling newspapers in the streets of San Francisco. Later, he signed on as a seaman aboard a sailing vessel, took a job as a mill hand in a jute mill, raided oyster beds, spent nights in jail, and then turned tramp, roaming over the greater part of the eastern United States.

Returning to his home town of Oakland, he managed to secure a place in the local high-school, became an avowed socialist, and then spent one term at the University of California before joining the frantic gold-rush to the Klondike. On his return in 1898, he found himself once again out of work, but he began writing of his experiences and was finally successful in selling a story in December that year to the *Overland Monthly*. Acceptance by *The Atlantic Monthly* of his *Odyssey of the North* in July 1899, and

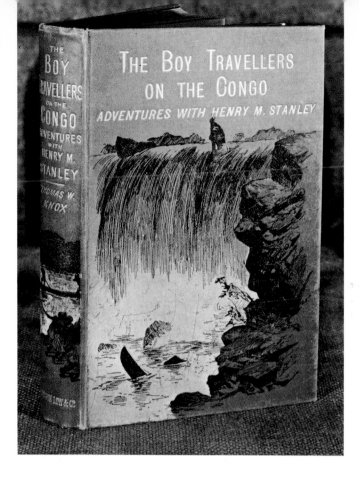

Published in 1888, by the American writer Colonel Thomas W. Knox, this travel and adventure book was based on H. M. Stanley's two-volume work *Through the Dark Continent*

First English editions of two of Jack London's most popular works, soon adopted by boys as their own

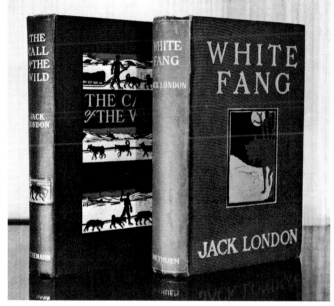

the publication of his first volume of stories *The Son of the Wolf*, 1900, convinced London that he had at last discovered his true vocation. Before long he had earned the title of 'the Kipling of the Klondike', and the international success of his best-selling novels *The Call of the Wild*, 1903; *The Sea Wolf*, 1904; and *White Fang*, 1906; all meant for an adult readership but avidly devoured by teenagers in both America and Britain, gave him the financial independence he had struggled for since boyhood.

London's earlier books, such as *Children of the Frost*, 1902; *God of his Fathers*, 1902; and *Cruise of the Dazzler*, 1902; were now being reprinted, and first London editions of his most popular tales were appearing in England under the imprint of William Heinemann and Methuen & Co. The majority of his fifty or so full-length novels do not concern us here as their subject matter contained little of interest to young people; but many read and enjoyed his *Cruise of the Snark*, 1911, and other of his seafaring tales. In 1912, London sailed round the Horn, returning to his native California to write *Smoke Bellew*, 1912, and *The Star Rover*, 1914. *John Barleycorn*, 1913, his semi-autobiographical novel, went some way to revealing his own problems of heavy drinking and extravagance. London's later work showed the deterioration of his mental powers brought on by his excesses, and, as he had forecast seven years earlier in *Martin Eden*, 1909, he ended his life by suicide.

Most of the first editions of London's books (all of which appeared under various American imprints) can still be purchased for quite moderate sums. His

most famous work, *The Call of the Wild*, published in New York, seldom exceeds £40 ($96) at auction, and this for the rare first issue, bound in vertically-ribbed pictorial cloth. There are issue points about several other of his titles, notably *The Sea Wolf*, the earliest issues of which are lettered in gold on the spine. After his death, his wife, Charmian London, published *The Book of Jack London*, 2 vols, 1921, New York; while *Sailor on Horseback*, 1938, by I. Stone, is another valuable source of biographical detail.

Some of the early stories of Francis Bret Harte (1836–1902), many of which first appeared in his own paper *The Overland Monthly*, were short sketches of mining life. *The Luck of Roaring Camp*, 1870, first published in book form in Boston, became almost as popular a favourite with young people as it was with adults; while his famous humorous poem *Plain Language from Truthful James*, 1870, known universally under the title of its refrain 'The Heathen Chinee', was recited with the gusto it deserved by hundreds of teenage voices. Joseph Hull of Chicago produced a set of nine lithographed cards depicting scenes from the ballad, in which a bland Oriental makes rings around two irate Western cardsharpers and beats them handsomely at their own crooked game. Collectors of early children's books also look for Harte's *The Queen of the Pirate Isle* (1886), published undated by Chatto and Windus, London, in which little Wan Lee, a Chinese boy, leads Polly and her cousin, Hickory Hunt, together with Patsey, the son of a neighbour, on a piratical expedition through the Californian foothills:

The actual, prosaic house in which the Pirates
apparently lived, was a mile from a mining
settlement on a beautiful ridge of pine woods
sloping gently towards a valley on the one side, and
on the other falling abruptly into a dark deep olive
gulf of pine trees, rocks, and patches of red soil.
Beautiful as the slope was, looking over to the
distant snow peaks which seemed to be in another
world than theirs, the children found a greater
attraction in the fascinating depths of a mysterious
gulf, or 'cañon', as it was called, whose very name
filled their ears with a weird music.

To creep to the edge of the cliff, to sit upon the
brown branches of some fallen pine, and putting
aside the dried tassels to look down upon the backs
of wheeling hawks that seemed to hang in mid-air
was a never failing delight. Here Polly would try
to trace the winding red ribbon of road that was
continually losing itself among the dense pines of the
opposite mountains; here she would listen to the far
off strokes of a woodman's axe, or the rattle of some
heavy waggon, miles away, crossing the pebbles of
a dried up water course. There were no frowning
rocks to depress the children's fancy, but everywhere
along the ridge pure white quartz bared itself
through the red earth like smiling teeth, the very
pebbles they played with were streaked with
shining mica like bits of looking-glass. The distance
was always green and summer-like, but the colour
they most loved, and which was most familiar to
them, was the dark red of the ground beneath their
feet everywhere. It showed itself in the roadside
bushes; its red dust pervaded the leaves of the

overhanging laurel, it coloured their shoes and pinafores; I am afraid it was often seen in Indian-like patches on their faces and hands. That it may have often given a sanguinary tone to their fancies, I have every reason to believe.

Bret Harte was a first-class story-teller, yet despite the excellent quality of his descriptive prose and the vivid picture he portrayed of adventurous Californian children in the latter half of the nineteenth century, *The Queen of the Pirate Isle* is sought by collectors much more for the Kate Greenaway illustrations than for the text. This is understandable, for this little quarto-sized volume contains some of Miss Greenaway's finest and most enchanting pictures of children. On receiving his presentation copy from the illustrator, his close friend, John Ruskin wrote to her: '. . . it is lovely. The best thing you have ever done – it is so *real* and natural . . . it is all delightful . . .'. Fine copies of this slim little volume, in their original pictorially-printed buckram bindings, are now seldom priced at less than £50 ($120) in the catalogues of antiquarian booksellers.

Finally, a place must be found for a writer whose books for boys, preaching the comforting philosophy that virtuous living, and a healthy respect for established Christian religion, is invariably rewarded with wealth, have left a deeper mark on the American character than the talented works of many a greater mind. Horatio Alger (1832–99), was born at Revere, Massachusetts, and his first recorded work is *Bertha's Christmas Vision: an autumn sheaf*, 1856, issued bearing a Boston imprint (as were nearly all his early titles). In 1860, Alger graduated at Harvard Divinity School, and was ordained as a minister, but resigned his living six years later and moved to New York. By this time he had already published *Frank's campaign; or, What boys can do on the farm*, 1864; and his novel *Helen Ford*, 1866; and he became determined to establish a career as a writer. He had taken lodgings not far from the Newsboys' Lodging House in New York, and he was soon taking an almost morbid interest in the half-starved young inmates of this juvenile doss-house for the penniless street urchins of the city. He soon established a close, and often charitable, association with the teenage boys there, and he turned this to good account with the publication of his first best-seller *Ragged Dick*, a sensationally successful work that was published undated in Boston in 1868. From that time onwards Alger produced several books for boys every year, the majority of which had as their theme from-rags-to-riches, or how a little street arab can rise to millionaire. *Rough and ready; or, Life among the New York newsboys* (1869); *Luck and pluck; or, John Oakley's inheritance* (1869); *Mark the match boy*, 1869; *Ben, the luggage boy; or, among the wharves* (1870); and *Sink or swim; or, Harry Walton's resolve* (1870); were the first of a rapid succession of titles all of which carried the same message. He sentimentalised and idealised the life of the under-privileged young waifs and strays of New York; later widening his net to include such titles as *Julius; or, the street boy out West* (1874); *The young miner; or, Tom Nelson in California* (1879); and *Bob Burton; or, the young ranchman of Missouri* (1888). He sometimes varied his theme by producing idealised versions of the biographies of famous men, such as *Abraham Lincoln; the backwoods boy* (1883); but to the end of his life he continued the same reiterated story of the penniless newspaper seller who ultimately achieves riches. *Do and dare; or, a brave boy's fight for fortune* (1884); *Adrift in the city; or, Oliver Conrad's plucky fight* (1895); *Adrift in New York; or, Tom and Florence braving the world* (1900), the latter part of the title later being changed to 'Dodger and Florence braving the world'; *Adventures of a New York telegraph boy; or, 'Number 91'* (1900), one of the few books he published under the pseudonym 'Arthur Lee Putnam'; and finally back to the Lodging House with the posthumous title *Ben Bruce. Scenes in the life of a Bowery newsboy* (1901).

Alger is known to have written a total of one hundred and forty two titles, nearly all of which were books for boys. Seventy different American publishing houses gave their imprint to his works, and fifty of these issued his books in the format of pictorially-printed paper-wrappers in the style of the *Dime Novels* that E. S. Ellis so often used. Joseph deMello,

writing in the American magazine *Western Collector*, has estimated that there are well over four thousand known collectors of the first and early editions of Horatio Alger's works, so it is hardly surprising that these now command higher prices at auction and in booksellers' catalogues than the work of almost any other juvenile author of the period. No comprehensive bibliography of his works exists, and the difficulties inherent in tracking down and dating the first and other important editions he wrote are made much greater by the fact that most of his books were issued without bearing dates on their title-pages. The ephemeral nature of their bindings, many being issued in flimsy paper-wrappers, resulted in their expectation of life being only a few weeks or months, and those that have come down to us in reasonably good condition after a hundred years must owe their preservation to a series of fortuitous circumstances.

The English writer 'Hesba Stretton', can be said to have earned the title of 'Mother of the street arab school'. In December 1867, the Religious Tract Society published what was destined to be her most famous book, *Jessica's First Prayer*, a title that had been serialised in the magazine *Sunday at Home* the previous year. 'Hesba Stretton' was the pseudonym of Sarah Smith (1832–1911), and she achieved fame and fortune by this book alone, a title which sold well over a million and a half copies. With this and her many subsequent books written in much the same vein, the Victorian seal of approval was set on uplifting juvenile works dealing with the sorrows of the poor. Hesba Stretton established a taste for stories dealing with the plight of homeless children who strove virtuously and honestly to earn their daily bread by overcoming seemingly insurmountable difficulties. Often their reward was a comfortable, even a wealthy, old age, in a station in life a little above that for which God had originally intended them. Many other authors followed the trend she had set, and typical of these was *Dusty Diamonds cut and polished – A tale of City-Arab life and adventure*, 1884, by R. M. Ballantyne. In the United States of America there can be no doubt that Horatio Alger well deserves the title of 'Father' of the same fraternity.

The Tide of Adventure

By the mid-1870's, the literate population of Britain was growing at a pace that must have gladdened the hearts of all those concerned with the book-publishing trade. The increasing use of the steam-driven printing-press and other labour-saving innovations was gradually bringing down the price of books to a level that made them readily accessible to an ever-widening circle of readers, while the number of members of the subscription and circulating libraries was growing by leaps and bounds. The passing of the Elementary Education Act of 1870, and the consequent hunger for books by the increasing number of children who could now read and write, led to expansion and prosperity for publishing houses in general, but had the greatest effect on those specialising in the production of children's books and teenage novels. The demand for school text-books, school prizes in book form, library books for schools, and a host of other literary needs created a thriving seller's market.

Publishers began to understand more clearly the contrasting and varying needs of boys and girls in different age groups, and within a few years increasing specialisation had caused the sub-division of the industry into a number of distinct fields. Publishers who produced only works for the juvenile market had existed since the days of John Newbery in the mid-eighteenth century; but there now came into being houses who concentrated nearly the whole of their output in one particular age-group. For the teenage market, bindings were restyled, with spines and covers pictorially blocked in gold and vivid colours on a rainbow of contrasting backgrounds. New book-cloths were devised, and publishers vied with one another to create eye-catching formats to attract customers in the teenage market; a class of readers who could now be expected to make their own choice of titles. The calibre of writing of many children's authors improved to a degree that gave the world a host of titles that are now household names and classics of juvenile English literature.

Two great landmarks in the annals of children's books were separated in time by nearly twenty years; but each marked a decisive victory over the now scattered exponents of moral earnestness. The appear-

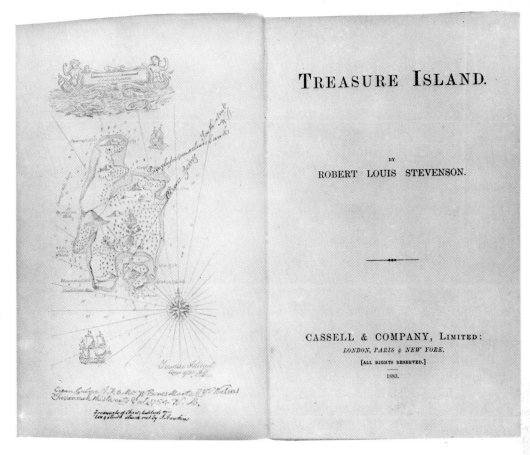

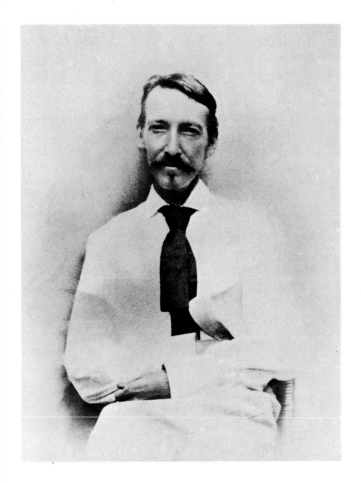

ance of *Alice in Wonderland*, 1865, by 'Lewis Carroll'
(Rev. C. L. Dodgson, 1832–98), showed that fairy
tale and fantasy had reached their culminating point
of triumph with this 'children's book for grown-ups'
and its companion volume, *Through the Looking-Glass*,
1872. The battle for juvenile emancipation in the
literary field was finally won with the publication of
that immortal classic *Treasure Island*, 1883, by Robert
Louis Stevenson (1850–94). Young people could
identify themselves with the Jim Hawkins of the
apple-barrel perhaps more easily than Alice in her
dream-world of fantasy and make-believe, but both
were rational human beings who became as easily
excited, bored, irritated and bad-tempered as the boy
or girl who turned the pages of their books.

Stevenson's love of the islands of the South Seas
stemmed from his first reading of Ballantyne's *The
Coral Island*, a story related earlier in this work. From
the time he first met his hero at the age of fifteen,
Stevenson had made a number of attempts to write a
novel, but each effort had ultimately been abandoned.
'The succession of defeats lasted unbroken till I was
thirty one,' he told his readers later. His earlier travel
books and collections of essays achieved only moderate
sales, *New Arabian Nights*, 2 vols, 1882, being the one
title accorded the distinction of appearing in a second
edition.

Yet the origin of the book which was to bring him

both fame and fortune was unpremeditated and quite accidental. Stevenson, with his wife and step-son Lloyd Osbourne, then twelve years old, was spending a cold, damp holiday with his parents at Braemar in August, 1881. During a particularly wet day, he set out to amuse the boy by drawing a detailed and complicated map of a South Sea island, which he outlined in water-colour. He named it Treasure Island, and legended the inlets, capes, bays, hills and harbours with romantic names, such as 'Haulbowline Head', 'Spyglass Hill', 'Rum Cove', and 'Skeleton Island'. The home-made chart fired not only his step-son's imagination, but Stevenson's as well, the idea of an adventure story of buried treasure and buccaneers coming to him in a flash. 'The next thing I knew,' he wrote later, 'I had some paper before me and was writing out a list of chapters.'

The next morning he had finished the first chapter and read it aloud to the family as soon as they had finished lunch. Their enthusiasm was greater than he had expected, his father taking an active interest in the future progress of the plot by drawing up an inventory of the contents of Billy Bones' sea-chest, and providing his son with the idea of the apple-barrel as a hiding place for young Jim Hawkins. On the advice of friends, Stevenson submitted the story to a Mr Henderson, the editor of a boys' magazine called *Young Folks*. It was in this obscure periodical that the story made its appearance as a serial, under the title 'The Sea Cook; or, Treasure Island', the author hiding behind the pseudonym of 'Captain George North'. The story ran from the issue dated 1st October, 1881, to that of 28th January, 1882; but it was not until Cassell & Company, London, issued the tale as *Treasure Island*, 1883, in book form, complete with a frontispiece showing the famous map, that the work suddenly became popular and Stevenson discovered himself the author of one of the best-selling novels of all time. Within a few years the story had been translated into nearly every European language, and in the U.S.A. it was as popular with young people as it was in Britain.

The book is rich in Stevenson's own observations on life and personal experiences, but also reflects the good use to which he put his early reading. Woven into the fabric of the story we can recognise the stockade and blockhouse from *Masterman Ready*, the skeleton pointer from the pages of Edgar Allan Poe, and the history of Billy Bones from a tale by Washington Irving. As Dennis Butts has observed in his *R. L. Stevenson*, 1966 (Bodley Head), 'the real quality of the book lies in its almost perfect combination and integration of characters and incidents to illustrate and embody motives and themes, for if it is in one sense a richly-exciting narrative of a search for buried treasure, it is also a serious exploration of such moral questions as conscience, loyalty and treachery; and the study of an adolescent coming to terms with the world of adult behaviour'.

What imaginative boy could resist a protracted encounter with an adventure novel whose opening sentence heralds thrills and excitements too strong to be resisted. From the moment when Jim Hawkins opens the tale as the narrator of events with these beckoning words, we are lost to the everyday world:

Squire Trelawney, Dr Livesey, and the rest of these gentlemen having asked me to write down the whole particulars about Treasure Island, from the beginning to the end, keeping nothing back but the bearings of the island, and that only because there is still treasure not yet lifted, I take up my pen in the year of grace 17—, and go back to the time when my father kept the 'Admiral Benbow' inn, and the brown old seaman, with the sabre cut, first took up his lodging under our roof.

Surely, one of the best and most compelling opening sentences in any novel yet written!

The book was issued in four different cloth colours, none of which denote any particular priority of issue. As has been pointed out in *The Collector's Book of Books*, the commercial binders stocked bolts of bookbinders' cloth in the hues selected by the author himself, or his publishers. As one bolt was used up, another was taken down for use, and this could well be of a contrasting colour to that previously used. It is known from letters of authors in the late-Victorian era that they sometimes selected as many as four cloth colours for the binding of their works, and the random use of these by the craftsmen employed in the bindery meant that the volumes went to the bookshops and circulating libraries in a variety of hues. *Treasure Island* appeared dressed in blue, olive-green, or red diagonal-ribbed cloth, lettered in gold on the spine, each with inserted publisher's advertisement leaves at the end of the text. These inserted advertisement leaves usually bear coded dates, those with the letters '5G-783' (i.e. 7th month, 1883) printed at the foot of the first page being in the earliest issues of the first edition. Other issues have dates such as '5R-1083' or '5R- 12.83', and denote later issues of the work. A copy of the earliest issue, in good condition in the original publisher's cloth binding, might well be worth as much as £200 ($480) at present-day market values. The first illustrated edition, dated 1885 (Cassell & Co), was published at six shillings, and contained the chart and some twenty five other illustrations. The most sought after of the hundreds of later editions are those of 1927, containing a suite of twelve coloured plates and other illustrations by the artist Edmund Dulac (1882–1953); and the issue of the Limited Editions Club, 1941, with hand-printed lithographs signed by the artist. Copies of either of these two editions would now be priced at over £30 ($72).

Of Stevenson's other works, two of the most popular with young people were *Kidnapped – being Memoirs and Adventures of David Balfour in the year 1751*, 1886, issued with a folding map-frontispiece; and its sequel *Catriona*, 1895; the central incident in the plot being the murder of Colin Campbell, the 'Red Fox of Glenure', an actual historical event. David Balfour and Alan Breck are witnesses to the crime, and suspicion falls on them; but, after a perilous journey across the Highlands, they manage to escape across the Forth. The sequel is principally occupied with the unsuccessful attempt of David Balfour to secure, at the risk of his own life, the acquittal of James Stewart of the Glens, who has been falsely accused, from political motives, of the murder of Colin Campbell.

Moonfleet, 1898, by John Meade Falkner (1858–1932), established itself as a near classic adventure story in the tradition of Stevenson's *Treasure Island*. The latter's *Black Arrow*, 1888, was originally conceived as a serial for *Young Folks*

Kidnapped was a book Stevenson was justifiably proud of having written, for it contains some of the finest of his creative writing. He seemed aware of this when he wrote a presentation inscription in a copy he gave to a friend:

Here is the one sound page in all my writing,
The one I'm proud of and that I delight in.

The Black Arrow: a tale of two roses, 1888, was originally conceived as a serial for *Young Folks*; and was followed by *The Master of Ballantrae: a winter's tale*, 1889. *The Wrong Box*, 1889, a highly successful satire with overtones of detective fiction; *The Wrecker*, 1892; and *The Ebb-Tide*, 1894; were a trio written in collaboration with his step-son, Lloyd Osbourne. Yet of all his books, with the notable exception of *Treasure Island*, possibly none appealed to teenage boys as much as the *Strange Case of Dr Jekyll and Mr Hyde*, 1886. It was a work that first appeared in a humble binding of paper-wrappers, printed in red and blue, and priced at one shilling a copy, yet it proved to be Stevenson's first popular success in the adult market; soon being discovered by inquisitive schoolboys intrigued by the horrific possibilities conjured up by the author's portrayal of dual personality. It was a work they commandeered as their own, in much the same way that an earlier generation had demanded cheaply-produced yet lavishly illustrated copies of *Uncle Tom's Cabin*, by Harriet Beecher Stowe (1811–96). When her two-volume work, dated 1852, first appeared in book form under the imprint of John P. Jewett & Company, Boston, Miss Stowe never for one moment imagined that teenagers the world over would adopt it as one of their own favourite novels, yet such was the demand from readers of all ages that over twenty different editions, bearing as many rival imprints, were issued in Britain within a few months of the book's first appearance in America. Numerous examples can be cited of works primarily or wholly intended by their authors for an adult readership that soon became best-sellers in the juvenile field. Stevenson discovered that *Strange Case of Dr Jekyll and Mr Hyde* was relished as much by teenage boys, with their seemingly insatiable love of the macabre, as it was by their parents.

His love of the islands of the Pacific led him and his wife to make their home in Samoa, and it was here that Stevenson bought the 'Vailima' property which became his permanent home in April, 1890. And it was here, at the age of forty-four, that the author of *Treasure Island* and so many other well-loved books, was suddenly struck down by cerebral haemorrhage on 3rd December, 1894, dying a few hours later. The next day he was buried in a romantic site on a hill near Apia; his grave has long been a place of pilgrimage. The book he considered his masterpiece was left unfinished at his death, but the completed chapters are acknowledged by critics to include much of his finest and most powerful writing. It was published as *Weir of Hermiston: an unfinished romance*, 1896, the final chapters to complete the work having been supplied by Arthur Quiller-Couch.

Collectors who manage to acquire a first or early edition of *Treasure Island* may notice that the first line of the buccaneer's song is printed with a deficiency of capital letters:

Fifteen men on the dead man's chest –
Yo-ho-ho, and a bottle of rum!

I remember puzzling over this line as a boy, wondering whether the pirates swigging their rum were crowded together like so many sardines on an extra big sea-chest, once the property of a dead comrade; or were they in some way seated on or around his corpse? In fact, Stevenson had taken the name, with all its sinister suggestiveness, from Charles Kingsley's *At Last: a Christmas in the West Indies*, 2 vols, 1871, in which a small islet in the Caribbean Sea, formerly the haunt of pirates, is named as Dead Man's Chest Island. It was some time before Stevenson noticed this printer's error, but it was corrected in later editions.

Among the Samoans, who still cherish his memory to this present day, he was their friend Tusitala – 'the teller of tales', and it is with the same affection that young people the world over remember the author of the adventure book that still takes pride of place on their shelves. Stevenson imparted an artistic quality to what until then had been the humble adventure story for teenage boys, realising their thirst for believable dramatic adventure peopled with characters whose motives were clear and understandable to the logical minds of youth. *Treasure Island*, with the vivid intensity of its action-filled plot blends in a mixture of moral originality, especially in the character of that likeable rogue Long John Silver, while its dramatic progress to a seemingly logical conclusion makes an instant imaginative appeal to boys of all ages. It is a story that has never been surpassed as a tale of adventure, unmoralised and unashamed.

The 1870's and the decade which followed produced no literary figure in the same field of anything like comparable stature; but it was the period that witnessed the publication of some of the earliest works of authors who were later to achieve fame as writers of the increasingly-popular juvenile adventure novel. Chief amongst these was undoubtedly George Alfred Henty (1832–1902), a man who had been ridiculed by his classmates for writing poetry while a pupil at Westminster School. Born at Trumpington, near Cambridge, the son of a wealthy mine-owner, he enlisted in the Hospital Commissariat soon after the outbreak of the Crimean War, later acting as a freelance agent of the *Morning Advertiser* as one of the newspaper world's first war-correspondents. His dramatic letters describing the siege of Sebastopol received prominent treatment in its columns, and the success of his stories of the war decided Henty, in 1865, on making journalism his full-time career. During the decade that followed, he was employed by *The Standard* and found himself in the thick of several minor European wars and almost a dozen colonial campaigns of varying degrees of bloodiness. The crushing of native tribes in revolt against the British Raj, and the constant flag-planting and empire building that accompanied the military expeditions to their far-flung outposts, he mirrored in many historical novels written during the final quarter of the nineteenth century.

His earliest attempts as a writer of the type of romantic three-volume novels called for by the circulating and subscription libraries failed miserably. Throughout his career he was never able to make the slightest impact on an adult readership, and one has only to attempt to wade through the introductory chapters of any of his novels of serious intent to understand instantly why this was so. His first book, *A Search for a Secret*, 3 vols, 1867, is typical of the rest of his output intended for adults; page after page of turgid prose and interminable descriptive passages intended to give 'atmosphere' to a tale whose flimsy plot is unable to sustain the characters he so painstakingly created. His next novel, *All but Lost*, 3 vols, 1869, fared just as badly; as did his later work in the same field: *Rujub the Juggler*, 3 vols, 1893; *Dorothy's Double*, 3 vols, 1894; and *The Queen's Cup*, 3 vols, 1897. Nevertheless, present day collectors of his works are prepared to pay several hundreds of pounds to obtain copies of these all but unreadable novels at auctions, and I have seen *A Search for a Secret* catalogued as high as £750 ($1,800) in the list of a London antiquarian bookseller.

Autobiographical accounts of his experiences as a war-correspondent were given in *The March to Magdala*, 1868; and *The March to Coomassie*, 1874. But it is with his adventure stories for boys that Henty's reputation as a writer stands or falls. Late in 1870 he started to write a juvenile novel, modelling the plot on an updated variation of *The Swiss Family Robinson*. *Out on the Pampas*, 1871, appeared under the imprint of Griffith and Farran, London, complete with a series of four full-page illustrations by J. B. Zwecker, and was the first of nearly a hundred tales for young people.

From the start of the tale the author made it clear that his heroes were not to be penniless emigrants seeking to find wealth and fortune in far off foreign lands, or castaways washed up on some remote yet idyllic coral strand. The head of his family of middle-class adventurers, a prosperous architect 'whose father had recently died, leaving him the sum of £3,000' ($7,200), Mr Frank Harvey decides to try his luck in the Argentine Republic, taking his wife

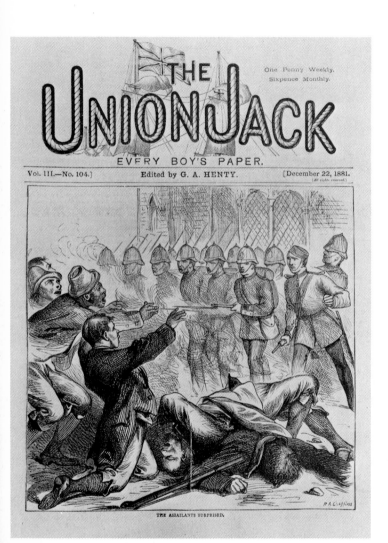

The troubles in Ireland received prominent treatment in the 1880's from the writers of boys' adventure stories. The picture shown was to illustrate *Christmas Eve on Detachment*, by J. Percy Groves, which ran as a serial in *The Union Jack*

and family with him. Mrs Clara Harvey, and her four growing children, Charley and Hubert, aged fifteen and fourteen respectively, Maud, twelve, and Ethel, eleven, have a Spanish teacher specially engaged for them, and for nine months take daily lessons in the language. The boys have a small armoury of weapons purchased for them, including Colt revolvers, rifles and shotguns, 'and many a dead blackbird soon attested to their improving skill'. After nearly a year of careful preparation, the family embark at Liverpool, taking with them their housemaid, Sarah, and a vast accumulation of cabin trunks, hat-boxes, and various impedimenta. Henty was making quite sure that none of the characters in his tale would have to rough it in the manner of the lower orders then emigrating in their thousands to the Americas, and the whole saga of the adventures of the Hardy family is permeated with a comforting sense of well-being and self-satisfied prosperity.

Soon after they arrive in Argentina, Mr Hardy purchases a parcel of some 25,000 acres of land by auction at an average price of '6d an acre', and it is here that the family set up their ranch 'Mount Pleasant'. A gang of native labourers is employed in the building of the house and stockade, but the two boys work hard at their carpenters' lathes, making tables and chairs and supplying the family with food by their hunting expeditions. Before long the inevitable happens, and a raid by Indian tribes deprives them of most of their livestock. The many battles with the rustlers that follow are particularly well told, and it is here that Henty for the first time displayed his talent for writing vividly descriptive accounts of hand-to-hand fighting, authentic-sounding tales of night raids on enemy emplacements, and seemingly factual descriptions of mounted skirmishes and set-piece battles with a courageous foe. This was a formula used in countless books that flowed so readily from his pen in later years, but it was in the pages of *Out on the Pampas* that his young readers were first able to sample the real-life experiences of this hardened campaigner and seasoned war-correspondent carefully woven into a fictional tale of adventure and romance. All ends happily, with each of the young members of

the family marrying well at a time when Mr Hardy computes that the ranch and livestock have increased to the value of some £40,000 ($96,000). Before sailing for England, he tells his sons that they can 'save £5,000 ($12,000) each in ten years, and you will receive another £10,000 ($24,000) each as your share of the estate. You will consequently, boys, at the age of thirty-one and thirty-two, be able to settle down in England in very comfortable circumstances . . .'. And the author concludes the tale by telling his readers that: 'Everything prospered at Mount Pleasant, and at the sale it was broken up into lots and fetched rather a larger sum than Mr Hardy had calculated'.

Henty's first book for boys was, in essence, a tale of British commercial enterprise and middle-class pioneering spirit in the hostile environment of a sparsely-populated foreign land. As an exercise in social and political propaganda on behalf of Victorian established ideals of commercial acumen and attention to business inevitably leading to capital appreciation and a prosperous old age, the book could hardly have been bettered. The fact that the wealth of the Hardy family was accumulated through ruthless pioneering in foreign parts lent an aura of valour that both young and old applauded. Although set in the year 1851, the story in no way relied on historical interest as a background for its plot, and this first juvenile adventure tale was an experiment in straightforward narrative set against a geographical background in the manner of R. M. Ballantyne. From that time onwards Henty turned to the historical novel as a vehicle for his romances, using Sir Walter Scott as his mentor and guide.

Almost immediately after the publication of *Out on the Pampas* he evolved the technique he employed continuously for the rest of his literary career, setting his stories of adventure against what then passed for a well-researched historical background of facts and figures. *The Young Franc-Tireurs and their adventures in the Franco-Prussian War*, 1872 (Griffiths and Farran), informed his readers that he was still 'Special Correspondent of *The Standard*', and had in fact reported the war from both Berlin and Paris to the readers of

the newspaper in Britain. Yet despite its historical accuracy, drawn from the author's first-hand knowledge of events, *The Young Franc-Tireurs* was no more successful as a juvenile novel than *Out on the Pampas*. Both sold moderately well, but neither appeared as a second edition until well after Henty had established himself as a popular editor of boys' magazines that carried his stories into thousands of homes throughout the land.

The turning point in his career as an author came with the illness and subsequent death of W. H. G. Kingston, editor and founder of *The Union Jack*. In May, 1880, Henty took his place as editor, and at the end of that year his first really successful book for boys appeared, again under the Griffith and Farran imprint. *The Young Buglers. A Tale of the Peninsular War*, 1880, was issued with eight full-page illustrations by John Proctor, and no less than eleven folding plans of battles, an unheard of bonus in a book specially written for teenagers. Coupled with the fact that Henty made sure that the title-page of the magazine always carried, under the editor's name, the legend: 'Author of . . .' followed by a list of his latest book titles, *The Young Buglers* could hardly fail to sell well. His next book, *In Times of Peril – A Tale of India*, 1881, was first printed as a serial in *The Union Jack*, appearing in each weekly number until its

conclusion in issue No. 40, on 30th September, 1880. By this time *The Cornet of Horse*, 1881, was already in the bookshops, published by Sampson Low, Marston, Searle & Rivington, the firm who had taken over the ownership of *The Union Jack* from Cecil Brooks & Co., who had themselves acquired the magazine from its original owners Griffiths and Farran. From that time onwards Henty's name became a household word amongst younger members of the community, juvenile historical novels issuing from his pen at the rate of two or three a year right up to the time of his death in 1902.

The Young Franc-Tireurs was revived and ran as a serial in *The Union Jack* from May, 1881; *Winning his Spurs*, 1882, told the tale of the Crusades; while *Jack Archer*, 1883, gave a thinly disguised account of the author's own experiences during the Crimean War. But it was with the appearance of *Facing Death; or, The Hero of the Vaughan Pit, A Tale of the Coal Mines*, 1882, that Henty formed the business connection that finally set the seal on his literary career. Not being satisfied with the financial terms offered by Griffiths and Farran, or with the payments received from Sampson Low, he submitted the manuscript of *Facing Death* to Blackie & Son, at their offices at 49, Old Bailey, London. Terms were agreed on the basis of a ten per cent royalty on all sales up to five thousand

"BEFORE HE COULD STRIKE AGAIN, I HAD RUN HIM THROUGH." [*p. 13*]

copies, increasing thereafter to a maximum of fifteen per cent. A substantial advance was made to the author, and a business friendship cemented that continued without interruption for the rest of his life. He had used as a drop-title at the head of the first chapter the words 'Facing Death: or, How Stokebridge was civilized'; and the book drew largely on his own experiences of visits to his father's coal mines in Staffordshire when still a boy at school. Blackie & Son had procured the services of a first-class book-illustrator for the work in the shape of Gordon Browne (1858–1932), the son of the famous Hablot K. Browne (1815–1882), whose pseudonym 'Phiz' (complementing the author's 'Boz') first appeared on the copperplate engravings used to illustrate *Pickwick Papers* by Charles Dickens. The combination of a lively text, detailing the adventures of pit-boy Jack Simpson from the age of six years until his final ownership of the Vaughan Pit and retirement to a wealthy old age, and Browne's action-filled illustrations, ensured the book's success. The second edition (so marked on the title-page, information always lacking on later titles) was published within a few months, this time dated '1883', and the book continued in print until well into the first quarter of the twentieth century. *Under Drake's Flag: A tale of the Spanish Main*, 1883, continued the Blackie connection, and the firm instituted the device of dating at the foot of the title-page first editions only. Later issues of the first edition (after the first substantial printing was exhausted) omitted this date, as did all subsequent editions, so the collector has an obvious clue to guide him when assessing a volume's worth. From 1883 onwards, Blackie & Son made it an almost invariable house-rule that only first issues of the first edition of any particular title were dated on the title-page: should this date be lacking (although the volume may otherwise appear exactly the same in both text and format) then it is almost certainly a re-issue. The advertisement leaves found inserted at the end of the book, changing by being brought up to date in later issues, are another means of dating the volume.

Henty had by this time settled into his stride as a best-selling author of boys' adventure stories and title followed title in rapid succession. Only occasionally did he stray from the Blackie fold: *Friends, Though Divided – A Tale of the Civil War*, 1883, had been promised to Griffith and Farran earlier; while *The Young Colonists*, 1885 (George Routledge & Sons); and *A Women of the Commune*, 1895 (F. V. White & Co.); were exceptions to the general rule. These out of sequence titles, and his earliest works for Griffith and Farran, are now the most difficult of his juvenile first editions to discover in acceptable condition. All command high prices on the few occasions when they are offered for sale.

It was in 1883 that Blackie & Son first used the attractive device of olivine edges on their books for boys. Henty's *By Sheer Pluck: A Tale of the Ashanti War*, 1884, had been published in the summer of 1883 (dated forward to the following year), and in early December came his *With Clive in India*, 1884, a work which proved to be the most successful of his novels to date. It was on this volume that the experiment of coating the outer edges of the leaves of the book with an opaque and shiny varnish was first tried. This new embellishment, coupled with other innovations such as casing the volumes in a binding of heavy bevelled boards (against the straight-cut edges previously employed), while retaining the vivid pictorial-cloth brightly blocked in gold and colours, proved extremely attractive to young would-be purchasers. Within a few months re-issues of Henty's earlier titles were appearing in a similar format (omitting the dates upon their title-pages), and the sales figures were so encouraging that Blackie & Son made this style of binding mandatory for all their better-class teenage novels.

With Clive in India was highly praised by the critics for its historical accuracy, and was soon in firm demand by schoolmasters and teachers as a prize to reward their most deserving pupils. The author, in his preface to the work, emphasised that the facts he had presented in the novel had been checked with the most reliable authorities; telling his readers:

In the following pages I have endeavoured to give you a vivid picture of the wonderful events of the ten years, which at their commencement saw Madras in the hands of the French, Calcutta at the mercy of the Nabob of Bengal, and English influence apparently at the point of extinction in India, and which ended in the final triumph of the English both in Bengal and Madras.

There were yet great battles to be fought, great efforts to be made before the vast empire of India fell altogether into British hands; but these were the sequence of the events I have described. The historical details are, throughout the story, strictly accurate, and for them I am indebted to the history of these events written by Mr Orme, who lived at that time, to the *Life of Lord Clive*, recently published by Lt. Col. Malleson, and to other standard authorities.

In this book I have devoted a somewhat smaller space to the personal adventures of my hero than in my other historical tales, but the events themselves were of such a thrilling and exciting nature that no deeds of fiction could surpass them.

From that time onwards nearly every book Henty wrote followed the same set pattern, and to scan his list of titles reveals immediately his determination to exploit to the full the potential of the historical novel as a juvenile best-seller. Within a few years his list of

"HUGH, SEIZING A POKER, SPRANG AT HIS UNCLE."

credits included: *In Freedom's Cause: A story of Wallace and Bruce*, 1885; *St George for England: A tale of Cressy and Poitiers*, 1885; *The Lion of the North: A tale of the times of Gustavus Adolphus and the Wars of Religion*, 1886; *Through the Fray: A tale of the Luddite Riots*, 1886; *The Dragon and the Raven: or, The days of King Alfred*, 1886; *The Bravest of the Brave: or with Peterborough in Spain*, 1887; *Bonnie Prince Charlie: A tale of Fontenoy and Culloden*, 1888; and *With Lee in Virginia: A story of the American Civil War*, 1890. In each case the book was prefaced by the author's acknowledgement of the debt he owed to writers who had published historical surveys of the period covered in his novel, and to those biographers whose lives of distinguished patriots and military commanders he had used as a factual background for his plot and characters.

Henty was now the most important member in Blackie's stable of authors, and the publishers made sure that the foremost names in the world of book illustration were pressed into service on his behalf. Gordon Browne remained a firm favourite; but Maynard Brown, G. C. Hindley, W. H. Margetson, W. H. Overend, H. M. Paget, Wal Paget, W. Parkinson, Ralph Peacock, Alfred Pearse, William Rainey, Charles M. Sheldon, John Schönberg, C. J. Staniland, Stanley Wood, and W. B. Wollen, were all employed during the succeeding years. The format of his full-length books remained constant

A pictorial binding
calculated to attract young
people. Dated 1898, the
lettering was blocked in
silver and gold and outlined
in red. Size of front cover
23.5 × 17 cm.

from 1883 until well into the Edwardian era, and the style proved so attractive to young purchasers that almost every publishing house specializing in books for teenagers copied Blackie's original design.

Henty's later works rapidly became stereotyped in both content and format, even the titles having a similar ring. *Through the Fray*, mentioned above, was followed by *Through the Sikh War*, 1894; *Through Russian Snows*, 1896; *Through Fire and Storm*, 1898; and *Through Three Campaigns*, 1904; while the earlier *Under Drake's Flag*, was complimented by *Under Wellington's Command*, 1899. A further series started with *With Clive in India*, and continued: *With Wolfe in Canada*, 1887; *With Lee in Virginia*, 1890; *With Cochrane the Dauntless*, 1897; *With Moore at Corunna*, 1898; *With Frederick the Great*, 1898; *With Buller in Natal*, 1901; *With Roberts to Pretoria*, 1902; *With the British Legion*, 1903; *With Kitchener in the Soudan*, 1903; and *With the Allies to Pekin*, 1904.

The debt the late-Victorian and Edwardian educationalists owed to G. A. Henty as a popular historian was often acknowledged in later years, when the boys who had devoured his historical romances and adventure tales had grown to manhood. The present writer well remembers the interest stimulated in Indian history when, as a boy of twelve, he first read *With Clive in India*; and how his knowledge of the African empire-building campaigns, presented in a dry-as-dust catalogue of dates and battle names at school, was increased in a painless and most enjoyable fashion as he read title after title from Henty's seemingly endless list of works. R. M. Ballantyne rendered an equal service to the young by broadening their knowledge of parts of the world unknown and unvisited, with descriptions of the exotic fauna and flora thrown in for good measure. Between them, Ballantyne and Henty fostered an early and invincible love of reading amongst thousands of teenage boys, and the basic facts and figures they presented in sugar-coated fashion stuck in the memory long after their insubstantial plots and characters had faded and been forgotten.

Henty's life was well documented by his friend and colleague George Manville Fenn (1831–1909) whose

George Alfred Henty – The Story of an Active Life, 1907, appeared as a second edition (with extra illustrations) in 1911. He reveals that Henty's books brought him a substantial income in later life, enabling him to indulge his hobby of yachting to the full. And it was on his yacht *Egret*, the last of a line of similar but less expensive sailing-vessels he had owned, that Henty died. In the autumn of 1902 he had suffered a stroke which had left him partly paralysed; but he had insisted on another short cruise in his schooner. She had anchored in Weymouth harbour on her return from sea, and it was there, after contracting pneumonia, that one of the most popular authors of books for boys was found dead in his bunk on 16th November, 1902. He was buried in Brompton cemetery.

Henty's biographer had himself graduated into authorship through the medium of a journalistic career. Manville Fenn was born in Pimlico, London, and studied at the Battersea Training College hoping to qualify for a post as a teacher. For a few years he was junior master at a small school at Alford, Lincolnshire, only to lose his job in 1854. He returned to London and entered the printing trade, and by May, 1862, he had saved enough to start his own poetical magazine *Modern Metre*. Two years later he bought an interest in the *Herts and Essex Observer*, a small provincial newspaper published at Bishop's Stortford.

But in 1864 Fenn determined to relegate journalism to second place as a means of livelihood after his story *In Jeopardy* was accepted by Charles Dickens for inclusion in *All the Year Round*. From that time onwards he concentrated all his energies into making a name as an author; but he was never able wholly to abandon journalism, and in 1870, in order to augment his income, he accepted the post of editor of *Cassell's Magazine*.

It is as the author of a long list of boys' adventure stories and teenage novels that Fenn is remembered today. His first full-length book in this field, *Hollowdell Grange; or, Holiday Hours in a Country House*, 1866, is now a sought-after collector's item, and one of the most difficult of his first editions to find in acceptable condition. Like his friend and colleague G. A. Henty, Fenn made several attempts to establish himself as a novelist of the type subscribed for by members of Mudie's and W. H. Smith's. *Thereby Hangs a Tale*, 3 vols, 1876 (Tinsley Brothers); *King of the Castle*, 3 vols, 1892; *In an Alpine Valley*, 3 vols, 1894; and several other three-deckers, were followed by the single-volume novels of the Edwardian era, such as *Blind Policy*, 1904. He also wrote several detective fiction tales, of which one of the best was *The Vibart Affair*, 1899.

His boys' adventure stories consumed much the greater part of his literary output, and he had the knack of choosing intriguing titles that must have stimulated the interest of potential purchasers to a marked degree. *The Golden Magnet*, 1884; *Quicksilver; or, The Boy with no Skid to his Wheel*, 1889; *The Rajah of Dah*, 1891; *Sawn Off*, 1891; *Real Gold*, 1894; *Draw Swords!*, 1898; *Walsh, The Wonder Worker*, 1903; and *Marcus: The Young Centurian* (1908) figure among his hundred or more juvenile novels. As a writer he was far closer to R. M. Ballantyne than G. A. Henty, and several of his titles, such as *Menhardoc: A Story of the Cornish Nets and Mines*, 1885, owe a considerable debt to his rival. Fenn's first editions are not always easy to identify, for a great many made their earliest appearance undated, especially those issued under the Ernest Nister imprint, or that of the S.P.C.K.

I would certainly not be forgiven if I made no mention of the stories teenage boys adopted as their own from the canon of work of Sir Henry Rider Haggard (1856–1925). He started his literary career with a biographical account of the Zulu chieftain, entitled *Cetywayo and his White Neighbours*, 1882, published at a time when Cetywayo had been brought to England as a prisoner before being restored as king of the Zulus the following year. But it was with his novels *Dawn*, 3 vols, 1884; and *The Witch's Head*, 3 vols, 1885; that his name first became known to a

CLARE FINDS THE ADVANTAGE OF A POWERFUL FRIEND.

wide public. *King Solomon's Mines*, 1885, followed almost immediately, and became a firm favourite with teenagers within a few months of publication. The large folding coloured frontispiece was enough to intrigue any boy lucky enough to obtain a copy, with its legend that it was a facsimile 'of the Map of the Route to King Solomon's Mines, now in the Possession of Allan Quatermain, Esq., drawn by the Dom José da Silvestra, in his own blood, upon a Fragment of Linen, in the year 1590'; while the book itself, with the never-to-be-forgotten witch-like figure of the sorceress Gagool shuffling through its pages, was one of the most gripping adventure stories ever written. Haggard's book *She – A History of Adventure*, 1887, was another teenage favourite; as were *Allan Quatermain*, 1887; *Ayesha: the return of She*, 1905; and *Queen Sheba's ring*, 1910.

An important contemporary of both Stevenson and Henty was George MacDonald (1824–1905), although his literary fame stems largely from his gift of writing fairy stories rather than books of adventure. His *Phantastes: a Faerie Romance for Men and Women*, 1858, was followed later by *Dealings with the Fairies*, 1867; but he contributed some important titles to the list of Victorian juvenile novels. The most successful of these was *At the Back of the North Wind*, 1871, a story that made its first appearance as a serial in the magazine *Good Words for the Young*. It was illustrated in a sensitive and intuitive fashion by Arthur Hughes (1832–1915), a well-known member of the pre-Raphaelite Brotherhood, with a series of pictures that exactly fitted the mood of the book. MacDonald had written the novel as a religious allegory (he was at one time a congregational minister), and told how his young hero Diamond, the half-starved son of a coachman, lives out his harsh and straitened existence in working-class London. Each night reality dissolves into a dream-world in which he finds peace and happiness by travelling with the North Wind. The wind appears in the shape of a kind and beautiful woman with streaming long black hair. In this, the boy Diamond shelters from the cruelties of the world and finally dies, finding sanctuary at last 'at the back of the North Wind'. MacDonald's other books for young

people included *Ranald Bannerman's boyhood*, 1871; *The Princess and the Goblin*, 1872; *Gutta Percha Willie: the Working Genius*, 1873; *The Princess and Curdie*, 1883; and *The Light Princess, and other Fairy Stories*, 1890. None of his first editions are easy to find, and all command high prices; but all his juvenile titles were later re-issued under the Blackie imprint.

Sir Samuel W. Baker (1821–93), famous for his discoveries detailed in *The Albert N'yanza and Exploration of the Nile Sources*, 2 vols, 1866; turned for light relief to writing at least one successful book for boys. *Cast up by the Sea*, 1869 (Macmillan), with illustrations by Huard, contained a preface by the author-explorer in which he set out his reasons for producing the work:

Since the publication of the *Albert N'yanza*, and the *Nile Tributaries of Abyssinia*, I have received numerous letters from boys to whom I was entirely unknown, and who are at this moment unknown to me except through their spontaneous correspondence. Their letters were written in the youthful enthusiasm of the moment, when, having shared in the excitement of our African journeys, they closed the book, and, full of sympathy, they wrote to me effusions which I prize as the outburst of boyish admiration for a successful struggle against difficulties.

As a proof of the value that I attach to these warm expressions of interest taken by the young in our past adventures, I now dedicate to all boys (from eight years old to eighty) a story of fiction, combined with certain facts, that will, I trust, relieve the dreariness of a long Christmas evening.

At the same time that I have endeavoured to avoid all improbabilities, I must apologize for having taken an astronomical liberty, in producing an eclipse of the sun which is not in the Almanac.

Set on the rock-strewn north coast of Cornwall in 1791, *Cast up by the Sea* relates the activities of the wreckers who lure the unfortunate crews of ships to their doom by putting out false lights on every stormy night. A variation introduced by Baker was the accidental drenching in lamp-oil of one of the principal wreckers, an old hag named Mother Lee. The ship selected as a victim is within a few hundred feet of the rocks, believing the two lighted beacons mark the entrance of a sheltered harbour, when Mother Lee trips over her keg of lamp-oil, soaking her hessian skirt. The gale blows the beacon flames towards her and she quickly becomes a human torch, falling screaming onto the rocks below. The captain puts the helm hard over, drops his anchors, and the good ship *Polly*, with the hero of the tale on board, is saved in the nick of time. *Cast up by the Sea* passed through several editions, later being issued by Gall & Inglis with a coloured pictorial-frontispiece that was repeated as an inset illustration on the front-cover of the volume.

Verney Lovett Cameron (1844–94) was another African explorer who later took pleasure in writing stories for boys, being prompted to do so, he told his readers, by the number of letters received from young people who had read his *Across Africa*, 2 vols, 1877. *In Savage Africa*, 1887; and *Among the Turks*, 1889; both issued under the Nelson imprint, are representative of his boys' adventure stories, while *The Adventures of Herbert Massey in Eastern Africa*, 1888, with illustrations by A. W. Cooper, was probably his most popular boys' story.

The Orchid Seekers – A Story of Adventure in Borneo, 1893, was the result of collaboration between Ashmore Russan and Frederick Boyle. Russan had applied to Sander & Company, St Albans, the premier importers and growers of orchids at that time, for information on orchid-collecting abroad for a story he proposed to write for the *Boy's Own Paper*. He was put in touch with the explorer and successful orchid species collector Frederick Boyle, and together they wrote *The Orchid Seekers*. Boyle supplied most of the scientific facts and figures and details of the geographical background, while Russan produced the plot and the characters of the tale. The book was so successful that the joint authors wrote a sequel: *The Riders – or Through Forest and Savannah with 'The Red Cockades'*, 1896, which again passed through several editions.

The final exponents of the now swiftly-flowing tide of adventure to find places in this chapter must be James F. Cobb (1829 – *c*. 1895), and David Ker (1842–1914). Cobb achieved a measure of fame with his *The Watchers on the Longships*, 1878, a tale of adventure in the lighthouses that dot our coasts, and a book that went through at least twenty editions before the turn of the century. *Silent Jim; A Cornish Story* (1871); and *Off to California* (1884) (the latter a free translation from the Dutch of Hendrik Conscience's *Het Goudland*, 1862), were less successful, and *Martin the Skipper*, 1883, appears to be his only other boys' story. David Ker specialised in adventure stories set in the wilder and unexplored regions of the earth, and typical of his titles are: *On the Road to Kiva*, 1874; *The Boy Slave of Bokhara*, 1875; *Lost Among White Africans*, 1886; and *O'er Tartar Deserts*, 1898.

By the time this last title appeared, all the well-known writers in the genre were being crowded and jostled by an eager throng of newcomers, while the number of publishing houses who issued nothing but adventure stories for boys, and diverse assortments of juvenile novels, had increased four-fold in the last decade. It was only the outbreak of World War I that temporarily stemmed the tide of adventure stories that now constituted an important part of late nineteenth century literary output; but the war itself was to generate a new style of teenage novel.

The Public School Saga

With one notable exception, school stories for teenage boys did not make their appearance until the 1840's; but by the latter half of the Victorian era they had established themselves as one of the most popular forms of juvenile literature.

The eighteenth century had drawn to a close with the publication of an anonymous work: *The Parent's Assistant; or, Stories for Children*, 3 vols, 1795. This collection of short stories had been written by Maria Edgeworth (1767–1849), with the purpose of exemplifying the principles later expounded in her *Practical Education*, 2 vols, 1798, a work written in conjunction with her father Richard Lovell Edgeworth (1744–1817). The original edition of *The Parent's Assistant* contained the stories of *The Little Dog Trusty*, *The False Key*, *The Purple Jar*, *The Bracelets*, *The Birthday Present*, and *The Mimic*, among several others. It is a work of the utmost rarity, and surviving copies of the two-volume second edition of 1796 can be counted in single figures.

It is this second edition which concerns us here, for the author added to it her story of *The Barring Out*. This was not only a tale of public school life that exactly fitted the tradition of firm-chinned loyalties and unswerving devotion to one's gentlemanly code of ethics, later accepted as symptomatic of the whole stereotyped genre of school stories; but it was also the so-far unacknowledged archetype of the countless tales of school life that poured from the presses of publishing houses throughout Britain some three-quarters of a century later. Maria Edgeworth had unconsciously devised a new literary art form that was later to become the stock-in-trade of several generations of writers who used practically no other medium of expression. Yet for several decades no use whatsoever was made of her original idea, and it was the 1850's before full-length stories of the trials and tribulations of life in the boarding schools of Britain first made their appearance.

The Barring Out told how the arrival of the wealthy young Mr Archer as a pupil at Dr Middleton's boarding school immediately divides the loyalties of the boys into two separate camps. Archer becomes the bitter rival of the head-boy De Grey (we are not told the Christian names of any of the boys), and when Dr Middleton refuses permission for the school amateur theatricals to be held in one of the outbuildings on the playing-fields, the division into two camps is complete. Many of the pupils side with young Archer, and he devises a scheme for barring all the windows on the inside and thus effectively locking out the headmaster.

A battle takes place between the De Grey faction and the boys loyal to Archer, with watering-cans being used to deluge the rebels barricaded in the school hall below. Dr Middleton and his staff strike back by cutting off the food supplies, but Archer and his drenched and hungry gang manage to hold out for two nights, keeping up their spirits by singing 'Rule Britannia!' Finally, some of his adherents mutiny and Archer is tied hand and foot. De Grey obtains admittance, bringing a basket of food; Archer repents his sins, and Dr Middleton strides purposefully into the barred and bolted school hall:

His steady step was heard approaching nearer and nearer. Archer threw open the door, and Dr Middleton entered. Fisher instantly fell on his knees.

'It is no delight to me to see people on their knees; stand up Mr Fisher. I hope in all conscious that you have done no wrong.'

'Sir,' said Archer, 'they are conscious that they have done wrong, and so am I. I am the ringleader – punish me as you think proper – I submit. Your punishments, your vengeance, ought to fall on me alone.'

'Sir,' said Dr Middleton, calmly, 'I perceive that, whatever else you may have learned in the course of your education, you have not been taught the meaning of the word Punishment. Punishment and vengeance do not, with us, mean the same thing. *Punishment* is pain given, with the reasonable hope of preventing those, on whom it is inflicted, from doing *in future* what will hurt themselves or others. *Vengeance* never looks to the *future*; but it is the expression of anger for an injury that is past. I feel no anger – you have done me no injury.'

Here many of the little boys looked timidly at the windows.

'Yes; I see that you have broken my windows, that is a small evil.'

'O Sir, how good! how merciful!' exclaimed those who had been most panic-struck – 'he forgives us!'

'Stay,' resumed Dr Middleton; 'I cannot forgive you – I shall never revenge, but it is my duty to punish. You have rebelled against the just authority which is necessary to conduct and govern you, whilst you have not sufficient reason to govern and conduct yourselves. Without obedience to your master, as children, you cannot be educated. Without obedience to the laws,' added he, turning to Archer, 'as men, you cannot be suffered in society. . . . This is a long sermon, Mr Archer, not preached to show my own eloquence, but to convince your understanding. Now, as to your punishment!'

'Name it, Sir,' said Archer; 'whatever it is, I will cheerfully submit to it.'

In the event, Archer and his followers are let off lightly, losing most of their pocket-money and having to report back to school early from play for the next two months. A bell will summon them to start their penance each evening.

'O Sir, we will come the instant, the very instant, the bell rings – you shall have confidence in us,' they cried, eagerly.

'I deserve your confidence, I hope,' said Dr Middleton, 'for it is my first wish to make you all happy. You do not know the pain that it has cost me to deprive you of food for so many hours.'

And he reveals that his only reason for forbidding the boys to use the outbuildings in the school playing fields for a theatre, was for their own protection. A party of gipsies had broken in and been sleeping there, some of whom had since contracted 'a putrid fever'.

'De Grey, you were in the right,' whispered Archer, 'and it was I that was unjust.'

And the two boys silently clasp hands. From then on they remain firm friends, their only rivalry being on the sports field. Both care for and protect the younger boys of the school and, under the wise superintendence of Dr Middleton, they prosper and do well in the world.

The Barring Out, written in the late eighteenth century, embodied many of the ideas on education propounded by Jean-Jacques Rousseau (1712–78); but still managed to tell an intriguing story of boarding school life and the jealousies and rivalries so often discovered there. It was not until the appearance of *The Crofton Boys*, by Harriet Martineau (1802–76), that any comparable work was written for young people. It is perhaps significant that two of the earliest public school stories we know of were both written by women, whereas in later years this field was almost exclusively a masculine preserve.

The Crofton Boys was first published in 1841 as the last of the four volumes of a series of tales called *The Playfellow*, and it was issued as a separate work in 1856. Shortly afterwards, within a period of only twelve months, two books appeared that were destined for international fame. Between them they caused school stories to take the prominent place in teenage literature they held for close on a hundred years. The first introduced us to one of the most acceptable of mid-Victorian schoolboy heroes, set, most appropriately, in the Rugby of the redoubtable Dr Arnold, at the dawn of the golden age of the British public school.

Tom Brown's School Days, 1857, issued by Macmillan & Company, over a Cambridge imprint, was published anonymously as being by 'An Old Boy'. The author was Thomas Hughes (1822–96), a barrister and Christian socialist, who had himself been a pupil at Rugby School at a time when Arnold was still headmaster there. And it was the Rugby of his own schooldays that he described so faithfully through the lips of Tom Brown. He told his readers that his purpose was to write 'a real novel for boys – not didactic, like *Sandford and Merton* – written in the right spirit, but distinctly aiming at being amusing'. The plot is too well known to bear further repetition, and was deservedly immensely popular from the book's first appearance. It has more than once been suggested that, between them, Dr Arnold and the story of *Tom Brown's School Days* made the modern public school. The battles fought on the playing fields were mirrored in Hughes' novel, and in the jingoistic school song shouted to the rafters by generations of teenage voices:

God gives us bases to guard and beleaguer,
Games to play out, whether earnest or fun,
Fights for the fearless and goals for the eager,
Twenty and thirty and forty years on!

Three more editions of *Tom Brown's School Days* appeared during 1857, its first year of issue, and a few months later the work was in its sixth edition. It was to this sixth edition that the author added a preface in which he quoted from the letter of an anonymous correspondent:

My dear Hughes,

I blame myself for not having earlier suggested whether you could not, in another edition of *Tom Brown*, or another story, denounce more decidely the evils of *bullying* at schools. You have indeed done so, and in the best way, by making Flashman the bully the most contemptible character; but in the scene of the *tossing*, and similar passages, you hardly suggest that such things should be stopped – and do not suggest any means of putting an end to them.

This subject has been on my mind for years. It fills me with grief and misery to think what weak and nervous children go through at school – how their health and character for life are destroyed by rough and brutal treatment. . . .

There ought to be a certain amount of supervision by the master at those times when there are special occasions for bullying, e.g. in the long winter evenings, and when the boys are congregated together in the bedrooms. Surely it cannot be an impossibility to keep order, and protect the weak at such times.

Whatever evils might arise from supervision, they could hardly be greater than those produced by a system which divides boys into despots and slaves.

Literally hundreds of letters poured in to the publisher's offices congratulating Hughes for exposing some of the worst evils of the public school system, and within a few years boards of governors at leading boarding schools were introducing reforms aimed at eradicating many of the excesses and humiliations their younger pupils were exposed to.

Good copies of the first edition of *Tom Brown's School Days* in the original publisher's cloth binding, complete with the twenty four pages of inserted advertisements dated February, 1857, are now priced at about £100 ($240). Rebound copies, more commonly met with for this very popular text, fetch less than half this price, and an even lower figure should the half-title be missing. The first illustrated edition, 1869, with its portrait frontispiece, is now a £25 ($60) book; but the best of the later editions is that dated 1878, with its series of full-page and other illustrations by Arthur Hughes and Sydney Prior Hall.

Thomas Hughes' sequel to his juvenile best-seller was *Tom Brown at Oxford*, 3 vols, 1861, a work that was much less purposive and direct in its impact. It never achieved anything approaching the success of the earlier work; but, as a Victorian three-decker, is sought by collectors at sums ranging up to £120 ($288). It was issued in a cloth binding under Macmillan's Cambridge imprint, and the earliest issues contained twenty four pages of advertisements in Vol I, plus a single leaf of advertisements in Vol II. Half-titles are called for in all three volumes. *Tom Brown at Oxford* made its original appearance in a series of ten, monthly, paper-wrapped parts of some four hundred and eighty four pages, issued under a Boston, U.S.A. imprint dated 1859–60; an edition seldom met with.

The only other of Hughes' books with any appeal to young people was *The Scouring of the White Horse; or, The Long Vacation Ramble of a London Clerk*, 1859, containing a delightful series of illustrations by Richard Doyle (1824–83), known affectionately as 'Dickie' Doyle. He designed the original front-cover for *Punch* magazine, and was an artist employed on numerous children's books. *The Scouring of the White Horse* was a book read by older children with a deal of amusement, and today copies of the first edition are collected as much by those interested in the evolution of publishers' binding styles and book illustration, as by those seeking an early copy of the text. Doyle also designed the striking gold-blocked pictorial binding.

Within a few months of the publication of *Tom Brown's School Days* the second notable title depicting Victorian boarding-school life appeared. *Eric or Little by Little – A Tale of Roslyn School*, 1858, by Frederick W. Farrar (1831–1903), was published by Adam & Charles Black, Edinburgh. It was the future Dean of Canterbury's first book and one that brought him immediate and lasting fame. Written when he was still a master at Harrow School, the work had little to do with the muscular Christianity of Hughes' earlier tale.

Farrar had used the title 'little by little' to sum up the gradual decline into sinful ways of the hero, Eric Williams, while a boarder at a public school. Before the story has progressed very far Eric starts to use words that scandalise his ultra-virtuous and up-right friend and companion Edwin Russell:

One day as the two were walking together in the green playground, Mr Gordon passed by; and as the boys touched their caps, he nodded and smiled pleasantly at Russell, but hardly noticed, and did not return Eric's salute. He had begun to dislike the latter more and more, and had given him up altogether as one of the reprobates.

'What a surly devil that is,' said Eric, when he had passed; 'did you see how he purposely cut me?'

'A surly . . .? Oh Eric, that's the first time I ever heard you swear.'

Eric blushed. He hadn't meant the word to slip out in Russell's hearing, though similar expressions were common enough in his talk with other boys. But he didn't like to be reproved, even by Russell, and in the ready spirit of self-defence, he answered –

'Pooh, Edwin, you don't call that swearing, do you? You're so strict, so religious, you know. I love

you for it, but then, there are none like you. Nobody thinks anything of swearing here.'

Russell was silent.

'Besides, what can be the harm of it? It means nothing. I was thinking the other night, and I concluded that you and Owen are the only two fellows here who don't swear.'

Russell still said nothing.

'And, after all, I didn't swear; I only called that fellow a surly devil.'

'O, hush! Eric, hush!' said Russell sadly, 'You wouldn't have said so half-a-year ago.'

Once started on the downward path, Eric slips from grace with startling rapidity. Before long, to Russell's intense distress, he starts secretly to smoke. Next term he downs pints of porter in a low pothouse, punches a master on the nose, steals pigeons from a loft, and almost (but not quite) purloins some cash. Wrongly suspected of theft the lad runs away to sea, to conditions of the utmost cruelty. The author had already regaled his readers with several flogging and whipping incidents; but now, having delivered his boy hero into the hands of a crew of seafaring men, his powers of description, when telling of the cruelties the lad endured, seem perceptively heightened.

After Eric has almost broken his leg he is ordered by the brutal captain of the ship to help the rest of the crew hoist sail, but collapses under the effort. He is immediately tied up, his shirt is ripped from his back, and then the captain and the crew stand in a semi-circle around the unresisting young boy while the author allows his imagination full play:

Again the rope whistled in the air, again it grided across the boy's naked back, and once more the crimson furrow bore witness to the violent laceration. A sharp shriek of inexpressible agony rang from his lips, so shrill, so heartrending, that it sounded long in the memory of all who heard it. But the brute who administered the torture was untouched. Once more, and again, the rope rose and fell, and under its marks the blood first dribbled, and then streamed from the white and tender skin.

This passage was suppressed in later editions; but it gives us something of the flavour of this remarkable work. It is a vivid example of the obsession with the physical characteristics and attendant discomforts corporal punishment visited on the heads (or, rather, the behinds) of young boys that so intrigued the clergymen and other masculine writers of this type of school story. The majority of public school masters of the day were in fact men of the cloth, and their delight in telling of the chastisements devised for their pupils in the fictional school stories so many of them wrote was most marked. *Pueris Reverentia: A Story for Boys and Masters*, 1892, by Rev. Henry William Pullen (1836–1903), himself the son of a rector, and, in early life, choir-master at York Minster, is typical of several others. He first sprang to fame with his pamphlet *The Fight at Dame Europa's School*, 1870, a satire on the German invasion of France and published a month after their investment of Paris. It was an inconsequential work which nevertheless sold over two hundred thousand copies and netted its author well over £3,000 ($7,200) in royalties. He then turned his hand to school stories, such as *Tom Pippin's Wedding*, 1871; and *The Ground Ash*, 1874; but it was with his *Pueris Reverentia* that he really gave vent to his feelings. Published at Salisbury, under the imprint of Brown & Company, the story tells of the adventures of a young pupil taken on a European sight-seeing tour in company of his form master, a clerical gentleman named, appropriately enough, Mr Fiddlebags. During term time, this master sends the boy, Charlie Tremlett, to the head for punishment. The author tells his readers that 'the schoolmaster of modern days is a gentleman, and his punishments are refined. Dr Ajax was not cruel, but he was hard – desperately hard . . .'. It was not the first time that Charlie had been birched 'by any means – and he turned his great brown eyes on the head in an attempt to avert his punishment'. But all in vain:

. . . two prefects, specially told off for the purpose, were in readiness to hold him down; and after a few unimportant observations from the Doctor, condemnatory of his disgraceful idleness and general reckless character of his career, he was desired to assume a condition of disordered garments, and group himself for the chastisement he so richly deserved. The prefects fell upon him gently and led him to a chair, assisting his unwilling fingers, with equal gentleness, to make things convenient for the Doctor. And very convenient indeed were all things made.

Charlie lent gracefully forwards upon the soft leathern seat of the high-backed chair, clutching the chamfered edge of the old-fashioned furniture with the desperation of one who feels that he is going to have a rough time of it, and would like at least to hang on to something. The prefects stood solemnly beside him, like supporters in a heraldic shield, each keeping Charlie at the proper angle with one hand, while the fingers of the other held up and twisted daintily the corners of the poor boy's shirt, lest the fluttering linen should get itself entangled with the twigs of the avenging rod, and temper the violence of the stroke to the shorn lamb. Dr Ajax, who was propriety itself, waited half a minute or so until all things were decently adjusted, coughing in a guttural whisper within himself, as if he wanted to make his throat believe that he had never seen such a thing in his life before, and that it rather shocked him.

He then unlocked a drawer, and took out from its inner depths two long wiry birches of a rich autumnal brown, most picturesquely knotted and fashioned with consummate skill. . . .

Dr Ajax tucked the right side of his gown behind his back, measured his distance with approximate accuracy, and dealt the first blow. Poor Charlie winced, and shrank, and shuddered, but uttered not a sound. The prefects stood clear, bending the victim's body still further forward towards the back of the chair, that the Doctor's arm might have fair play. The birch went hissing through the air and fell once more, raising a long red-freckled line. Charlie bit clean through the toffee till it stuck to his teeth like glue, and looked at the Head Master out of his great brown eyes, as if he would like to say: 'All right, old fellow, hit away. It hurts rather,

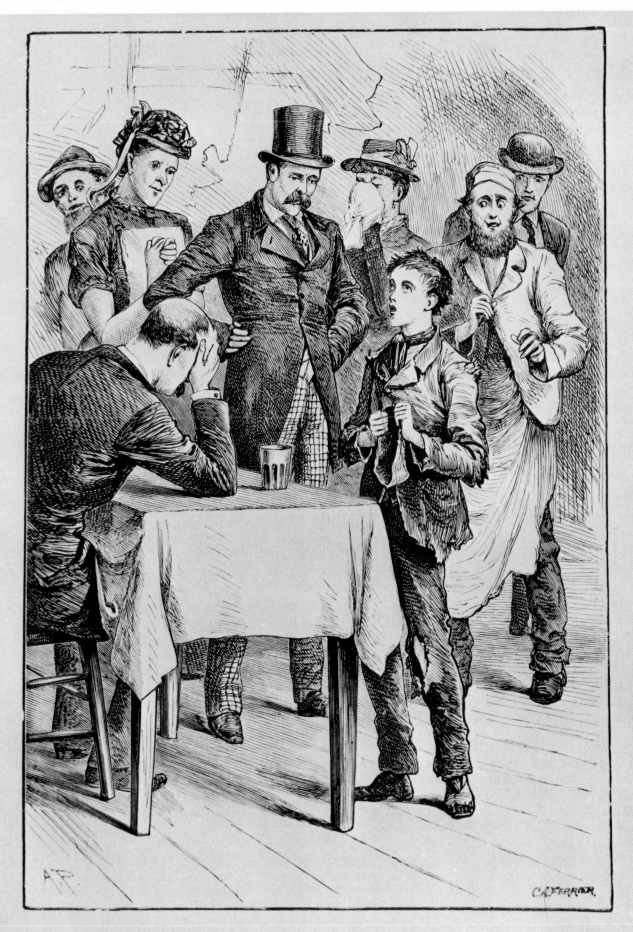

DIBS BEGAN TO SING IN A CLEAR, SWEET VOICE.

but never mind. I daresay you think I deserve it. I differ from you of course, but I don't bear you any malice . . .'. What would be the use of a Schoolmaster who could be moved by any such ridiculous appeal? It is well understood that a boy of thirteen is simply a troublesome young brat. . . .

When nine cuts had been delivered the Doctor paused for a few seconds to examine the birch; and observing that the knots had worn off, and the extremities of the twigs had peeled, giving the brush end of the instrument an altogether ragged and disreputable appearance, he changed the weapon, and fell to again. The boy is either very obstinate or very tough,' said he to himself; 'in either case, another half a dozen strokes won't hurt him, and he shall have them well laid on.' The new birch stung most cruelly, cutting crisp into the blistered wounds. It was as much as ever Charlie could do to keep quiet; and, struggle as he would, he could not restrain his tears. They ran down his cheeks in streams; and when the two prefects, who understood boys rather better than the Doctor did, saw how keenly the poor child was suffering, and how pluckily he was bearing up, they looked first at one another, and then at the Head Master in so very significant a way that the latter became uneasy, and stayed his hand.

After their holiday in Italy together, Mr Fiddlebags regrets the flogging he ordered the boy to undergo, and he begs Charlie's forgiveness:

'Oh please, sir, don't,' said the boy, beginning to sob. 'I haven't thought of it for a month or more. And it served me jolly well right; and it's all over now.'

'It isn't all over, Charlie, for the marks are on you still, I saw them when you jumped into the water at Lucerne, and they have haunted me ever since.'

This was the descriptive style of relished anecdotes of whippings and floggings which in part caused the French to invent the phrase 'maladie d'anglais' for

'NOW, MASTER TADPOLE, HERE'S YOUR INK.' [See p. 34.

types of sexual sadism. In *Eric or Little by Little*, the future Dean of Canterbury was so carried away by his chastisement of his young victim that he allowed him only just to survive his whipping. Eric finally returns home to learn that he is forgiven. Later, like his friend Russell, he dies, repenting his sins and 'with a smile playing gently around his lips'.

Farrar's other novels for youth include *Julian Home; A Tale of College Life*, 1859; *St Winifred's; or, The World of School*, 1862; and, *The Three Homes; A Tale of Fathers and Sons*, 1873, issued under the pseudonym of 'F.T.L.'. None achieved the success accorded to *Eric*, a book which, as a first edition, now commands about £60 ($144) for copies in the original publisher's cloth binding. The present writer has seen only a single copy in all his years of book-collecting, and it appears to be considerably rarer than first editions of *Tom Brown's School Days*.

Two works kept on the same shelf as the well-known titles just described are *The Collegian's Guide: or Recollections of College Days*, 1845, by Rev. James Pycroft (second edition 1858); and *Etonia Ancient and Modern*, 1865, by Rev. William Lucas Collins (1817–87); both of which exhibit, in milder form, similar interests to those which so engrossed their colleagues.

Another, but dissimilar, exponent of the saga of school life was Talbot Baines Reed (1852–93), an author who reacted strongly against the sentiments of both Hughes and Farrar. Born the third son of Sir Charles Reed (1819–81), chairman of the London

An illustration epitomising
the cruelty of an earlier
public school era. From *Fifth
Form at St. Dominic's*, 1887, by
Talbot Baines Reed

right
P. G. Wodehouse's first
book, the start of a very
long line of over two
hundred novels. Published
in 1902, when he specialised
in public school stories for
inclusion in *The Captain* and
other boys' magazines, *The
Pothunters* gives little
indication of the style that
would later make the
'Jeeves' books world famous

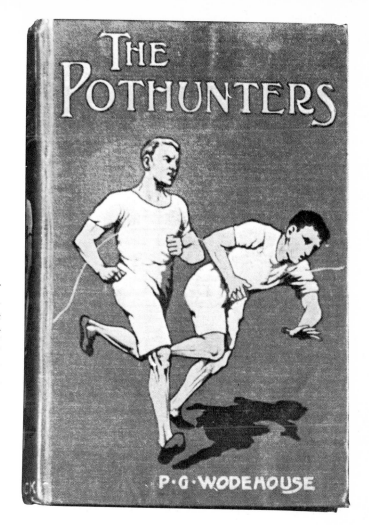

School Board, he joined his father's firm of type-founders and ultimately became managing director. As the founder of the Bibliographical Society, and the author of a number of books about books, including the authoritative *History of the Old English Letter-Foundries*, 1887, he would already have been well-known to bibliophiles even had he not written several influential juvenile novels. From its inception, Reed was a regular contributor to the *Boy's Own Paper*, and his personal collection of early children's books was one of the best in private hands. His most famous work: *The Adventures of a Three Guinea Watch*, published undated in 1883 by The Religious Tract Society as No. 1 in their series of cloth-bound volumes of *The Boy's Own Bookshelf*, had made its first appearance as a serial in the *Boy's Own Paper*. It ran from October 2nd, 1880, to April 16th, 1881, and when it was issued as a book the paper's editor, G. A. Henty, supplied a preface. The volume, which has all its full-page and other illustrations by Gordon Browne printed on the text paper, was published in the unusual format of a tall, square-rigged octavo, blocked pictorially in gold and silver on its front-cover and spine, and pictorially in black on the rear cover. It has always been a most difficult first edition to find in anything approaching original condition, a tribute to its popularity in its first few years of life.

The story of *The Adventures of a Three Guinea Watch* is related by the watch itself, a narrative device first used long before Charles Johnstone wrote *Chrysal; or, The Adventures of a Guinea*, 4 vols, 1860–65, in which the inanimate object of the title chronicles the events for the reader. Most members of the animal and bird kingdom have at some time been pressed into similar service by the writers of children's books in the style of *Black Beauty* (1877), by Anna Sewell (1820–78). One has only to recall such titles as *The Rambles of a Rat*, 1857, by 'A.L.O.E.' (i.e. Charlotte Maria Tucker, 1823–93); or *The Life and Perambulations of a Mouse* (1783), by Dorothy Kilner (1755–1836), to realise how early this method found favour with story-tellers. Talbot Baines Reed's book proved an instant success, and passed through numerous editions before the turn of the century.

His tales of boarding school life were hardly less popular, and *The Fifth Form at St Dominic's*, 1887; *The Cock-House at Fellsgarth* (1893); and *The Master of the Shell* (1894), all became best-sellers in their day. Others in the same vein were '*Follow my Leader*'; or, *The boys of Templeton*, 1885; *Tom, Dick, and Harry* (1894); and *The Willoughby captains; A school story*, 1887, none of which make more than a few pounds apiece as first editions.

The increasing interest in tales of public school life, coupled with the wide sales commonly achieved by such stories, persuaded dozens of hopeful writers to try their hand at similar schoolboy yarns. Many of these would-be professional writers were themselves schoolmasters, and almost without exception had once suffered the dubious honour of being boarders in such establishments.

A glance along my own shelves reveals a diversity of talent amongst a wide variety of titles and authors. Almost without exception they have long-since sunk without trace, their only monument being the names gold-blocked on the spines of the stories they hopefully penned in the late-Victorian and Edwardian eras. Yet their stories of school life are symptomatic of the middle and upper class society of their day, and were read as greedily by working-class boys as they were by the Oxford-accented young characters they displayed in so British a fashion. Many wrote nothing *but* school stories; some interspersed the drama of life in the lower fourth with adventure stories or tales of schoolboy detective fiction.

Lewis Hough was typical of a host of others that crowded publishers' tables with their bulky manuscripts, but he seems to have lost heart after writing *Phil Crawford*, 1882, and its sequel, *Dr Jolliffe's Boys: A Tale of Weston School*, 1884, both published by Blackie & Son. Andrew Home was more prolific, and a cross-section of his titles include: *From Fag to Monitor*, 1896; *Exiled from School*, 1897; *The Spy in the School*, 1899; *Story of a School Conspiracy*, 1900; *Jack and Black*, 1902; and *The Boys of Badminster*, 1905.

Charles H. Avery (1867–1943), who wrote under the name of 'Harold Avery', concentrated most of his output into tales of school life. *An Old Boy's Yarn*, 1895; *Frank's First Term; or, Making a Man of Him*, 1896; *The Dormitory Flag*, 1899; *Heads or Tails*, 1901; *A Toast-Fag*, 1901; *Sale's Sharpshooters*, 1903; *An Armchair Adventurer*, 1903; *The House on the Moor*, 1904; and *Off the Wicket*, (1910); were all published in vivid pictorial-cloth bindings, and his stories continued to appear until well into the 1930's. Walter Rhoades is now remembered almost solely for his *The Boy from Cuba – A School Story* (1900); although *For the Sake of His Chum*, 1909, appears to have achieved some success. Meredith Fletcher is another one-book man, with his *Every Inch a Briton*, 1901, illustrated by Sydney Cowell. Frederick J. Whishaw is listed by only a single title in the British Museum Catalogue; yet at one time he occupied an important position in the lists of subscription libraries such as Mudie Ltd, and W. H. Smith, where nearly sixty of his full-length novels were listed. *Lost in the African Jungles*, 1896; *The Three Scouts*, 1900; *The Boys of Brierley Grange*, 1906, with a fine series of illustrations by Harold Copping; *Gubbins Minor and some other fellows*, 1913; and *The Lion Cub – A Story of Peter the Great*, 1916, give a clear idea of Whishaw's type of story. *Ray: the boy who lost and won*, (1908), by J. Williams Butcher, is a difficult title to acquire, due to the author using as his publisher the obscure firm of Robert Culley Ltd, London, who had not the outlets of the larger pub-lishing houses. *The Senior Prefect; and other chronicles of Rossiter*, 1913, is the only other title of his I have been able to track down.

Stories of public schools found little favour in the U.S.A.; but a writer who achieved some success with tales of college life was Ralph Henry Barbour, whose *Winning his 'Y' – A Story of School Athletics*, 1910, passed through several editions. D. Appleton & Company, New York, published nearly twenty titles by this author, but I have been unable to discover any that appeared on this side of the Atlantic under a British imprint. Almost without exception, his stories were based on inter-school rivalries on the (American) football or baseball field, or on the running and athletics tracks.

F. Cowley Whitehouse wrote a successful story woven around the activities of a public school foot-ball team, under the unlikely-sounding title of *The Sniper*, 1907; while Charles Gleig's story *The Rebel Cadets*, 1908, centred around the adventures of a group of Dartmouth College naval cadets afloat on the training ship *Britannia*. Both these writers are credited with at least half a dozen other books for boys, all school or adventure stories.

Desmond Coke made a speciality of inter-school and inter-house rivalries. His book *Wilson's*, 1911, was later almost completely rewritten and enlarged, then published under the title of *The Worst House at Sherborough*, 1915, this time with a series of full-page coloured plates by H. M. Brock. The golden age of public school stories had passed its zenith when Gilbert L. Jessop wrote *Cresley of Cressingham*, 1924; but, as George Orwell pointed out in his famous article on 'Boys' Weeklies', printed in the magazine *Horizon*, Vol 1, No. 3, in March 1940, they were kept alive by the seemingly insatiable demand for serial stories of school life in magazines such as *The Gem*, *The Magnet*, and, to a lesser extent, the *Boy's Own Paper*.

It was left to Rudyard Kipling (1865–1936), to upset all the accepted traditions of school stories. His earlier series of short stories for teenage boys, collected in *The Jungle Book*, 1894, and *The Second Jungle Book*, 1895, were immensely popular. They have never since

Fine copies of the first
editions of Kipling's famous
series of Jungle Stories are
now valued at about £150
($360) a pair

Public school stories
published during the early
part of the twentieth century

This picture of the end of an
aerial dog-fight, by W. R. S.
Stott, appeared in *The Air
Scout* by Herbert Strang in
1912

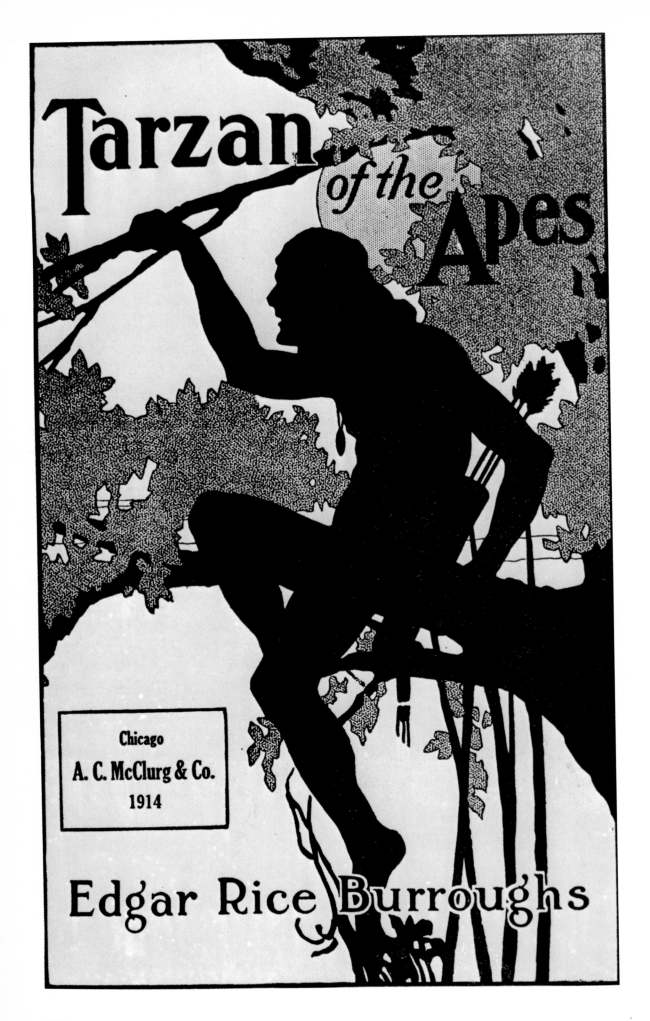

Tarzan
of the
Apes

Chicago
A. C. McClurg & Co.
1914

Edgar Rice Burroughs

The first issue of the first edition of a very long line of Tarzan books by the American author Edgar Rice Burroughs (1875–1950)

right
Scout Thurgate to the rescue! An illustration from the magazine *The Captain*, 1911, a periodical specialising in stories for grammar and public school boys

It was Thurgate's last chance. Relinquishing his grasp on the rail, he leant right over and made a great stab at the tyre. If his plan succeeded, the rescuing car might yet overtake them.

been out of print. Kipling told his young readers how the child Mowgli was brought up by the forest wolves, and how he was taught by Baloo, the bear. Bagheera, the black panther, schooled Mowgli in the law of the wild, and his adventurous life with his friends the animals of the jungle intrigued generations of boys. There was a strong affinity between the stories in the *Jungle Books* and the later remarkable adventures of *Tarzan of the Apes*, 1914, by Edgar Rice Burroughs (1875–1950), and the many sequels that fascinated tens of thousands of readers of all ages in America and Britain in the inter-war years.

The two *Jungle Books* will be given an honoured place in any collection devoted to the history of children's books. The first of the series is much the most difficult to find in good condition as a first edition, and a fine pair in the original publisher's cloth bindings now cost in the region of £100 ($240).

Kipling's other books for young people were also of importance, although, like the *Jungle Books*, they cannot rightfully claim a place in this chapter. *Just So Stories for Little Children*, 1902, was illustrated by the author, and the best of the many later editions was that of 1913, containing a fine series of coloured plates by J. M. Gleeson. *Puck of Pook's Hill*, 1906, and *Rewards and Fairies*, 1910, were deservedly popular, while '*Captains courageous*', a story of the Grand Banks, 1897, the only one of Kipling's books with a North American setting; and *Kim*, 1901, with illustrations by John Lockwood Kipling, the author's father; were also read by older children.

But it was with his memorable *Stalky & Co.*, 1899, a thinly-veiled autobiographical tale of his own teenage life while a pupil at the United Services College, North Devon, that Kipling really put the cat amongst the public school pigeons. It was a deliberately unsentimental series of stories, with three boy heroes who were later described by H. G. Wells as 'mucky little sadists'. One feels the remark well justified after reading how the lads trap and cold-bloodedly shoot the school cat. This they secrete beneath the floorboards of a rival dormitory in order that the slowly decomposing carcase will gradually make life unbearable for the boys in the beds above. This dubious

escapade is followed by a detailed, eight-page description of the slow torture of two tied-up bullies captured in a school ambush. Their cries and screams of pain are muffled by gags thrust into their mouths while Stalky, M'Turk and Beetle work their will, finishing an hour long session of kicks, scrubs and arm-twisting by a final cudgelling of their tear-stained and completely demoralised prisoners.

The uncompromising realism and the obvious condonement by the author of many of the schoolboy cruelties so starkly described in the pages of *Stalky & Co.*, had far-reaching effects on teenage literature, not least by seeming to expose the naïvete of all past and contemporary school stories for boys. The public school story was never quite the same again.

One related style of gregarious boyish activity beloved by later writers of school stories deserves a special mention. Robert S. Baden-Powell (1857–1941), later Lord Baden-Powell, hero of the siege of Mafeking during the Boer War, conceived his original idea for groups of highly-trained woodcraftsmen as early as 1899, when his *Aids to Scouting* first made its appearance. On his return from South Africa in 1903, he had been surprised to learn that the book had been extensively used by teachers in order to school their pupils in the arts of tracking and the delights of an outdoor life. The success of the young cadets at Mafeking encouraged a fatherly interest in the Boys' Brigade; but it was the publisher

C. Arthur Pearson who initially sponsored and partially financed Baden-Powell's separate organisation of Boy Scouts. A trial camp for boys of diverse social backgrounds was held on Brownsea Island in Poole Harbour in July and August 1907, and from that time onwards the Scout movement progressed from strength to strength.

Baden-Powell's *Scouting for Boys* made its original appearance under the Horace Cox imprint as a series of six fortnightly paper-wrappered parts from January to March 1908, and in book form in May 1908. By 1930, fifteen editions, each of several impressions, had been published, and well over five hundred thousand copies sold. The first edition has long been a sought-after collector's piece, and copies of the original paper-wrappered parts fetch high prices at auction on the few occasions when they are offered for sale. It was a work that in its context owed much to Kipling, but it resulted in an international world-wide movement that long survives its founder, and did much to encourage a love of the countryside and an outdoor life in the youth of towns and cities.

It also resulted in a crop of juvenile novels with scouting as their theme and with Boy Scouts and Wolf Cubs as their heroes. First in the field was John Finnemore, whose book *The Wolf Patrol – A Tale of Baden-Powell's Boy Scouts*, 1908, containing eight full-page coloured illustrations by H. M. Paget, was in the bookshops within a few months of the appearance of Baden-Powell's *Scouting for Boys*. In his preface to the work, Finnemore enthused on the speed with which the movement had spread:

No movement of recent years has so swiftly and so completely won the love of boys as the Boy-Scout movement founded by Lieutenant-General Baden-Powell. It has done so because it touches at once both the heart and the imagination. In its dress, its drill, its games, its objects, it jumps perfectly with the feelings of the boy who adores Robinson Crusoe, Chingachcook the Last of the Mohicans, Jim Hawkins, who sailed to Treasure Island, buccaneers, trappers of the backwoods, and all who sit about camp fires in lonely places of the earth.

It is a movement which aims at making all boys brothers and friends, and its end is good citizenship; it is a foe to none save the snob, the sneak, and the toady.

Amid the general chorus of congratulation on the success of the movement, only one dissentient whisper has been heard, and that has gathered about the word 'militarism'. But the Boy-Scout movement is no friend to militarism in any shape or form, and the murmur is only heard on the lips of people who have never looked into the matter, and never read the Scout Law. The movement is a peace movement pure and simple, and its only object is to make a boy hardy and strong, honest and brave, a better man, and a better citizen of a great Empire.

Within a year or two the Boy Scout movement was the happy hunting ground of dozens of writers of boys' adventure stories, with nearly every author of juvenile novels contributing at least one story of the exploits of the keen young lads with ash-staves and toggles, clasp-knives and windswept knees. John Finnemore followed up his success with *The Wolf Patrol* (reprinted by Blackie & Son several times), by producing *A Boy Scout in the Balkans*, 1913; and *A Boy Scout with the Russians*, 1915, amongst similar titles. Captain F. S. Brereton, whose works are discussed later, turned aside from his historical novels to write *Tom Stapleton – The Boy Scout*, 1911, containing a preface by Baden-Powell, to whom the author had dedicated the book. And within the space of a few years scouting stories and adventures in camp and under canvas were competing on almost equal terms with the seemingly endless sagas of public school life. They made a refreshing change.

Science Fiction Stories

Fictional tales of space travel and human encounters with the bizarre inhabitants of other, far distant, worlds have fascinated readers of all ages since science fiction stories first appeared in print. The earliest of these imaginary and spectacular accounts of dramatic technological and scientific advances in human knowledge, adventures in hostile environments or benevolent utopias, was much further back in time than is commonly realised. Some authorities go so far as to credit the Greek writer Lucian (c. A.D. 115 – c. 200), with being the founder of the movement, by producing in his *Vera Historia* (or, 'True History'), the first story of space travel. His hero is carried to the moon by a whirlwind and describes in detail his experiences with the strange inhabitants he finds there. Lucian's account of the huge mirror, by means of which every action on earth can be watched and monitored, seems to some extent to anticipate the present-day man-made television satellites hovering thousands of miles above our planet Earth.

Yet Lucian's imaginary history, like other narratives in the *Arabian Nights* tradition, is really a fairy story. It was in many ways a prototype of *Gulliver's Travels*. In fact elements common to science fiction can be discovered in the works of Homer, and folk-lore abounds with magical incidents that could possibly be given a sound scientific basis by filling in a few missing details. The demarcation line between pure fantasy and 'true' science fiction is blurred; but, as A. C. Clarke, the one-time chairman of The British Interplanetary Society, has pointed out, 'one may say that a story is science fiction when its fanciful elements are made to seem plausible in terms of contemporary knowledge – even if, as is often the case, the treatment is not strictly accurate'.

My own award for the first writer to fulfill these criteria goes to that distinguished seventeenth century prelate John Wilkins (1614–72), bishop of Chester. His father, Walter Wilkins, an Oxford goldsmith, was described as being 'a very ingeniose man with a very mechanical head. He was much for trying of experiments, and his head ran much upon the perpetuall motion'. Young John Wilkins received his earliest education from his father and grandfather,

From *The Log of the Flying Fish*, 1887, by Harry Collingwood. This science fiction adventure story passed through several editions

A steam-driven
interplanetary rocket. An
1873 illustration of a future
space-flight to the moon and
beyond

and proved himself so highly intelligent that he gained a place at Oxford University at the age of only thirteen. Ordained vicar in 1637, he devoted most of his energies to mathematics and scientific pursuits, and was later one of the founder members, and the first secretary, of the Royal Society.

It was in 1638 that he startled his contemporaries by the publication of the fore-runner of all works of science fiction, a book that had the distinction of passing through several enlarged editions during its author's lifetime. *The Discovery of a World in the Moone, or, A Discourse tending to Prove, that 'tis probable there may be another habitable World in that Planet*, 1638 was based on scientific theories that could be counted among the most advanced work current at that time. It should be remembered that Sir Isaac Newton (1642–1727), was not yet born, and his *Philosophiae Naturalis Principia Mathematica*, 1687, in which he propounded for the first time the law of gravity, was not to be published for nearly another fifty years. Wilkins was a century or more before his time, and his *Discovery of a World in the Moone*, must have been fascinating reading when it first appeared in the days of Charles I. That young people discovered its potentialities as an ultra-modern thriller of extra-terrestrial exploration seems more than likely, for the little book is replete with plans and diagrams to illustrate its author's theories, and the text itself makes fascinating reading. To prove some of his points, Wilkins delves back into mythology, but with others he is surprisingly prophetic in his observations. The moon, he thinks, may well be 'more inconvenient for habitation than our World', and he goes on to examine the possibilities of life there:

. . . since we know not the regions of that place, we
must be altogether ignorant of the inhabitants.
There hath not yet beene any such discovery
concerning these, upon which wee may build a
certainty, or good probability: well may we guesse
at them . . . that the inhabitants of that world,
are not men as we are, but some other kind of
creatures which beare some proportion and
likeness to our natures. . . .

He calls the moon creatures 'Selenites', and then conjectures that they were probably of 'divers dispositions, some desiring to live in the lower parts of the Moone, where they might looke downewards upon us, while others were more surely mounted aloft, all of them shining like the rayes of the Sunne . . . I dare not my selfe affirme any thing of these Selenites, because I know not any ground whereon to build any probable opinion. But I thinke that future ages will discover more; and our posterity, perhaps, may invent some meanes for our better acquaintance with these inhabitants. . . . 'Twas a great while ere the Planets were distinguished from the fixed stars, and some time after that ere the morning and evening starre were found to be the same, and in greater space I doubt not but this also, and farre greater mysteries will be discovered.'

Wilkins' book was published in March, 1638, a few months before the appearance of a similar work by the late Bishop Francis Godwin (1562–1633), published posthumously, but believed to have been written when Godwin was still a student at Oxford. *The Man in the Moone; or, A Discourse of a Voyage thither*, 1638, did not appear until August that year, but Wilkins may well have read the work while it was still in manuscript form. And whereas Godwin's work was a lighthearted satire, issued under the pseudonym of 'Domingo Gonsales, the Speedy Messenger', Wilkins' was a serious treatise in which he attempted to prove, by means of the scientific knowledge then available, that the moon was a habitable world. His *A Discourse concerning a new World: in two bookes*, 1640, followed soon afterwards, in which he discussed the possibilities of a manned landing on the moon, and the difficulties to be overcome to ensure 'a safe passage thither'. A French translation, entitled *Le Monde dans La Lune*, was published at Rouen, dated 1655, after circulating in manuscript for some time, and it was from this translation that Savinien Cyrano de Bergerac (1619–55) may well have derived much of his information for his satirical scientific romance *Histoires comiques des etats et empires de la lune*, 1654, a comical work of seventeenth century science fiction. Bergerac's work was translated into English in 1659, and again in 1687; finally appearing in modified form as *A Voyage to the Moon*, 1754, by Samuel Derrick (1724–69).

This, then, comprises the scanty historical background to the works of science fiction that emerged in the nineteenth century in the form we recognise today. The important astronomical discoveries of the seventeenth century, and the interest of the public, young and old, in the planets and stars and the heavens about them, gave the subject its initial impetus. There can be little doubt that intelligent teenagers read whatever popular scientific tracts they could lay their hands on, and the immediate and lasting vogue amongst young people for copies of *The Adventures of Baron Munchausen*, by Rudolph Erich Raspe (1737–94), a fantastic series of short stories containing exaggerations of supposed adventures of the grossest and most improbable kind, can be at least partly attributed to the science fiction element running through many of the tales. Raspe worked in the spirit of Lucian and Rabelais, borrowing certain episodes from *Vera Historia*, but salting the whole with anecdotes in the modern idiom. Dozens of early nineteenth century editions were specially prepared for young people, and the work was added to and

One of the fantastic tales told by Rudolph Erich Raspe in his *Adventures of Baron Munchausen*, a collection of wild exaggerations that delighted teenage boys in the late eighteenth century

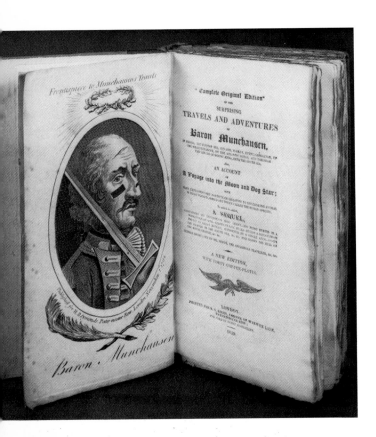

enlarged by publishers' hacks employed by Thomas Tegg, George Kearsley, R. S. Kirby, and others. Raspe's tales of Munchhausen's voyages through space to the Moon and Dog Star were amongst the most popular. His descriptions of the humanoid creatures met with on the former, all about thirty six feet high and riding on domesticated three-headed vultures, might well have been lifted from a modern SF novel:

Everything in this world is of extraordinary magnitude; a common flea being much larger than one of our sheep. . . . Some of the natives of the Dog Star are to be seen here; commerce tempts them to ramble: their faces are like large mastiffs, with their eyes near the lower end or tip of their noses; they have no eye-lids, but cover their eyes with the end of their tongues when they go to sleep: they are generally twenty feet high. As to the natives of the Moon, none of them are less in stature than thirty six feet: they are not called the human species but the cooking animals, for they all dress their food by fire, as we do, but lose no time at their meals, as they open their left side, and place the whole quantity at once in their stomach, then shut it again till the same day in the next month; for they never indulge themselves with food more than twelve times a year, or once a month. . . . When they grow old, they do not die, but turn into air, and dissolve like smoke! As for their drink, they need none; the only evacuations they have are insensible, and by their breath. They have but one finger upon each hand, with which they perform every thing in as perfect a manner as we do who have four besides the thumb. Their heads are placed under their right arm. . . .

And so on! So popular did the book become that at one time it outsold nearly every other published work, and acquired such world-wide fame that, according to Raspe's biographer in the *Dictionary of National Biography*, it 'has probably been translated into more languages than any English book, with the exception of *The Pilgrim's Progress*, *Robinson Crusoe*, and *Gulliver's Travels*'.

As popular with young people as it was with adults, *The Adventures of Munchausen*, shown here by the 1819 edition in its original boarded binding with uncut leaf-edges, remained in print throughout the nineteenth century and beyond

The work was originally published as a series of
five adventures under the title of *Baron Munchausen's
Narrative of his Marvelous Travels and Campaigns in
Russia*, 1786, but, according to contemporary
accounts, 'the first edition, for want of more matter,
was comparatively slow in sale'. This first edition was
solely Raspe's creation. It was not until George
Kearsley, 46, Fleet Street, London, re-issued the work
as a series of monthly parts during the period 20th
April, 1786, to 23rd December, 1786, embellished
with seven full-page folding copperplate engravings,
that the public took real notice and sales started to
soar. Edition followed edition, and more chapters
were added by hack-writers in Kearsley's employ.
The work was taken over by H. D. Symonds, Pater-
noster Row, who commissioned a second volume of
adventures, the whole being issued in December,
1792, with a total of twenty eight full-page plates,
including a portrait frontispiece of the Baron himself.
From that time onwards the work established itself
as an eighteenth century best-seller, attracting
parodies and imitations, such as *Gulliver and Munchhausen Outdone*, 1807, by 'Peter Vandergoose', and a
host of juvenile versions well into the nineteenth
century. It was nicknamed 'The Liar's Monitor',
and coined the phrase 'That's a Munchhausen' for any
long-bowed flight of fancy. But it also created fresh
interest in adult and juvenile minds in the possibility
of life existing on other planets and a vogue for
stories of moon exploration and flights to outer space.

Another hundred years was to elapse, however,
before the appearance of the first works of a writer
who handled the theme of science fiction with an
acceptable degree of scientific realism. It was left to
Jules Verne (1828–1905) to popularise internationally
a new style of novel in which almost every kind of
plausible scientific discovery was made the basis for
thrilling fictional adventures of the most extravagant
description. He was the first to master the art of
fending off fantasy by basing his novels of space travel
and terrestrial (and celestial) exploration on what
could be accepted by the layman as scientific
principles.

Born at Nantes, France, he studied in Paris as a

law student, staying on when he had passed his
Finals in the hope of earning something better than a
precarious living as a writer and journalist. In this
he was disappointed for many years, only a slender
income from his father, Pierre, enabling him to
continue to live in the capital. During 1848, his
earliest stories made their appearance in the periodical
Musée des familles; but success did not come until
the publication of the first of his many scientific
novels, *Cinq semaines en Ballon*, 1863. This was later
translated by W. H. G. Kingston, and appeared as a
serial as *Five Weeks in a Balloon*, in the magazine
Youth's Play-Hour during 1871, having been issued in
book form by Chapman & Hall, London, dated
1870. Within five years a further six English editions
had been issued, together with translations of each of

Verne's continuing series of *Les Voyages Extraordinaires*
as his science fiction tales had been dubbed.

His greatest success at home came with the publication of *De la Terre à la Lune*, 1865, although this did
not appear in English as *From the Earth to the Moon
direct in 97 hours 20 minutes*, 1873, for nearly eight years.
By this time his name was becoming as well known in
Britain and the U.S.A. as it was in his native France,
and by the end of the 1870's nearly every book he
had written to that date had appeared in translation
in both countries. *Voyage au centre de la Terre*, 1864,
appeared as *A Journey to the centre of the Earth*, 1872
(Griffiths & Farran), with illustrations by the French
artist Riou; while *Vingt milles lieues sous les Mers*,
1870, passed through numerous editions after its
first English appearance as *Twenty Thousand Leagues*

series of translations they called *The Jules Verne Library*, with abridged and modified texts to appeal more strongly to boys, and they ran such titles as *The Moon-Voyage* and *Among the Cannibals* for well over twenty years.

There was a wealth of imitators following in the wake of Jules Verne's best-selling comets, but none achieved anything like the master's success in the field of science fiction until the advent of our own H. G. Wells (1866–1946). Born the son of a small-time shopkeeper and professional cricketer, young Herbert George Wells was apprenticed to a draper in early

under the Sea, 1872 (Sampson Low & Co).

All these titles were immensely popular with teenage readers, as well as adults, and *Le Tour du Monde en quatre-vingts jours*, 1873, in its English version of *Around the World in Eighty Days*, 1874, has never been out of print from that day to this. *Hector Servadac*, 1878, sub-titled 'or the career of a Comet', was another title popular with young people, and Sampson Low & Company brought out a companion volume *The Giant Raft; or, Eight hundred leagues of the Amazon*, 1881. Ward, Lock & Company started a successful

The satellite in lunar orbit. A prophetic illustration that appeared in Jules Verne's *From the Earth to the Moon* in 1873

right
An illustration from the serial issue of *The War in the Air* by H. G. Wells, on its appearance in *The Pall Mall Magazine* in January, 1908

right
Science fiction stories for boys had become commonplace by the 1930's. This was the frontispiece of *Adrift in the Stratosphere*, 1937, by A. M. Low

life, memories of which may be seen reflected in his novels *The Wheels of Chance*, 1896; *Kipps*, 1905; and *The History of Mr Polly*, 1910. None of these were tales for boys, and the author intended all his science fiction novels to appeal to a similar adult readership. But it did not take young people long to discover the attraction of such titles as *The Time Machine*, 1895; *The Wonderful Visit*, 1895, in which human life is surveyed through an angel's eyes; *The Invisible Man*, 1897; *The War of the Worlds*, 1898; and *The First Men in the Moon*, 1901. They developed an almost equal interest, at least amongst older teenagers, in

his stories *The Food of the Gods and how it came to Earth*, 1904; and his prophetic *The War in the Air*, 1908; stories that gave rise to numerous juvenile imitations in the pages of boys' weekly papers. *Men like Gods*, 1923, a utopian story, also attracted youthful attention, and Wells' book *The Shape of Things to Come*, 1933, produced as a full-length cinema film in 1936, ensured his popularity with schoolboys who were shortly to experience in real life the horrors the author so accurately predicted.

Wells' books included many themes dominant in later science fiction tales: invasion from outer space

in *The War of the Worlds*; biological catastrophe in *The Food of the Gods*; travel through space and time in *The Time Machine*; and aerial warfare and mass bombing of cities in *The War in the Air* and *The Shape of Things to Come*. Half a century earlier, Jules Verne had correctly anticipated the arrival of the submarine and helicopter, both of which featured in tales for boys from that time onwards.

Science fiction, as a literary art form, gained a new respectability with the appearance in the 1920's of several magazines exclusively devoted to the genre. The American publisher, Hugo Gernsback, a pioneer of his craft, was almost solely responsible for their success and ever-increasing circulation. Meanwhile, in Europe, one of the few Czech writers to win an international reputation as an author, Karel Čapek (1890–1938), gained immediate fame by the staging of his play *Rossum's Universal Robots* in 1920. As a book it appeared as *R.U.R.*, and coined the name 'robot' for any automated machine-servant or press-button workman. This theme of human power over an obedient mechanical device with humanoid qualities delighted generations of teenage boys. Their interest seemed insatiable, and stories of the adventures of their popular heroes, assisted or attacked by pre-Dalek robots in a diversity of ingenious guises, were soon making almost weekly appearances in teenage magazines such as *The Wizard*, *The Bull's-eye*, *The Hotspur*, *The Champion*, *The Rover*, *The Triumph*, and even *The Wild West Weekly*. Čapek's high reputation as a dramatist ensured a wide circulation for his novels, many of which show the influence of H. G. Wells, especially his clever satire *War with the Newts*, 1937.

Science fiction novels set in the future, such as the brilliantly-conceived fantasy *First and Last Men*, 1930, by Olaf Stapledon, soon had their influence on contemporary and later writers in the field. *Adrift in the Stratosphere*, 1937, by A. M. Low, and dozens of similar titles, many issued under the imprint of Blackie & Son, crowded the library bookshelves in the late 1930's. After World War II, with its V2 rockets and the harnessing of atomic energy as a weapon of war, science fiction stories took on a fresh lease of life.

133

First editions of two
Edwardian science fiction
stories

Fictional trips to the planets and our own humble satellite became commonplace long before the first manned landing on the moon in July, 1969.

Today, more than a score of adult magazines, and several juvenile versions of the same periodicals, now cater for the needs of readers of science fiction. Many attain a high technical and scientific quality, and have as contributors well-known names in the world of literature. The appetite of young people for science fiction adventure novels is growing rather than diminishing. Their impatient demand for well-written stories devoted to space-travel and the exploration of the expanding cosmos is reflected in the output of high-quality juvenile novels of this type by some of the best-known publishing houses in Britain and the U.S.A.

The Minors and the Moderns

Early in their careers, neither Ballantyne nor Kingston suffered from the competition of would-be literary rivals to any serious extent: they were exploring a comparatively new terrain whose horizon was as wide as their imaginations cared to make it. They were breaking a trail where only a handful of literary pioneers had so far ventured; but it was not long before dozens of other eager explorers were tracing the same route. In a few years the situation had radically changed, and by the time that G. A. Henty was established as a successful author of boys' adventure stories, a swelling concourse of writers, all hoping to make a living, if not a fortune, by the same means, were hanging on to his coat-tails.

Most of these minor *literati* had little new to say, preferring variations on the themes already composed so effectively by their better-known rivals. Those who were successful in seeing their books in print often acknowledged their indebtedness to the masters on whose works they modelled their tales for youth. Occasionally their novels were prefaced with notes of thanks, or were dedicated to their more successful rivals-in-trade. Bernard Heldmann decided to do both:

St Helier's – May, 1882

My dear Henty,
I am already very greatly in your debt; and by accepting the Dedication of this little story you will place me under a still further obligation.
Yours very faithfully,
Bernard Helmann.

This note appeared in his book *The Mutiny on board the ship 'Leander'*, 1882, and Henty was of further service to the impecunious Heldmann by first offering him the post of editorial assistant on his magazine *The Union Jack*, and later, in its last ill-fated year, promoting him to joint-editorship.

Writers who had done their best to emulate the success of R. M. Ballantyne by setting their plots against what they believed to be a well-researched background of historical or territorial facts and figures, wrote to him personally or printed thankful acknowledgements in the pages of their books. It was a genteel and well-mannered age in this respect, and their public appreciation of the help received was a reflection of the manner in which Henty had earlier gratefully saluted the memory of Walter Scott, Ballantyne his mentor Fenimore Cooper, and Kingston his one-time hero Frederick Marryat.

The profusion of authors who specialised in the juvenile novel during the period 1890–1940, makes any literary historian's task of selection an extremely difficult one. Whom to include in a representative list of writers of boys' adventure stories during this fifty year period, and whom to disregard in a history of the genre with only limited space, is a problem which can only be solved by arbitary choice among the minor authors. The major names have already carved a niche in literary history and are discussed elsewhere. It is the long-forgotten names that concern us here, and a vast sea of faces we have to choose from. For, by the 1890's, the incessant demand by teenage boys for adventure novels had caused a mushroom growth of specialist publishing houses who concentrated almost their entire output into the narrow field of the juvenile adventure novel.

To fill this need, writers of almost every degree of literary quality were recruited, from the highest to close on the lowest. Their novels jostled on the booksellers' shelves, many writing two, three, or even four, full-length adventure stories every twelve months, usually for a lump sum of well under £100 ($240) a book. Some of these shadowy figures were early casualties, falling by the wayside after an initial hopeful burst of activity, their tales appearing serially in boys' magazines before being issued in book form, then being heard of no more. Others achieved fame of a sort, and some whose work appeared in the early 1900's were still producing their annual Christmas offering for the boys of Britain until well into the 1940's.

Little of importance these minor writers so painstakingly produced is remembered today, even by bibliographers and students of literary history. But their influence on late-Victorian and Edwardian

youth, including our own fathers and grandfathers, must have been considerable. Sheer weight of numbers had its effect: the latest Ballantyne and Henty titles were on the shelves, but they were flanked by scores of intriguing titles by little-known names dressed in almost exactly similar format. Their tales of cliffhanging danger and manly heroism in the face of overwhelming odds were read and absorbed by boys eager to learn the pitfalls and perils of the wide, wide world. Their universal glorification of the majestic benevolence of the all-powerful British Raj was only equalled by their constant appeals to the patriotic fervour of clean-living British youth. It was well-meaning propaganda that ultimately left its mark on the soil of Flanders and in the far-flung outposts of a still expanding empire beyond the seas.

Boys' adventure stories published during this period were issued in some of the brightest pictorial-cloth bindings ever commissioned by our conservative-minded publishing houses. Rival firms vied with each other as to who could produce the most arresting and compelling formats for their juvenile novels, many of which can be seen illustrated in the pages of this present work. The paper-salvage drives of two world wars accounted for many thousands – in fact many

hundreds of thousands – of volumes that today would be eagerly sought-after collectors' pieces. Even today, copies are occasionally discovered in almost pristine condition. Their sparkling condition is usually a tribute to some youthful prizewinner's loving care; the volume presented to him on speech-day at school having been wrapped in light-excluding brown paper after the book's initial reading and preserved through manhood and marriage, to be ultimately sold with the rest of the household effects after his death. Copies such as these now form a colourful display on lucky present-day owners' walls, their gilt spines challenging the imagination with titles as intriguing as the illustrations they contain. From those before me now, I have selected a wide diversity of talent. The list gives some indication of the almost unlimited range of plots and counter-plots the young men of the period were able to choose from on their visits with benevolent parents, aunts and uncles to booksellers' shops. They still glitter and beckon today. How they must have dazzled the eyes when presented brand-new for sale, fresh from the printers and binders, their olivine edges catching the light, and the only barrier to possession the five-shilling piece needed for purchase.

A TITANIC COMBAT

man, 1889; *With Airship and Submarine*, 1908; and *A Middy of the Slave Squadron*, 1911. Army and naval officers on retired pay crowded the publishers' lists, while some of those still playing an active military role noted any promotion in the service on the title-pages of their books. One of these was Frederick Sadleir Brereton (1872–1957), a close relative of G. A. Henty, in whose steps he closely followed as a writer of boys' historical adventure stories. In his earlier books his named appeared as 'Captain F. S. Brereton', but before the close of his literary career it was being printed as 'Lt-Colonel Brereton'. His first books for boys, such as *With Shield and Assegai*, 1900; *In the King's Service – A Tale of Cromwell's Invasion of Ireland*, 1901; and *With Rifle and Bayonet – A Story of the Boer War*, 1901; are now difficult to find, although un-dated reprints can still be acquired fairly easily. *Under the Spangled Banner; A Tale of the Spanish-American War*, 1903, is amongst the most readable of his stories; while *The Great Aeroplane*, 1911, and its sister volume, *The Great Airship*, 1914, are sought for their dramatic illustrations of early flying-machines. A long list of First World War books came from his pen, and *The Armoured-car Scouts*, 1918; *With Allenby in Palestine* (1919); and *With the Allies to the Rhine* (1919), are typical of these titles. Every book written by Brereton was issued under the imprint of Blackie & Son, London, a total of well over forty titles.

Yet another military gentleman, Captain Charles Gilson (1878–1943), wrote *The Lost Column*, 1909; *The Lost Empire*, 1910; *The Lost Island*, 1911; and then switched his titles by producing *The Spy – A Tale of the Peninsular War*, 1911; *The Race Round the World*, 1914; *Submarine U-93*, 1916; *In Arms for Russia*, 1918, with a fine series of full-page coloured illustrations by C. E. Brock; and *In the Power of the Pygmies*, 1919. His books for boys continued to appear almost up to his death in 1943.

A particular favourite of mine was Percy F. Westerman (1876–1959), who left Portsmouth Grammar School at the age of eighteen hoping for a naval career. Poor eyesight put an end to these hopes, and he spent much of his early life as a clerk in Portsmouth dockyards. He was thirty two before he

Typical in many ways of the boys' authors of the period we have been discussing was W. J. C. Lancaster (1851–1922), a writer known to his young readers only under his pen-name of 'Harry Collingwood'. He produced his first book for boys, now a much sought-after collector's piece, *The Secret of the Sands*, in 1879. Although the majority of his tales were about the sea (he was an ex-naval officer) he is remembered for writing some of the earliest adventure stories featuring aerial warfare and bombing attacks. The best amongst his long list of titles are *The Pirate Island*, 1885; *The Congo Rovers*, 1886; *The Log of the 'Flying Fish'*, 1887; *The Log of a Privateersman*, 1897; *The Missing Merchant-*

had his first full-length story for boys accepted by Blackie & Son, and it was published as *A Lad of Grit*, 1909, starting a literary career which spanned over fifty years. His early books were historical novels in the Henty tradition, such as *The Winning of the Golden Spurs*, 1911; and *The Young Cavalier*, 1911. The main interest in his works today lies in his series of naval and military books, issued under titles such as *The Flying Submarine*, 1912; *The Sea Monarch*, 1912; *The Rival Submarines*, 1913; *The Sea-Girt Fortress*, 1914; *The Secret Battle-plane*, 1916; *The Secret Channel*, 1918; *A Sub and a Submarine*, 1919; *The War of the Wireless Waves*, 1923; and many others. The outbreak of World War II brought a resurgence of similar activity, with titles such as *The War – and Alan Carr*, 1940; *With the Commandos* (1943); and *Squadron Leader* (1946). His series of scouting books passed through several editions; typical titles were *The Scouts of Seal Island*, 1913; *The Sea Scouts of the 'Petrel'*, 1914; *Sea Scouts All* (1920); *Sea Scouts up-Channel* (1922); etc. Westerman was writing almost up to the week of his death, and throughout the 1950's further titles made regular appearances. Two of his last books were *The Ju-Ju Hand*, 1954; and *Jack Craddock's Commission*, 1958, bringing his total of full-length works to almost two hundred titles. Today he is almost forgotten, yet in the 1930's he easily headed in juvenile popularity a long list of writers of boys' adventure stories compiled by the *Daily Sketch*. *Sic transit gloria mundi!*

Robert Leighton (1859–1934), wrote an interesting series of boys' stories, finishing with a total of nearly fifty titles. Amongst the best were *The Pilots of Pomona: a Story of the Orkney Islands*, 1892; *Wreck of the Golden Fleece – The Story of a North Sea Fisher-boy*, 1894; *In the land of the Ju-Ju; a tale of Benin, the City of Blood* (1903); and *Gildersley's Tenderfoot – A Story of Redskin and Prairie*, 1914, this latter title one of a series he wrote under the C. Arthur Pearson imprint for their matching set of books entitled *The Scout Library*. Leighton achieved fame with his book *Convict 99*, 1898, a work written in collaboration with his wife Marie Connor Leighton. Their *Michael Dred, Detective*, 1899, is thought to be the first story in which the murderer turns out to be the detective himself.

A collector of many years standing who runs his eye along the shelves devoted to his first editions of boys' adventure stories is made instantly aware of the impossibility of putting together anything more comprehensive than a small cross-section of the thousands of titles produced during the Golden Age of the juvenile adventure novel. Titles and authors crowd my own shelves, and hundreds of brightly-hued spines, blocked pictorially in gold and vivid colours, tempt me to include each and every one I have slowly collected from the catalogues and from the dusty shelves of antiquarian and secondhand booksellers throughout the British Isles. This is impossible in an illustrated work of this length, so my selection of the minor and long-forgotten names must depend on acquaintance with the stories inside the late-Victorian and Edwardian covers, or on the measure of literary success the author attained in his own day and age.

Even a drastically-weeded alphabetical list, with only a few titles of each selected author quoted, has had to be shortened; but my friendly rivals, collectors in the same wide-ranging field, will be able to add their own favourite authors and titles to those listed in the index of this present work. Few biographical details are available for the names quoted, despite months of research, and the majority of the writers I have resurrected appear to have left no other mark in the annals of English literature and national affairs than the titles of the books here quoted. By no means all the titles listed have been read or even dipped into other than in a cursory manner, but all, I believe, are symptomatic of the age in which they were written. Their original publishers' cloth bindings delight the eye, and their dramatic series of tipped-in full-page illustrations are some of the best ever to appear in teenage novels.

Master of his Fate, 1886, by the Swedish writer A. Blanche, stands next to a book that appeared in the catalogues the same year: *Spunyarn and Spindrift*, 1886, by Robert Brown, several of whose titles eventually found their way into Mudie's list. I was pleased to find a copy of the first edition of *Vandrad the Viking*,

1898, the first book from the pen of J. Storer Clouston (1870–1944), who later became famous with his series of 'Lunatic' stories, including *The Lunatic at Large*, 1899. His *Carrington's Cases*, 1920, has become one of the most sought-after collections of detective short stories, but his earliest works were in the field of juvenile fiction. *Sons of Victory*, 1904, by O. V. Caine; and *Among the Zulus*, (1892), by Maj. General A. W. Drayson, are two titles well worth looking out for; while the works of Henry Frith (*b.* 1840), such as *Jack O' Lanthorn*, 1884; *The 'Saucy May'; or, The Adventures of a Stowaway*, 1889; *The Lost Trader*, 1894; and *In the Yellow Sea* (1898), rank amongst some of the best seafaring yarns of the period. Herbert Hayens was another prolific writer in the same field, with *Under the Lone Star*, 1896, taking pride of place in half a shelf-ful of his works. He was strongly influenced by G. A. Henty, and his historical adventure novels included: *Clevely Sahib – A Tale of the Khyber Pass*, 1897; *Paris at Bay*, 1898; *The British Legion – A Tale of the Carlist War*, 1898; *Scouting for Buller*, 1902; and *For the Colours*, 1902.

Andrew Hilliard is represented by only a single title: *Under the Black Eagle*, 1896; as is William Johnston with *One of Buller's Horse*, 1900. Thomas W. Knox specialised in travel stories, and gave us *The Boy Travellers in the Congo*, 1888; and *John Boyd's Adventures*, 1893. Alexander Macdonald went even further afield, with *The Island Traders – A Tale of the South Seas*, 1908; *The Quest of the Black Opals*, 1908; and *Through the Heart of Tibet*, 1910. His namesake, Robert M. Macdonald, wrote his first book, *The Great White Chief*, 1908, advertised as 'a story of adventure in unknown New Guinea', after returning home to England from exploring expeditions in the Far East. *The Rival Treasure Hunters*, 1910, is another from his pen, and both are still well worth reading today. The American writer Kirk Munroe, specialised in stories of the struggles between the Redskins and Palefaces, in such titles as *The Flamingo Feather*, 1888; *At War with Pontiac*, 1896 and *Longfeather the Peacemaker – or, The Belt of the Seven Totems*, 1901.

To conclude with a few names from the lower shelves, mention can be made of Bertram Mitford,

May Wynne's books probably had more of an appeal to girls than boys. The title shown is dated 1918

Juvenile novels published between 1880–1920 are collected as much for their colourful and evocative bindings as for the stories they contain. The two shown are dated 1918 and 1907 respectively

Typical pictorial cloth
bindings of the Edwardian
era

Four of the best known titles
which W. J. C. Lancaster
published under his
nom-de-plume of Harry
Collingwood

whose *The Luck of Gerard Ridgeley*, 1894, passed through
several editions, although his next book *A Veldt
Official*, 1895, was intended for an adult audience.
James Macdonald Oxley (1855–1907), gave his
readers *Fergus MacTavish; or, A Boy's Will*, 1893; *Up
among the Ice-floes*, 1894, which told the story of a boy's
adventures aboard a steam-whaler in the Canadian
Arctic; and *Baffling the Blockade*, 1896; while Herbert
Russell, is represented by only *The Longshoreman*, 1896.
S. Walkey achieved distinction with his *Rogues of the
Fiery Cross*, 1897; and also wrote *Kidnapped by Pirates*,
1906, very much in the Stevenson tradition. And right
at the bottom of both shelf and alphabet I have a
couple of titles by R. Egerton Young, who graduated
from missionary tales for the young, such as
*Oowikapum; or, How the Gospel reached the Nelson River
Indians*, 1895; to a collection of bloodthirsty stories of
inter-tribal strife called *Algonquin Indian Tales*, 1903.

I have omitted the names and titles of well over
fifty writers of boys' adventure stories that form part
of my collection of first editions covering the period
1880–1920; but there are two authors who, between
them, span these years. Their works remained firm
favourites with more than one generation of teenage
boys. The first was William Gordon Stables (1840–
1910), a full list of whose books would total well into
three figures. While still a medical student, he
voyaged to the Arctic, later achieving the rank of
naval surgeon. Soon after his retirement from the sea
in 1871 he settled down, like so many other half-pay
naval and military men, to writing adventure stories
for boys, a large number of which contain an autobiographical flavour. He stepped up his average to
between three and four full-length books a year, one
of his earliest successes being *The Cruise of the Snowbird*,
1882, a title constantly re-issued during the next ten
years. *Harry Milvaine; or, The Wanderings of a Wayward
Boy*, 1887; *Wild Life in the Land of the Giants*, 1888;
By Sea and Land – A Tale of the Blue and Scarlet, 1890;
Rocked in the Cradle of the Deep, 1890; *To Greenland and
the Pole*, 1895; *Our Home in the Silver West* (1896);
How Jack Mackenzie won his Epaulettes, 1896 (often re-
issued, with later dated title-pages); and *The Cruise
of the Rover Caravan*. 1896, are only a few of his vast

A FIERCE ENCOUNTER

left
An illustration from *A Sturdy Young Canadian*, 1915, by Captain Brereton, a work which combined the elements of detective fiction with a wartime adventure story. The front cover of the book is shown below

right
Two difficult first editions to discover in good condition. The more popular stories were literally 'read to death' by their young owners, the bindings disintegrating within a few years of their first appearance

A STURDY YOUNG CANADIAN
BY CAPT BRERETON

left
The artist Stanley L. Wood gained the reputation of instilling more movement and action into his pictures than any other book illustrator of the period. Much in demand for juvenile novels, he drew the picture shown for *A Hero of Sedan*, 1910, by Captain F. S. Brereton

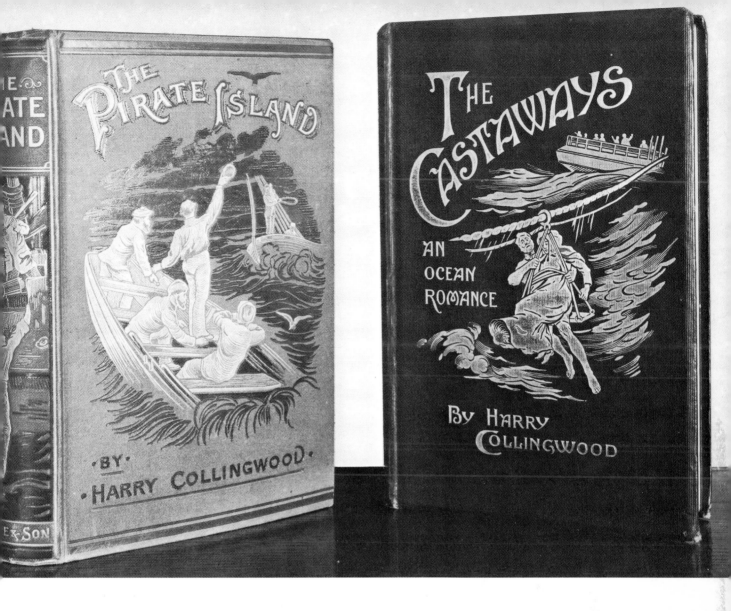

output before 1900. He also wrote a long series of books about cats, *Shireen and Her Friends – Pages from the Life of a Persian Cat*, 1895, illustrated by Harrison Weir, being in the style of several others. As his canon of work contains such a diversity of titles, Gordon Stables is an interesting man to collect, but to attempt to amass a complete set of his first editions, or even a complete set of his texts, would be an all-but impossible task.

A name famous in the early part of the twentieth century, and which no bibliographer or literary historian would be forgiven for omitting from any list of boys' adventure story writers, is that of 'Herbert Strang'. This was the pseudonym that disguised a partnership between two writers, George Herbert Ely (died 1958), and James L'Estrange (died 1947), who wrote their long series of juvenile adventure novels in collaboration. Their first book, *Tom Burnaby*, 1904, was the forerunner of well over fifty full-length stories, covering the field of historical novels, science-fiction, military and naval epics, adventures in the Wild West and the Frozen North, school stories, and almost every other teenage interest. *Boys of the Light Brigade*, 1905; *Kobo – A Story of the Russo-Japanese War*, 1905; and *The Adventures of Harry Rochester*, 1906, between

them brought forth a host of admiring comments from the critics, several of whom drew attention to the gap left by G. A. Henty's death in the field of juvenile fiction. Blackie & Son, having lost their best-selling author, were quick to print these comments on the front fly-leaves of the Herbert Strang books:

Mr. Henty's mantle may most worthily be worn by Mr. Herbert Strang . . . *Truth Magazine*

Now that boys have had the last of Henty's books they will be looking round for a suitable successor; and I have no doubt but that that successor will be Herbert Strang . . . *Books of To-day*

Herbert Strang will undoubtedly do much to fill the gap in boys' lives left by Mr. Henty . . . *Bookman*

Three such successes as Mr. Strang has now achieved definitely establish his position, and should fully reassure those who despondingly wondered when and where a worthy successor to Mr. Henty would appear . . . *Glasgow Herald*

That Ely and L'Estrange conceived the idea, soon

after Henty's death in 1902, of approaching Blackie &
Son with a literary replacement scheme appears
quite possible. The partnership between the two men
was cemented during the writing of *Tom Burnaby* in
the early part of 1903 (Henty having died at the end
of 1902). Soon afterwards, Blackie & Son invested a
considerable sum in advertising this book and their
subsequent titles, while at the same time keeping
secure the secret of the dual-personality of the writer
'Herbert Strang'. After the four stories listed above,
the same publishers issued *Brown of Moukden*, 1906,
again sub-titled 'A Story of the Russo-Japanese War'.
In the preface the authors were at pains to advise
their readers that 'while in *Kobo* the struggle was
viewed from the Japanese stand-point, in *Brown of
Moukden* (which is in no sense a sequel) you will find
yourself among the Russians, looking at their side of
the shield. It is not the romancer's business to be a
partisan; and we British people were at first, perhaps,
a little blind to the fact that the bravery, the endur-
ance, the heroism, have not been all on the one side'.

What happened subsequently is not clear; but a
rift appeared between the publishing house of Blackie
& Son and the Herbert Strang partnership concerning
the American rights of their books. The two men wrote
no more for Blackie, offering their next novels to
Hodder and Stoughton, London, with the American
editions being separately published by the Bobbs-
Merrill Company, U.S.A. *One of Clive's Heroes*, 1906;
and *Samba – A Story of the Rubber Slaves of the Congo*,
1906, both appeared under these imprints. Hodder
and Stoughton did their best to outshine Blackie &
Son in their praise of Herbert Strang as the new-
found successor to the great G. A. Henty, filling the
preliminary leaves of their boys' books with critical
opinions which emphasised this aspect of their work:

It has become a commonplace of criticism to
describe Mr. Strang as the wearer of the mantle of
the late G. A. Henty . . . we will go further, and
say that the disciple is greater than the master.
The Standard

We rank Mr. Strang above Henty in many respects.
The Academy

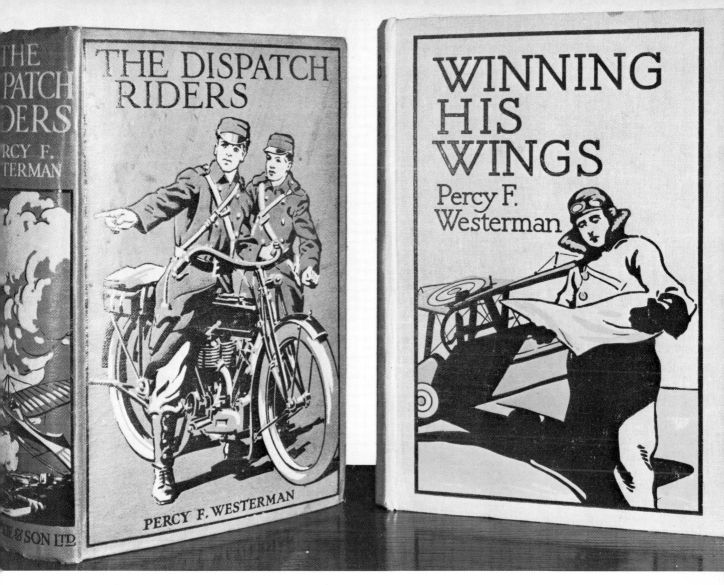

Two of Percy F. Westerman's many titles with a World War I setting

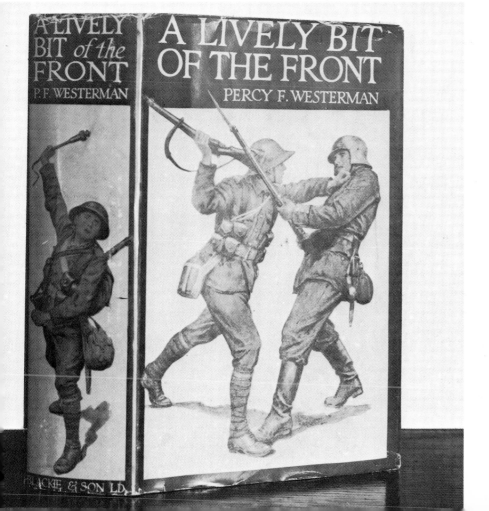

Once again the British straight left proves itself more than a match for a German bayonet. The dust jacket, designed by Wal Paget, of an undated (1918) first edition

Mr. Henty was the ancient master in this kind; the present master, Mr. Herbert Strang, has ten times his historical knowledge and fully twenty times more narrative skill.

Manchester Guardian

Poor Henty must have turned in his grave; but Ely and L'Estrange went from strength to strength. They achieved the unique distinction of having several of their adventure stories for boys issued in special limited editions as large-paper copies. These were published simultaneously with the ordinary trade editions, and included *Rob the Ranger – A Story of the Fight for Canada*, 1908; *Humphrey Bold – His Chances and Mischances by Land and Sea*, 1909; and *A Gentleman-at-Arms; being passages in the Life of Sir Christopher Rudd, Knight*, 1914. All were issued under the joint imprint of Henry Frowde, London, and Hodder and Stoughton, London, with the American rights once again invested in Bobbs Merrill Company, U.S.A. It was the 1920's before the two writers changed to another publishing house, all their titles until that date continuing to be published by the same joint London imprint.

It was not long before their success led to a widening of their literary enterprises. *Herbert Strang's Annual for Boys* was on sale in the bookshops during November, 1907 (dated 1908), and was still making its appearance in the 1930's. The two men also co-operated in producing *Herbert Strang's Historical Series*, a most successful list of supplementary school readers, that were also available, at slightly extra cost, in pictorial cloth bindings. Each of these well-written fictional tales was set in the reign of a different English monarch, thus teaching young people history while they enjoyed the adventure story. *With the Black Prince – A Story of the Reign of Edward III*, 1908; *In the New Forest – A Story of the Reign of William the Conqueror*, 1910, written in collaboration with John Aston; *One of Rupert's Horse – A Story of the Reign of Charles I*; and *With Marlborough to Malplaquet – A Story of the Reign of Queen Anne*, 1910, were typical of the rest of this series of titles. The historical accuracy of each story was checked by Richard Stead, Fellow of the Royal Historical Society,

and other experts. It was not long before this attractive and inexpensive series of easy-to-read historical textbooks gained a reputation for accuracy. They proved a most profitable enterprise for Ely and L'Estrange, and continued in production until the outbreak of World War I.

Meanwhile, their full-length adventure novels continued to appear at regular intervals, each employing the talents of a first-class artist as illustrator. Each had a suite of full-page tipped-in coloured-plates, and were bought as the annual Christmas present for deserving sons and nephews in tens of thousands of homes throughout the land. Early in 1906, Ely conceived the idea of a series of teenage novels in the Jules Verne tradition, with the plots woven into a background of modern scientific invention. Most of them bordered on the realms of science-fiction, and the influence of H. G. Wells was not difficult to discern. The authors' prediction of the coming of inter-continental flight was revealed some two years before Bleriot attempted his flight across the English Channel, with the appearance of their book *King of the Air; or, to Morocco on an Aeroplane*, 1907, the use of the words '*on* an Aeroplane', rather than '*in* an Aeroplane', giving some conception of the type of machine they conjured up for the trip. The book has a memorable coloured frontispiece and other illustrations by W. E. Webster, and was followed by an equally exciting series of other science-fiction titles.

Amongst those I have on my own shelves are *Lord of the Seas – A Story of a Submarine*, 1909; *The Cruise of the Gyro-car*, 1911, surely one of the best juvenile science-fiction stories ever written; *Swift and Sure – The Story of a Hydroplane*, 1910, in which, according to the publisher's blurb, 'Mr Strang shows that he is a new Jules Verne'; *Round the World in Seven Days*, 1911, with a large folding map as well as the usual full-page coloured illustrations; *The Flying Boat*, 1912; and *The Motor Scout – A Story of Adventure in South America*, 1913.

Two of the last stories in this series were amongst the best they had written, and their publishers conferred on them the distinction of issuing both volumes in a specially-prepared thicker and taller demy-octavo format than those of the books written by the

rest of their stable of authors. They were titled *The Air Scout – A Story of National Defence*, 1912, containing some graphic coloured illustrations of aerial dog-fights; and *The Air Patrol – A Story of the North-West Frontier*, 1913, with a series of coloured plates by Cyrus Cuneo, one of which contains the first pictorial representation of an aerial bombing attack by a conventional (as opposed to a science-fiction) aeroplane. It was in this book that the authors turned to their young readers in their preface, telling them of the shapes of things to come in future wars:

It needs no gift of prophecy to foretell that in the not distant future the fate of empires will be decided neither on land nor on the sea, but in the air. We have already reached the stage in the evolution of the aeroplane and airship at which a slight superiority in aircraft may turn the scale in battle. Our imperial destinies may hinge upon the early or later recognition of the importance of a large, well-equipped, and well-manned aerial fleet.

The outbreak of World War I caused Ely and L'Estrange to move the location of their stories to the battlefronts, with tales like *A Hero of Liége – A Story of the Great War*, 1914; *Frank Forester – A Story of the Dardanelles*, 1915; *Through the Enemy's Lines – A Story of Mesopotamia*, 1916; and *With Haig on the Somme*, 1918; amongst many others. After the end of the war they switched their allegiance to the London publishing house of Henry Milford Ltd., at the Oxford University Press, issuing a series of stories illustrated by C. E. Brock, such as *Dan Bolton's Discovery*, 1926, together with a host of others. The same firm started a long-running series entitled *Herbert Strang's Library*, in which the two men acted as joint editors of an extended list of famous juvenile texts.

A few years ago, almost any of these titles could have been bought for the equivalent of 50p ($1·20) to £1 ($2·40) apiece – good copies with the text firm and unsprung and resplendent in their original publisher's pictorial cloth bindings. Today, these dated first editions, with their fantastic pictures of early submarines, wood and wire aeroplanes, gyro-cars, hydrofoils, rockets, balloons, and airships, change hands at up to £10 ($24) each, and the time is not far

The text and illustrations of
both volumes are the same,
and both are dated '1897'.
The first issue of the first
edition is shown on the left
of the picture; the other is a
remainder binding not
issued until 1903

right
The outbreak of World War I
resulted in a spate of
teenage novels devoted to the
Allied cause. A typical series
of first editions of the period
are shown above

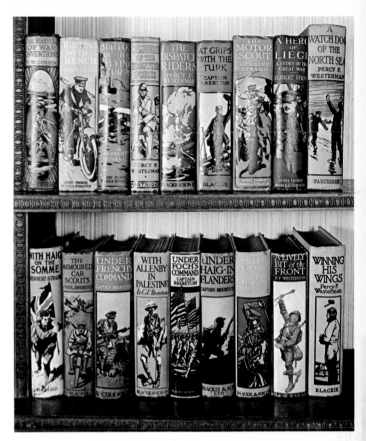

below
Historical novels and
romanticized histories were
as popular with young
people on the Continent as
they were with the teenagers
of Britain. *Richelieu*, 1901, by
Theodore Cahu, was
published as a large folio
volume with illustrations by
Maurice Leloir

distant when this price will be doubled and trebled. Until quite recently, these boys' adventure stories, blended into a background of scientific invention and futuristic mechanical devices, were almost totally disregarded by collectors; only the well-known names, such as Ballantyne and Henty, Mayne Reid and Marryat, commanding more than a pound or so apiece. Jules Verne and H. G. Wells titles always sold well, but the minor authors, and those writing in the early part of this present century, were seldom, if ever, catalogued by antiquarian booksellers. If they made the auction rooms at all, they appeared there unlisted in a stack of fifty or more titles as 'a bundle of boys' books, including many first editions'. Our present age of space travel, and the virtual disappearance of the first editions of the major writers in the genre, has changed all that. Collectors today are seeking out each and every title of authors of the calibre of Harry Collingwood, Gordon Stables, and 'Herbert Strang', before their shelves, too, become as empty as their distinguished predecessors.

The 1920's turned out to be the lean and hungry years in the annals of children's literature, and this was especially evident in the small number of well-written teenage novels produced during this period. Publishers seemed content to resurrect texts that had already passed through six or more editions, issuing many of them as cheaply-produced 'reward' books. A vogue was started for Christmas 'bumper books', massive-looking but very lightweight productions, printed in large type on what looked like and felt like blotting paper, thus giving a thick and satisfying feel to the volume. These swamped the bookshops at each year's end, turning them into literary bargain basements; but they contained little that was new or refreshing in either text or pictures.

In the field of boys' adventure stories the title of Erich Maria Remarque's famous book *Im Westen nichts Neues* summed up the literary scene. This interregnum was a tribute to the number of talented writers, actual and potential, who had been silenced forever on the battlefields of Europe. The glum young heroes were gone, 'lost in Flanders by medalled commanders', as C. Day Lewis put it; and their loss was to be felt in the arts and the world of books for a generation and more.

Many of the older writers survived the war, and Walter de la Mare (1876–1956), remembered for his animal story book *The Three Mulla-Mulgars*, 1910, later re-named *The Three Royal Monkeys*, was still producing delightful stories for young people. Such enterprise as there was seemed confined to fantasy and fairy stories and tales for younger children. Four unforgettable books of stories and verse were contributed by A. A. Milne (1882–1956), and *When we were very young*, 1924; *Winnie-the-Pooh*, 1926; *Now we are Six*, 1927; and *The House at Pooh Corner*, 1928, illustrated in memorable fashion by E. H. Shepard, have never since been out of print. But the decade of strife and trouble which followed the war had merged into the 1930's before any new and important development in the history of the juvenile novel could be recorded.

The principal architect of the new-style juvenile novel was Arthur Ransome (1884–1967), who inaugurated a fresh and exciting trend in children's literature with the appearance of his *Swallows and Amazons*, 1930. Written when he was already forty six years old, and with a quarter of a century's writing already behind him, this first of his school-holidays adventure stories captured a wide audience of both boys and girls. The first edition had no illustrations and caused little stir; but the publication of the second edition, with illustrations by Clifford Webb and end-paper maps by Steven Spurrier, was praised by reviewers for its realistic portrayal of the scenes and the characters so vividly depicted. Arthur Ransome's triumph was his seemingly effortless ability to wake to life juvenile characters who were almost more realistic than the boisterous children of the everyday world. His Swallows and Amazons, and their adventures ashore and afloat, continued to fascinate teenagers through the whole series of twelve titles. *Swallowdale*, 1931; *Peter Duck*, 1932; and *Winter Holiday*, 1933; were read by girls at least as much as boys, and yet have earned a place in any representative collection of boys' adventure stories for the influence they exerted over contemporary and later writers in this field. *Coot Club*, 1934; *Pigeon Post*, 1936; *We Didn't Mean to Go to Sea*, 1937; *Secret Water*, 1939; *The Big Six*, 1940; *Missee Lee*, 1941; *The Picts and the Martyrs*, 1943; and *Great Northern?*, 1947; complete the collection, and it is a fortunate man who has been able to acquire the whole set in first edition form.

The long series of 'William' books from the pen of Miss Richmal Crompton Lamburn (1890–1969), who wrote under the name of Richmal Crompton, are still genuinely alive in the sense of being reprinted for modern reading. Originally a school-teacher, she started her career as a writer by submitting schoolboy stories to the *Home Magazine* in 1920, and later to the more popular *Happy Magazine*. The publishers, Newnes, decided to issue a collection of her stories in book form. *Just William*, 1922, was the first title in a series that continued for over forty-five years (36 different stories were published by the end of 1966), and brought their authoress both fame and fortune. *More William*, 1922; *William again*, 1923; and *William the Fourth*, 1924, are typical of a series of hilarious tales about a mischievous and irrepressible schoolboy that have now sold well over ten million copies.

Mention must also be made of the extremely popular

A boys' adventure annual of 1910. Size 26.6 × 20 cm.

See page 211.

TRICK CINEMATOGRAPHY—THE AUTOMOBILE ACCIDENT.

The producer giving instructions to the principal actor and his double, the legless cripple.
The dummy legs in the foreground. – *See page 211.*

Frontispiece

and successful series of 'Biggles' books created by William Earl Johns (1893–1968). *Wings: a book of flying adventures* (1931), and *The Camels are coming* (1932), set the pace, followed by *The cruise of the Condor* (1933). With the appearance of *'Biggles' of the Camel Squadron* (1934), his success was assured, and the series of similar tales featuring his hero continued well into the 1960's.

Adventure stories of the 1930's were not all confined to tales of contemporary life. The changed values of the age were reflected in the radical (and anti-romantic) historical novels of Geoffrey Trease (*b.* 1909), whose *Bows Against the Barons*, 1934, with its gruesome frontispiece that exactly matched the grim realism of the narrative, after a hesitant start

later attained the respectability of special school editions. George Orwell gave Trease every encouragement, and *Comrades for the Charter*, 1935; *Call to Arms*, 1935; *Mystery of the Moors*, 1937; *Cue for Treason*, 1940; *The Grey Adventurer*, 1942; *Black Night, Red Morning*, 1944; and a host of still continuing titles, were amongst the best boys' adventure stories written during the period bounded by the end of World War II.

The revival of interest in children's literature during the latter half of the twentieth century, both here in Britain and in the U.S.A., is shown by the institution of medals and awards for writers and others concerned in the production of children's books. The

U.S.A. has the Newbery Medal, awarded annually to the author of the most distinguished contribution to literature for children in that country. The first two winners were Hendrik Willem van Loon for his *The Story of Mankind*, 1921; and Hugh Lofting for his *The Voyages of Dr Dolittle*, 1922. The Caldecott Medal has been awarded annually since 1938 to the best American picture book for children. Britain has two principal awards in the field of children's books, both presented annually by the Library Association. The Carnegie Medal has been awarded since 1936 (when it was won by Arthur Ransome with *Pigeon Post*) for an outstanding book for children published during the preceding year and written by a British subject living in the country. The Kate Greenaway Medal, inaugurated in 1955, is awarded to the British artist who produced the most distinguished work in the illustration of children's books during the preceding year. The first winner was Edward Ardizzone, for his book, *Tim All Alone*. And the magazine *The Junior Bookshelf* has been a most successful and useful publication since its first number in 1936.

There is no award in any English-speaking country specifically for the best teenage novel, in which category boys' adventure stories play a major role. I am hopeful that this present history of the genre may stimulate sufficient interest in the adventure novel, and a growing awareness of the important part it has played in moulding the minds of generations of teenage youth, to make such an award of merit a distinct possibility in the near future.

Bibliography

The bibliographical works listed below form a selective reference background that a collector of juvenile novels and boys' adventure stories needs to consult. A few of the best-known writers for juveniles have their own individual bibliographies which can be bought and consulted separately as your interest dictates, and these are not included in this general list.

Book-Auction Records 1902 to present day. 69 annual volumes; Dawsons Ltd., Pall Mall, London

Boys will be Boys by E. S. Turner (magazines and penny dreadfuls). Collins, Toronto 1948

Cambridge Bibliography of English Literature edited by George Watson, 5 vols, Cambridge University Press 1969–75 (printing)

Cambridge History of English Literature edited by A. W. Ward and A. R. Waller. 15 vols, revised. Cambridge University Press, 1907–33 (at present under revision – but also issued in single volume concise form, 1970)

Cassell's Encyclopaedia of Literature edited by S. H. Steinberg, 2 vols, Cassell, London 1953

Children's Books in England by F. H. Darton, Cambridge University Press, 1970 (second edition, reprinted)

Collector's Book of Books by Eric Quayle; Studio Vista, London 1971

Collector's Book of Children's Books by Eric Quayle; Studio Vista, London 1971

Early American Children's Books by A. S. W. Rosenbach. Kraus Reprint Corporation, New York 1966

English Children's Books by Percy Muir. Batsford Ltd., London 1954

Les Livres de L'Enfance, 2 vols. Gumuchian & Cie, Paris 1930

Nineteenth-Century Children by Gillian Avery and Angela Bull, Hodder & Stoughton, London 1965

Osborne Collection of Early Children's Books, 1566–1910 edited by Judith St John. Toronto Public Library, Canada 1958

Written for Children by J. R. Townsend. Garnet Miller, London 1965

XIX Century Fiction by Michael Sadleir. Constable, London, 2 vols, 1951

Index